Dorothy B. Hughes and The Murder Room

>>> This title is part of The Murder Room, our series dedicated to making available out-of-print or hard-to-find titles by classic crime writers.

Crime fiction has always held up a mirror to society. The Victorians were fascinated by sensational murder and the emerging science of detection; now we are obsessed with the forensic detail of violent death. And no other genre has so captivated and enthralled readers.

Vast troves of classic crime writing have for a long time been unavailable to all but the most dedicated frequenters of second-hand bookshops. The advent of digital publishing means that we are now able to bring you the backlists of a huge range of titles by classic and contemporary crime writers, some of which have been out of print for decades.

From the genteel amateur private eyes of the Golden Age and the femmes fatales of pulp fiction, to the morally ambiguous hard-boiled detectives of mid twentieth-century America and their descendants who walk our twenty-first century streets, The Murder Room has it all. >>>

The Murder Room
Where Criminal Minds Meet

themurderroom.com

T0352510

Dorothy B. Hughes (1904–1993)

Dorothy B. Hughes was an acclaimed crime novelist and literary critic, her style falling into the hard-boiled and noir genres of mystery writing. Born in Kansas City, she studied journalism at the University of Missouri, and her initial literary output consisted of collections of poetry. Hughes' first mystery novel, *The So Blue Marble*, was published in 1940 and was hailed as the arrival of a great new talent in the field. Her writing proved to be both critically and commercially successful, and three of her novels – *The Fallen Sparrow, Ride the Pink Horse* and *In a Lonely Place* – were made into major films. Hughes' taught, suspenseful detective novels are reminiscent of the work of Elisabeth Sanxay Holding and fellow Murder Room author Margaret Millar. In 1951, Hughes was awarded an Edgar award for Outstanding Mystery Criticism and, in 1978, she received the Grand Master award from the Mystery Writers of America. She died in Oregon in 1993.

By Dorothy B. Hughes
(Select bibliography of titles published in The Murder Room)

The So Blue Marble (1940)
The Cross-Eyed Bear Murders (1940)
The Bamboo Blonde (1941)
The Fallen Sparrow (1942)
The Delicate Ape (1944)
Johnnie (1944)
Dread Journey (1945)
Ride the Pink Horse (1946)
The Candy Kid (1950)
The Davidian Report (1952)

The Cross-Eyed Bear Murders

Dorothy B. Hughes

An Orion book

Copyright © Dorothy B. Hughes 1940

This edition published by
The Orion Publishing Group Ltd
Orion House
5 Upper St Martin's Lane
London WC2H 9EA

An Hachette UK company
A CIP catalogue record for this book is available from the British Library

ISBN 978 1 4719 1727 1

www.orionbooks.co.uk

For Susan Amanda, who arrived two days before Fredi.

List of *Exciting* Chapters—

The Cross-Eyed Bear Murders

Chapter One: Danger's Bright Face

No ONE paid any attention to you in the subway. Ermine or rags, it didn't make any difference. She might have been wearing the shabby brown tweed as well as the black velvet evening coat, hood lined in white fur; beneath it the black evening gown, unornamented save for the one good clip at the breast line. It had been irresistible although she shouldn't have spent the money for it.

She couldn't endure staying in tonight, two days since her first utterly-alone Christmas. She had decided at six-fifteen to go out, alone as always, but at least pretending a part of the tinsel-wrapped holiday. There was valid reason to go. Eight months of search, haunting the theaters, the concert halls, the hotels, the right New York places where he might appear, a search limited by her meager income—eight months and to no avail. But some night she would see the man whose name she did not know; she would see him and she would begin to find out that which she must know. It might be this night.

Miraculously the small and dingy bathroom had been empty. She had bathed, dressed quickly, and left the apartment. She had considered a taxi but that was too much; she'd walked instead down to 116th, across to Broadway to the subway. She swayed in it now, watching the numerals appear on the underground walls. She got off at Columbus Circle, moved toward the theater district. Tonight she would attend the theater, not merely watch in the lobbies before and after curtain and during intermissions. A gala musical show, only that would suffice; only that could make her forget her loneliness, eight months alone in New York.

She entered the lobby of the theater. There was a small line ahead of her approaching the ticket-seller's cage. She waited, knowing there would be nothing available. She looked about idly, playing a little game—she was with those two men at the end of the line; they were all going to some luxurious hotel for dinner before the show and eat all they wanted to; she was merely standing aside while they bought the seats. She even listened to them, heard one saying amusedly, "Are you still running that melodramatic ad, Bill?"

And then she looked with consciousness at their black overcoats. She had seen those shoulders before, that unbelievably gargantuan back. A little shiver went through her, not the result of her walk in the night air; it was chilly, yes, but it was not that cold. She forced herself to move a bit closer to them.

The thinner one, the one she hadn't ever seen, answered, "Yes. I haven't found what I'm looking for," and then moving forward to the cage, "Reservations for tonight. Folker is the name—the Lorenzo phoned...."

The Lorenzo. That melodramatic ad.

They saw her standing there but they didn't see her. She was just another unknown face on a night in New York, someone waiting for tickets. But she had seen the corner of that ugly face before. It hadn't ever seen her.

This then was the end of the search. It had happened as she had known it must happen. But she knew the end was no more than the beginning. And she didn't know exactly what to do. Seeing him was not enough; she must discover who he was, some way she must meet him, know him. If, indeed, it were he.

She waited until the coats swept out again, then approached the cage. As she had known, no seats to be had; the clerk consented to sell her one standing room, impressing by his bored mouth that she was lucky to be allowed the privilege. She took it, paying out her precious dollars. Those two would return and she would get to see the one again, to make certain. But of course she was certain; there couldn't be duplications of those shoulders and ugly jaw.

She ate alone in one of the smaller hole-in-the-walls where turkeys roasted on a spit in the window; walked back again to the theater. She stood there in the foyer alone, cigarette in hand, as if expecting a dilatory escort. She watched the audience arrive, the formal dress for orchestra circle, the street lengths for balconies. And she saw those two moving their long legs through the door. Then she went in.

They brushed by her during intermission, took a place in a circlet with beautifully gilt women and the usual nondescript escorts. She stood apart; she could stare at them and they wouldn't know. She knew she had never seen the one. He was tall, a young forty, saffron blond, with that nice thinness that wasn't too thin, that length of face that didn't mean skinny shoulders. It was to him that the gilded women turned their predatory eyes. But he didn't look much interested; his own eyes were restless. Once she felt that they turned on her, although it was ridiculous; she had stationed herself sufficiently far away to watch unnoticed, as if anyone noticed anything in a crowd in New York. There was no reason to feel again that little chill; his face was a fine one. But something about him even at this distance and unknown made her feel unsure, unsafe. That was how it was.

It was the other man that would make you shiver, that angry face with the deep slashes around the mouth, and that build like a mammoth football player or a gorilla. He shouldn't have looked at home in tails as did the first man, but he did. He was the same: two years were as nothing; you could never forget the bulk, the ugliness.

The finale was on when they came up the aisle again, almost knocked against her in the dark. The good-looking one was saying, "We can meet her another time, Guard, but I want you to have a chance to see this fellow before the place gets too crowded. He won't admit it but——" and then, with a cold waft of air, they were gone into the lighted lobby.

Again the subway and return to her ash-heap, the morning papers under her arm, hurrying from Broadway toward Morningside. It was cold and late and there was the office in the morning. She hated the grubby little room in the drab apartment. She could actually reach across from the bed and touch the bureau. The box closet, closed by a faded chintz curtain, was too small to hold her trunk; that stood out in the room, half-shutting away the small window, but it didn't matter. Sun only came down the long shaft to the pane from ten-fifteen to ten-fifty of a morning. She had timed it one Sunday.

She hated the smell of the old carpet, always the odor of dust in every corner, and if you opened the door, of canned soup cooking. That was the snoopy older woman in the first room of the apartment, breaking rules. Liz-anne didn't break rules. She brought in milk and hard rolls for breakfast, sometimes for dinner, but she didn't cook. Neither did the Texas girl studying music in the second room, nor the fashionable girl studying something in the best room. She knew them by name and sight, occasionally a word. Those two didn't have to break rules; there were always men, some handsome, some not, but all well-dressed, waiting in the dark hallway for them.

Lizanne undressed and sat on the edge of that bed. Rooms didn't grow so small except in the city; in Vermont this would have made a second jam pantry. She held in her hand the check for seventeen dollars, beside it the office notice. It hadn't come as a blow. She was only substituting and the stenographer whose place she had taken was to return the first of the year: next week.

She hadn't paid last week's rent. Seven dollars must go for that; maybe she could eat on five this week, and then there was subway fare. One more of these seventeen dollars and no more. There wouldn't be even this ugly room to which to return. She wondered what happened to girls in Manhattan who had no room, no money, no job. It was all right to read about sleeping on a bench in Central Park; it didn't sound so dreadful, but reality was different stuff. What would she do with her trunk if she moved to a park bench? And what would she eat?

She knew the elusive way of jobs; she hadn't given up two seasons of summer stock, a winter of climbing long, dusty stairways, sitting day by day in producers' harsh anterooms, because she preferred stenography. She had tried what she wanted to do for those months before admitting failure and returning to Uncle Will's to help him sell stamps and sort the mail. But she had known she couldn't stay forever in that Vermont village. She had studied secretarial work by mail at nights preparing for a vague someday return to the city. She had thought it would be easier to find work at a typewriter. She must stay in New York; she'd work at anything to stay in New York. Nothing short of starvation would send her back to Vermont yet. If it came to that she would return and try it again later; she had too much sense to starve to death when Uncle Will's friends would welcome her return, feed her, find work for her, try to keep her safe. But she couldn't return after only eight months away. It might not be safe.

There was, of course, the Lorenzo ad. It had been running for several weeks now, not in the want ads but in the personal column. She read it again although she knew it almost by heart:

> Wanted: A beautiful girl. One not afraid to look on danger's bright face. Room 1000, The Lorenzo.

It might be only a message to someone who hadn't seen it thus far. If it were not that, she had been a little afraid of it. Of course, it must be legitimate. A great hotel wouldn't sponsor any kind of a racket under its roof. And yet, maybe they didn't know. It was such a strange ad.

She had been afraid of it. Not afraid of the danger part exactly; she could take care of herself here. Nothing was going to happen to her; nothing would happen to her until she'd finished what she had come to the city to finish. But you had to be careful alone in New York. It wasn't as if she had a family behind her. Uncle Will's death six months ago had severed her last close tie.

She was more afraid of it now. She excused herself anew from answering. She didn't qualify. "Wanted, a beautiful girl." She wasn't beautiful. She was all skin and bones; she always had been thin, it wasn't just not having enough to eat the past eight months. Her face was too tiny, and her round eyes, blue as china plates, diminished her features even more. Her eyes and her too-bright scarlet hair.

She didn't look bad, dressed up, but she couldn't wear black velvet to answer the ad, not even to pass as, not a beautiful girl, but one good-looking enough. She'd have to appear in the shabby brown tweed suit and coat, the brown sweater with the white collar, the old brogues.

She cut the item from the column, placed it in her purse. It wouldn't hurt to try this. She wouldn't have to take the job even if it were offered. Tomorrow was Saturday, half-day at the office. She could go in the afternoon. The saffron man had said, "The Lorenzo phoned...." He looked as if he might know danger intimately. Remembering him, he didn't look at all like one to be feared. The other one had faced danger; that she knew. And she wasn't afraid now. Tomorrow afternoon she would pretend to be "a beautiful girl."

She looked terrible. Although late, winter had arrived. A wet snow had started at noon, her brown felt was mashed to her ears and her hair straggled in her neck behind it; her feet were damp and uncomfortable. The Lorenzo lobby was, in its austerely marble beauteousness, just where she didn't belong. She wasn't going to give up now. She had her mind settled. She went straight to the marble desk as if she were going to rent the best suite, not deliver someone's hat.

She said, "I want to see the house detective."

The musical-comedy clerk, port-colored carnation and all, stared at her as if he wished she were not there.

She took a breath. "I'm not here to make a complaint. I just want to ask him a question."

The clerk wasn't reassured, but he spoke to the girl at the switchboard and said to Lizanne, "If you'll wait." He didn't motion her to the silver brocade chairs reserved for lobby elect and she didn't move toward them. She had no intention of insulting beauty with a damp tweed coat.

The house detective looked exactly as he should, the Lorenzo grandeur notwithstanding. He kept his hat on. He calmed Lizanne's nervousness even before the clerk spoke, "This young lady was inquiring for you, Mr. Simmons."

She had taken the clipping from her bag. "I'm about to answer an ad here and I just wanted to know if it's ... safe."

Mr. Simmons took it and the clerk peered over the desk at its words. The clerk began to titter. "That's Mr. Folker. Room one thousand."

She had thought it would be; how much she had hoped it she didn't know until he spoke the name. But she wasn't surprised.

Mr. Simmons was chuckling. "I should say it is all right, young lady. Mr. Folker's been living here a whole year almost and no complaints. He could buy you and me out like we'd buy a stick of chewing gum."

The clerk said—it was to Mr. Simmons—"He explained about the ad. He's writing a radio serial now and looking for copy. You should see the beauties that have been trailing in."

Lizanne felt dropped and left there. Nothing of romance or glitter, nothing that might pair with a slashed face and too wide shoulders, just an author looking for some unusual assistance. Her voice was small. "Shall I go up?"

"Certainly, go on up." The clerk had forgotten her. He glanced at her now and he looked amused, as if she must be pretty funny thinking she could compete with the trailing beauties. She set her chin and held out her hand for the clipping. At least none of them had been hired.

She left the crystal and gold elevator on the tenth floor. Room 1000 was the first at the right, a white paneled door. She was almost afraid to tap at it but she had to now. She'd come this far; she must finish.

A voice said, "Come," and she went inside. The room wasn't a bit fancy. It was like any well-dressed hotel room only there were a desk and files where beds usually stood, and a few extra chairs. There was a woman behind the typewriter at the desk. She looked tall even sitting down, her face was plain, her hair unfashionably drawn into a knot at the back of her head. She said, "Yes?"

Lizanne was almost ashamed to speak. Plain women recognized beauty; this one must have seen all those lovely women come and go. Her own voice was timid when she spoke, "I've come about the ad."

The woman looked her over. Naturally she wasn't impressed. She said, "Sit down. I'll speak to Mr. Folker."

Lizanne sat down on the edge of one of the chairs and the woman went through a door at the left. She felt like crying. She should never have come. But she blinked the sting out of her eyes. She could do it even if she weren't beautiful. She could help an author. And she wouldn't turn away sight unseen.

The woman returned and said, "Mr. Folker will see you." She held the door open. Her face looked placidly unhopeful.

The saffron man was on a chaise longue near the window, a heavy maroon throw over his knees. He wore a gray business suit and a dark maroon tie and his voice was pleasant. He said, "Pardon my not rising. I have to take it easy." His gray eyes were pleasant, too, but in back of them he was studying her as if she were an important map. She knew it. And she had known last night that this would happen, that he and the ad and the big man were together, and that some power unexplained and unexplainable had led her out of her room and on to West 52nd street at that certain hour. Yet she wasn't frightened. It was only in thinking about things that you were frightened, not in their actuality.

He smiled at her. "Sit down, Miss..."

"Lizanne Steffasson." But she couldn't put her damp coat on one of the oyster-white chairs. This room was all beautiful, maroon and oyster-white and glass. She said, "My coat's wet. It's snowing out."

He smiled again, touched a button on the arm of the chaise. The plain woman came in. "Lydia, will you take Miss Steffasson's coat and hang it up to dry? And her hat."

Lizanne removed them, not wanting to; her hair was a mess, she was certain, and her suit so shabby. The woman took the dampness away into the anteroom.

"Now, Miss Steffasson," he began, "suppose you tell me how you happened to answer the advertisement."

She met his eyes, just as if she had never laid her eyes on him before; just as if there were nothing in his, save amusement at such a one as she coming to him. "I need the job," she answered.

His eyebrows raised. "Is that the only reason?"

She didn't hesitate. Truth was self-evident. At the moment it was to her an important reason. "Yes."

"What does your family think of your answering it?"

10

She said, "I have no family."

He smiled faintly. "You must have someone."

She shook her head. "No. There is no one at all." It was true.

He looked her over. The smile had gone from his mouth; there was something else there, as if he were probing beyond the face and word she offered him. "What about the danger? You aren't afraid of danger?"

"Yes, I am," she answered honestly, more to herself than to him. "I'd be scared to death in real danger. I know I would."

"Yet you came." He was laughing at her now and she was angry.

"I'm in danger right now," she told him. He wasn't amused. "Danger of having no place to sleep and nothing to eat, having to walk the streets and sleep on a park bench——" She broke off. "Do you think any radio serial danger can frighten me when that's what I'm looking forward to next week?"

He didn't say anything for a moment and when he did he spoke with seriousness. "Suppose it weren't a radio serial?"

She answered without hesitation. "I need the job."

He looked at her steadily. Her eyes didn't waver. He began again, "You're not beautiful——"

"I know that," she interrupted. "I'm too thin and my face is too little and my hair's too red——"

"Orange," he corrected.

She bit her lip. It wasn't a color she'd prefer. "I look better dressed up," she confided.

"Yes. Dressed right." She might have been a dog he was examining. "You might do. I don't get around——"

She shouldn't have said it but she did. "I saw you at

the theater last night."

He raised his eyebrows again. "Did I see you?"

She didn't know. "I was wearing black velvet, in the lobby."

He said, "I believe I spoke to you. Didn't I say excuse me?"

"You didn't. But you nearly knocked me down twice." She didn't say anything about the man with him, just as if she hadn't noticed.

He laughed out loud at her. "I do believe you will do, Lizanne Steffasson. I don't get around much, as I started to say. My heart"—he touched his coat—"keeps me in. I need someone to do a little extra work. What sort have you been doing?"

She told him, and why she was leaving. "I couldn't start for another week." She held breath while he thought that over. If it would make a difference, she'd quit the other job at once, but when he spoke he said, "Naturally not—days. Perhaps you could do a little night work. If I needed you."

"Oh, yes. Anything."

He smiled at her. "You haven't even asked what the duties are to be, or hours."

She shook her head. It didn't matter.

"Or your salary. I will pay you one hundred a week." Miracle, sheer miracle.

"How long the job will last I can't tell you, but if you stay with it I promise you a bonus of five hundred dollars in lieu of the customary two weeks' notice."

It was wealth; daydream wealth.

"Your hours—I can't say. You will have to suit them to my convenience. Your duties—well, if you want the job, if you accept it, I'd like to tell you a little something of what it is all about. It is—strictly confidential."

Something in back of his face, something in the way he spoke, made a shiver pass through her. She ignored it. Whatever the confidences she must keep, it was worth it.

"How about it, Lizanne Steffasson?"

She shook her head as if to wake herself up. "Of course, I accept. It's—unbelievable." More so than he could know. Here, she would find out about the ugly man.

He laughed out loud again, pressed the button. "Lydia, have tea sent up, please." When the door was closed again he said, "You need something warm before you brave the snow." She saw now it was falling more thickly outside the pane. "I will explain a few things while you're having it." He was looking her over, in that steady unwavering way. "Have you ever heard of Knut Viljaas?"

She sat on the edge of the white chair, her toes pressed into the maroon rug. It wasn't just a question; he was waiting for an answer.

She muttered, "The Cross-Eyed Bear," and then she looked up, startled, into his searching eyes. She added quickly, "That's what the newspapers called him. He was the Swedish billionaire, wasn't he?"

"A Finn, not Swedish. Yes, they did call him that, and it was strangely apropos. He was like a northern bear, big and shaggy and white, and one eye crossed. He wouldn't wear glasses."

"You knew him?" She made her voice breathless, as if it were like a fairy tale that anyone should know him.

He looked at her again and deep inside she was like ice but he couldn't know. He answerd, "No. But I saw him, more than once. Did you ever know him?"

She shook her head, simulating amazement. "My, no!

I only read about him in the newspaper."

A waiter silently rolled in the tea cart. Folker dismissed him, said, "Serve yourself, Miss Steffasson. I'll have mine later. Right now I want to talk."

She obeyed.

"There were three Viljaas sons, Stefan, Lans, and Dene. To them, the father left three million dollars, unbelievably in cash. The money is on deposit, has been for about seven years now, at the National Bank. Viljaas, you may remember if you read of him, lived in the United States the last twenty-five years of his life, after his second marriage. The legacy was given in the form of a check, divided into three triangles, one for each son. This check could not be cashed until the twenty-first birthday of the youngest son, and only if the three sections were presented together. Each triangle contains not the son's name but Old Viljaas' seal of the cross-eyed bear. Furthermore, the check must be endorsed in triplicate with the cross-eyed bear."

Her eyes grew bigger and bigger by the moment but he couldn't see them. She had swooped on the hot buttered muffins, poured the hotter tea.

"Two years ago, shortly before his twenty-first birthday, Dene, the youngest boy, disappeared while on a hunting trip in the north woods. He's never been heard of, or from, since."

She went right on clearing the plates of food and gulping more tea. He couldn't know that not even the heat of the tea could stop her from shivering. It was as if a ghost had laid hand on her spine.

"The estate must be settled on the first of April of this year. That is as stipulated in the will, if anything should prevent the settlement before this date. I am here to find Dene Viljaas, sometimes known as Dene Thyg. He more frequently used a part of his grandmother's name. None of the sons kept the name Viljaas. It was too famous to permit a normal existence."

She made herself speak, chattily, the way a typist would. "You think he is here in New York? Maybe he was killed on the hunting trip, or got lost, or froze to death or something."

Folker said, "No body was ever found. He must be alive—purposely disappeared. It isn't an unusual trick of the Viljaases. Old Knut himself didn't tell anyone where he was when he first came to America. And before that when he left his native village and went to Copenhagen where he began the founding of his fortune, he didn't send word back for fifteen years."

She said slowly, "I can't see why this Dene would want to disappear with a million dollars waiting around for him. Suppose he isn't found. Then what?"

"Then the check cannot be cashed unless——"

She waited:

"Unless his triangle is found—and the cross-eyed bear."

"He had that?"

He shrugged. "No one knows who had it. It was given to one of the three brothers, but to which one old Knut didn't say. That part was secret."

She asked, "What happens if they aren't found? To the money?"

His face darkened and his gray eyes seemed to turn saffron as his hair. He said, "The money goes to a group of fool societies that the Old Bear favored."

She was silent a moment, then asked, "Where are the other brothers now?"

"Stefan, the eldest, is supposed to be in Sweden. Lans

is here in New York. He is, I believe, playing the piano at a second-rate night club on Fifty-third street. One called Jim and Jack's. He doesn't admit to being Lans Viljaas."

That was where Bill Folker and the ugly man had been going before the curtain fell last night. "Where does 'danger's bright face' come in, Mr. Folker?"

He waited so long she began to be afraid, to feel she should not have asked. But she kept her eyes round and innocent on him until he replied.

"If you are going to work for me, you may as well know. The legacy is only a small part of the Knut Viljaas estate. He owned a majority of the mines in the Norse countries. They are located at almost the northern outposts of Sweden and of Finland, too far north for the conquering nations to obtain them, as yet, by force. This fact, plus their belonging to American heirs, has kept them untouched. But their output is extremely important to warring nations. Although he left his native land as a young man, and was later naturalized in the United States, Knut was a nationalist in the way that only those of the old school have been. His contracts were so signed that only his own country and her allies could profit. These contracts lapse on April first of this year, which is the reason for the stipulation that the estate must be closed then. The Old Bear expected that his sons would renew the contracts in the same way, left memoranda almost dictating that. However, because of the wars, the mines are of more importance than ever, and certain other nations, in particular the Three, have entered their bids at a far higher price than Finland or her friends can begin to offer."

His eyes slanted. "If the sons are not on hand, the

executors will have no choice but to sign with the highest bidder. It is obviously, therefore, to the advantage of the Three that the sons do not appear to close the estate. We believe that Dene disappeared, not through his own volition. We know that Stefan and Lans are living in immediate danger. And unless we find Dene and the cross-eyed bear before this date, the estate must remain in the executors' hands. I am here to locate them."

"You want me to help find them."

"Exactly."

She said, "I won't know how to go about it."

"You'll simply do as I say," he told her. He was looking her over carefully. "You'll need clothes. Leave your name and address with Lydia outside. I'll have her mail you a check. Get yourself fixed up before you come back. If you haven't the right taste, put yourself in the hands of someone who knows. There's another thing, but it's up to you entirely. Think it over. Lydia is leaving, and I'd prefer if you'd take her quarters here in the suite. They're on the other side of the office. You are under no compulsion to do so, understand, but it would simplify matters for both of us in making reports and because of my odd hours."

She said, "I'll do it." He didn't know how delighted she would be to be out of the dark room. It would be better, too, to be here at hand where she could hear, see more. The fear she had smelled on first seeing him was almost non-existent now. His being on Viljaas business didn't mean she should necessarily be afraid of him.

"If I need you before next Saturday, I'll send word. If not, report to me then. You'll excuse my not seeing you out."

Her eyes were shiny blue. "Thank you for giving me

a chance, Mr. Folker. I'll work hard. I promise you." She walked out of the room on winged oxfords. She wasn't acting now. It was all too good to be true.

Lydia rose from behind the typewriter; wordless, she brought the coat and hat from the closet. When she handed them over, she said flatly, "He's going to hire you."

Lizanne nodded. She stood in front of the mirror, crammed the brown hat again on her head.

"You're making a mistake."

She turned, looking curiously at this woman. The plain face was unemotional, the voice quiet, conscious of that closed door and the man behind it.

"You think now I'm saying this because I'm disgruntled at your taking my place. You'll find that isn't true. If you'll only take my advice——" She broke off. "You won't, of course." And then she spoke with passion, If you only would, you'd never come near here again. It's dangerous. You're too young to be mixed up in it."

Lizanne had put on her coat. She didn't like this, didn't like its making her uneasy again. She answered, "I'm twenty-two and I'm used to working." She buttoned her coat and spoke again, normally now. "Mr. Folker told me to leave my name and address." She gave it and went out without looking back. The woman's eyes were warning her and she didn't want to be warned. Not with this miracle poured into her hands.

She didn't even want to think. The snow was thick swirls as she walked downtown again, looking into shop windows, keeping her mind empty, as empty as possible. A movie would be best for that. She took the subway up to 110th, better to be near home in such a storm. The mild winter had turned vicious. Again she window-shopped, stopping at the rental library for some mystery books, having a sandwich and cup of chocolate in the drugstore, buying a sack of candy at the confectioner's before entering for first show.

She was at home by nine-thirty; the little room even seemed cozy tonight with snow outside, books to read, tomorrow Sunday and late sleep. She laid her flowered flannelette pajamas on the foot of the bed. She undressed comfortably, hanging the tweed suit where it would shake out as it dried. Stripped, she stood for one brief moment, looking down at her body, looking at that figure branded, etched in acid, there beneath the curve of her left breast. The cross-eyed bear.

Shivering, she put on her pajamas quickly. She wouldn't think about it now. She wouldn't think about anything. She'd read the books and forget. She piled into bed, books, cigarettes, butterscotch at hand.

She wondered who Bill Folker was. She knew what he wanted. And she knew where it was.

The letter was in her box when she returned from work on Monday. She opened it in the little room, stared unbelievably at what it held. Five thousand dollars. For clothes. To get herself fixed up. There was a typewritten list enclosed with suggestions, what to buy, where to buy it. She couldn't spend all of this fortune—yet with two fur coats, the evening clothes, the shops named. . . . Tomorrow, Tuesday. Wednesday, New Year's day; stores closed; a short week to transform herself. Maybe she could take an afternoon off. She couldn't really do all of the shopping in lunch hours this week. She could make a start. And if Mr. Folker would give her some time off, she could finish up after she started to work for him.

Again, she couldn't stay in this room. She could be truly gala tonight even if she spent all of the eight dollars and forty-four cents remaining from last week's paycheck. Tomorrow she would bank this one. Mr. Folker surely wouldn't mind if it fed her this week as well as clothing her. She dressed in her one evening dress, the black velvet coat, this time taxied to the theater. She could afford a good seat now. She was able to get one. She didn't run into Bill Folker or the big ugly man.

After the curtain she didn't know why but she turned without willing it to 53rd street. There was the lighted neon sign, "Jim and Jack's." Monday night, night before New Year's Eve; it shouldn't be too crowded. And it was early as yet. She could pretend she was waiting for her escort, glimpse the pianist. She walked inside. The place was fairly empty, only a few tables occupied, no evening clothes save her own and the orchestral tuxedos. The head-waiter came up to her in the tiny foyer.

She spoke with just the right annoyance, "My friend—evidently hasn't arrived."

"Would you wish a table while you're waiting?"

She hesitated correctly, raised her head, and said, "Yes. Near the music." She followed him, allowed him to hold her chair. The pianist's back was to her.

"Do you care to order?"

She shook her head, then changed her mind. "You might have the boy bring me a glass of Sauterne while I'm waiting."

She had but a few steps to walk from her table to the orchestra platform. She waited until the number was finished, the few dancers returned to their tables. The pianist looked down at her with the blank waiting expression of the orchestra expecting a musical request.

She didn't know what to say. She could scarcely hear her own words. "I wanted to speak to you."

He said, "Yes," and when she still hesitated, repeated, "Yes," without interest.

She half-stammered, "May I ask you a question?"

"Yes." He wasn't helpful.

She couldn't come right out and ask him what she wished to know. Not with his black eyes, familiar eyes, staring at her with complete disinterest She began again, "You look like someone I used to know. Do you mind telling me your name?"

He continued to stare at her out of the black unwavering eyes. When he answered it was rudely, "My name is Vaught. V-A-U-G-H-T. Vaught." Then he deliberately turned his back on her before she could say anything else.

There was nothing to do but return to the table with that abashment brought on by utter failure. Her wine was there. She took a small sip and the music began again. She'd go as soon as she decently could; she couldn't afford to waste money on a second drink. Taxi, theater, now this, had cut down her little wad of bills. Besides she had never liked to drink.

She looked up in honest surprise when the girl came to her table. She was a tawdry little thing, too blonde hair, too curled, a pathetic face. Her body was half-starved but her breasts and buttocks were big beneath the tight black crepe dress with too much tinselly gilt on it. Her lipstick was too orange and too much. She didn't ask if she might sit down; she did, opposite Lizanne.

"You talked to my husband," she stated.

Lizanne's eyes widened. "Yes?" There was only the headwaiter and the pianist to choose between. She questioned, "You're——"

"I'm Sally Vaught." She had a whiny, feminine voice. Surely she was used to women in the club speaking to her husband. Perhaps not women alone.

Lizanne said, "I mistook him for someone else."

"Who did you think he was?"

There seemed no reason not to tell her. "I wondered if he weren't Lans Viljaas."

If the name meant anything, she didn't show it. She said, "He isn't. He's Lans Vaught."

"Lans?"

Sally was defiant. "More than one man has that name. I ought to know who my own husband is. It's on the marriage license."

Lizanne tried to soothe her. "I'm not doubting you. I made the mistake."

It wasn't enough for the girl. She asked, "Who is Lans Viljaas? Do you know him?"

Lizanne shook her head. "I've never laid eyes on him." She wasn't surprised that the pianist had come now to the table, sat down without asking.

Sally said, "I'm asking her who Lans Viljaas is, honey." She put her hand on his coat sleeve but he didn't pay any attention to her. His black eyes, Dene eyes, were on Lizanne's blue ones.

Lizanne explained, "Your wife asked if I knew him. I was telling her I'd never laid eyes on him in all my life."

Lans Vaught took out a pack of Luckies, shoved it to her, and helped himself. Sally waited for hers until he laid the pack on the table.

"Why all the interest then?"

She answered easily, "I'm working for a man who's looking for the brother, Dene Viljaas."

There was a little smile came to Lans's lips.

Sally said, "Maybe that's the man here the other night, hon. The one who thought you was this Viljaas fella." She mispronounced the name.

He ignored her. His stare hadn't left Lizanne's face. She felt uneasy, as if he could see beyond her eyes, enter her thoughts. She had to break the spell. Sally's words weren't doing anything, just spattering unheeded.

She opened her mouth but he spoke first. "You wouldn't mean Stefan Viljaas?"

She said quickly, "No," and she repeated, "No." She was like snow even to hear that name spoken. But she must not allow this cold fright to clench her whenever she heard, or thought, the name. Some day she must face him; when the time came it must be in angry courage, not in fear. And she didn't need to worry about it now; he was in Sweden. She said quietly, "No, I'm working for Bill Folker. Do you know him?"

He still wore that little smile and his eyes were inscrutable. "Never heard of him."

The orchestra had gathered again on the platform, were stirring cacophony of notes. Lans Vaught stood up. So did Sally Vaught. Lans leaned to Lizanne's chair. He was deliberately offensive. It was scrawled on his face. "Does Folker pay you for your night work?"

Fury came over her at the insinuation but he only laughed and went back to the piano. The wife hadn't heard. She'd returned to the table in the corner, looking sulkily across at Lizanne, as if Lizanne were as beautiful and glamorous as Bill Folker wished her to be.

Lizanne marched into the foyer, shut herself in the telephone booth, called Folker. She demanded violently, "Can you join me?"

He was a little skeptical. "Who is me?"

She had forgotten. He wouldn't know her voice. "It's Lizanne Steffasson. I'm at Jim and Jack's."

"You've met up with Viljaas?"

"He says he isn't."

There was a moment's hesitation. "You'd better come up here. I shouldn't risk it going out at this hour."

She didn't return to her table. She spoke to the same man who had ushered her in. "Will you get my wrap and call a cab for me? My friend is unable to come." She gave him one of the last of her precious dollars. But the pale green paper folded in her bag, marked in four figures, reassured her. The man handed her into her coat, said, "One moment, if you please. I get the cab."

He stepped to the door; she kept her back turned to where music sounded. She twirled to the voice. The pianist stood at her shoulder; he'd left his instrument. He asked, "Can you meet me after we close up?"

She answered with finality, "No."

He persisted, "It might be a good idea."

The man had returned. "Your cab, Miss."

Lans Vaught said, "In a minute, Jim," and waved him away. He asked again, "Will you?"

"You're not Lans Viljaas?"

"No."

"Then I don't see where it would help me any to talk with you." She started to the door. He followed, put his hand on her arm. She shook it off quickly. "My cab is waiting."

He didn't argue. But he told her, "It might be wiser if you would talk to me. I might know some things you'd like to know."

She went on into the night, directed the driver, "The

Lorenzo." Lans had Dene's eyes despite his denials.

Lydia opened the door for her, just as if it were day, not almost two in the morning. She said flatly, "You're to go in."

Bill Folker was pleasant. It was foolish to have that momentary gulp of panic every time she came to his door. She didn't know why she had come. Because a piano player in a cheap night club had been insulting.

She said, "I'm sorry I bothered you at this hour. I didn't realize how late it was. I'd been to the theater and I stopped at Jim and Jack's."

"You met the pianist?"

"I asked him if he were Lans Viljaas and he denied it. His wife denied it."

"He has a wife?" This seemed news to him.

"Yes. She said his name is Lans Vaught, on the marriage license." She leaned forward. "But he knows something, Mr. Folker."

He took a drink. "What makes you think that?"

She couldn't mention Dene's eyes. She fumbled, "I think he's a Viljaas."

Bill relaxed comfortably. "I'm sure of it. I wonder if he has the bear."

She didn't say anything. She was listening to noise in that outer room, the office room. It couldn't be Lydia flinging open a door, banging a door, raising her voice tyrannously. Lizanne looked curiously at Bill. There was something of surprise, of annoyance on his face, mingled with a disturbing anger and a surprising resignation.

The door between was flung wide. It wasn't Lydia, not the girl who stood swaying in the doorway, although there was a glimpse of the plain woman's face, frightened and apologetic, behind this one.

Bill said, "It's all right, Lydia. Go on back to bed," and to the newcomer, "Well, Alix."

She was superb. She was what he must have been asking for in "Wanted, a beautiful girl." Tall, she was easily as high as Bill Folker's shoulder; her body long and narrow, not hidden, not meant to be hidden, in the swathe of silver cloth tight from breasts to heel. Her hair, pale, almost powdered gold, was cut like a little boy's, ringleted all over her head, with a forelock falling to one golden eyebrow. Only a woman with perfection of face and feature, with perfection of throat and shoulder, would dare wear her hair cropped that short. As she swayed there, her eyes, colorless and cold as ice circlets, saw Lizanne. She demanded, "Who is that?"

Bill hadn't risen from his couch. His hands were tight to the arms, so tight his knuckles were bleached. But he answered quietly, "This is my secretary."

"And what is Lydia?" the girl cried insolently. She took a step into the room, letting the sable coat slide from her shoulders to the floor, slide and remain there, regal fur sprawled on the white and maroon rug.

He didn't answer her. He began, "If you'll just wait for a few moments in the other room, Alix, until Miss Steffasson and I finish our conference——"

"Conference!" she laughed shrilly. "Conference at two in the morning! I know you too well—you and women." Her eyes narrowed. "I won't go," she stated. She took another step, swayed again.

Lizanne knew his rage; it was in his hands, biting the white stuff of the chaise. It was in his eyes suddenly gone saffron. She was frightened at it. But she couldn't let the woman fall on her face here. He didn't stir.

She sprang up, said, "Sit here."

26

The woman mocked, "Lovely manners the child has. Who sold her to you?" She was deliberately insulting, as Lans Vaught had been, but she made it to the chair, swayed into it. She said, "You might give me a drink, Bill. You might say you're glad to see me. I've come straight to you." Even if she were drunk, there was something pathetic in the way she looked at Bill Folker.

He said without emotion, "You've had too much to drink. Where are you staying?"

She cried out, as if she were imparting a delightful surprise, "Here, darling!"

Still without emotion he said, "Not here. Where are your things?"

She wasn't so certain now. "Below. In the lobby."

"You'd better go to your apartment." He threw off the maroon rug and stood quietly. "Lizanne, call the desk. Ask them to get a cab for Mrs. Tinker. She will be down immediately." He put his fingers on Alix's upper arm. His voice said as quietly, "I'll come to you as soon as I'm free, Alix," but his knuckles were still colorless and she came out of the chair with her face gone ivory.

He was walking her toward the door. He said, "Pick up your coat and put it on." He didn't help her. He went out of the room with her and Lizanne replaced the phone. She came back to the chair and sat down again. She was cold as if the winter outside were in the room. Bill Folker's yellow eyes had held hate worse than any hate she'd seen.

She heard the outer door open, close. She sat with her hands clenched. She wanted to slip out, run away. She'd been right to be afraid of him. She knew it now that she had seen his eyes go amber, seen his fingers turn to pincers. She jumped when she heard a key turning; not

27

in that connecting door but the one leading to the corridor. She jumped and turned and stood there facing it, her hands tight together.

It wasn't Bill Folker who came in. It was the big ugly man who had been his companion at the theater.

She shivered but she stood without moving.

He was surprised to see her. His eyebrows winged. "Who are you?" He might have asked: Who the hell are you? He said it in that way.

She piped, "I'm Lizanne Steffasson," and then she knew that meant nothing. "I'm Mr. Folker's secretary."

He asked, "What about Lydia?" even as Alix had.

She didn't have to answer that for Bill Folker came in again. He walked to the small bar and poured himself half a tumbler of liquor, swallowed it before he spoke.

The ugly man waited until Bill set down the glass, then he began to take off his overcoat. "She's out again," he said.

Bill said, "You're a little late, Guard."

"She's been here?"

"I just ran her off."

The man called Guard flung his coat and hat on another white chair and poured himself a drink. "The irresistible Mr. Folker. What did she want?"

"Me, I gather."

Guard's laugh was sudden and boisterous. It stopped when he drank.

Bill Folker sat down but he didn't recline. He muttered, "She'd better stay away from me. She has to stay away from me. I haven't time for her now."

Guard roared again.

Bill looked up at him. "Tell her that."

"Tell her yourself," Guard said, and he bobbed his

28

head toward Lizanne as if she were a doll that couldn't understand. "Who's this kid that says she's your secretary?"

Bill said, "I forgot. Miss Steffasson." His smile turned charm on her just as if she hadn't seen anything that had taken place. "My friend, Mr. Croyden. Guard Croyden. Miss Steffasson is my secretary."

Guard didn't acknowledge the introduction. Instead he repeated, this time to Bill, "What about Lydia?"

"She's leaving me of her free will."

It was strange, that little trickle of apprehension that suddenly set on Guard Croyden's harsh mouth, but Bill's eyes were looking into his and it went away.

Guard took another drink. "I'm not keeping you, Bill?"

There was almost a flush on Bill Folker's cheekbones when he answered, "Not at all."

"You're not going to her?" It was mockery.

He seemed abashed. "Yes."

"What would Fredi say?"

"She isn't here." He half apologized, as if to himself. "I told Alix I'd come. If I don't, she'll return here. You know Alix."

"Yes." Only a syllable, but Guard Croyden's mouth tightened and he poured still another drink.

Lizanne wished they would remember she was there. She was growing sleepy. She wanted to go home. Besides she didn't belong in this. It was something between these two men and the beautiful swaying woman.

Then Guard said, and his voice was ugly as his face, "Yes. I know Alix. Sure, I know Alix. She's beautiful— my God, she's beautiful. Even if she weren't beautiful, she——" His teeth clamped.

And Bill said dryly, "She's not that good."

Guard was belligerent. "She is, and you damn well know it, Bill Folker." .

Bill ignored that, turning to Lizanne just as if there'd been no interruption in their conversation. "Do you think you might strike up a sort of—friendship with these Vaughts?"

She couldn't stand either of them nor they her.'She answered finally, "If it's part of the job, yes."

"Call it that." .

"There's one thing." She hesitated. "Someone will have to escort me. I can't keep going in there alone. Tonight I pretended I was waiting for a friend."

He thought it over. "I'll find somebody. I can't figure in this. Even if I could get around."

Guard asked, "What about Dinky? He's asked to help out, finding Dene."

Bill said, "Yes. It's about as much as Dink could do." He was thinking about it. "It wouldn't hurt to have him around. Dene may have given him the cross-eyed bear, or told him where it was."

The phone made a dull coppery sound. Lizanne should have realized that it would be Alix. The voice was insolent, "So you're still there. Inform *Mister* Folker I am on the phone."

Guard was saying, "Maybe. He was Dene's best friend. He may have joined him up north."

"But there was a girl with Dene."

"Dene didn't like girls."

"There's a girl figures in it somewhere, Guard. I know that." He saw Lizanne.

They didn't know her panic. She made her dry throat sound. "It's—it is she." She didn't know what to call her.

30

Bill strode to the phone. He said only monosyllables, and then, "I'm coming right away."

Guard said to Lizanne, "We might as well go home. The party's over."

She answered curtly to hide fear, "It's no party. I work here." She wasn't going with him. She was afraid. But she wouldn't let him know.

He looked at her for a moment. "Where do you live?"

She wouldn't tell him but his face commanded answer. After all, there wasn't any real reason for her fear, just because he looked like a killer didn't mean he was. And he didn't know she'd seen him before. There was no use being foolish; she hadn't enough money left for a taxi home; it was cold and late for the subway.

"West One Hundred Eighteenth street." She stated the number as he waited for it.

"I'll take you up." Before she could say anything, he said, "A kid can't go running around at this hour of the morning alone."

"I'm not a kid," was all she could say. She tried to say it with protest just as if she didn't fear those shoulders. She mustn't forget to play the part with him, too. She could do it with Bill Folker, even in the moments of panic. Because this man was more terrifying to her, she mustn't let herself forget the role.

Bill had coat and hat out of a hidden closet. "Come around tomorrow, Guard." He turned to Lizanne. "I'll get in touch with Dinky. He's in Washington. I'll send word to you." He went out the corridor door, leaving her there with Guard Croyden.

Guard took her velvet coat from the chair. "This yours?" She nodded. He held it for her, said, "Come on."

She repeated, "I'm no child. You needn't take me

home." It was absurd to hesitate. She couldn't just sit here while he waited. She had to obey. But she would rather take the subway.

She said nothing in the elevator nor in the cab. She didn't want to talk to him. He directed the driver, "Skip the park. Go over and up Broadway to One Hundred Eighteenth street." He spoke the number she had given.

The streets were almost deserted; dirty snow, like sleeping ghosts, was piled against the curbs on upper Broadway. At the apartment he told the driver, "Wait."

She said, "You needn't go in."

"I'm going."

You couldn't argue with the bulk of Guard Croyden. But surely if he'd been going to do anything to her he wouldn't have brought her here.

He started to the elevator. She told him, "It stops running at twelve."

"What floor are you?"

"Fifth."

He took her arm and walked with her to the narrow twisting ascent of the staircase. Silently they climbed until they were in the dim lighted hallway outside her door. She took out her key, inserted it.

He asked, "How do you come to know Bill?"

She was surprised. "Bill Folker?"

"Yes."

"I don't know him."

"Then what are you doing with him?"

She didn't understand any of this. "I told you. He told you. I'm working for him."

"Who steered you on to the job?"

She flared back, "I answered an ad." She was suddenly furious and she wasn't afraid of him now. Besides her door was open. Why should he be questioning her? What reason had he to be suspicious of her?

He stared down at her. It looked as if he wanted to laugh. "That fool ad!" But there was still suspicion when he said, "How did you happen to land the job?"

"I don't know." Actually she didn't. She hadn't qualified, not even to Bill Folker, yet she had succeeded where the hotel clerk's trail of mentioned beauties had failed. She felt a little chill again travel up her spine.

He was still staring at her. "You're sure you didn't know Bill Folker before?"

She met his eyes with her round china blue ones. "I answered that once. If you've any more questions you'll have to save them, Mr. Croyden. I must be at work at nine in the morning. I can't talk here all night." She pushed open the door, went inside, and without saying good night closed it in his face.

She wasn't quite so sure now of what she was getting into. Tonight had been—somewhat upsetting. Not that she had any intention of walking out on the bargain. She would stick until she found out who killed Dene.

Chapter Two: THE MARK ON HER BODY

THE TEXAS girl who studied music came to the doorway. She said, "Sammie told us you were leaving." Sammie was the San Juan hill negress who did the rooms. She was the carrier pigeon between the flabby landlady, two flights below, and the tenants.

The music girl's name was Janet. She wasn't missing anything, from the beaver coat and hood on the chair, to the shimmering shell satin of the nightdresses folded on the bed. You couldn't carry flannelette to The

Lorenzo.

"You have a better job?"

"Much better," Lizanne nodded. "Private secretary to a writer with a weak heart."

"Where are you moving to?"

It seemed wise to tell her, that someone in New York might know her whereabouts, if only an almost stranger. "The Lorenzo."

Janet whistled. "Some people do have luck," and she added, "Your room's already rented. How she does it I don't know. The prices she asks for these holes."

Lizanne said, "I hope it will be a lucky move." She couldn't tell this stranger her panic over going there. But she'd burned bridges, spending his money.

Sunday to move. Lizanne hadn't heard from Bill Folker. There'd been no answer to her call Saturday. She called again now from the pay phone in the inner hallway. She knew Lydia's flat voice.

Mr. Folker was out. Lydia said, 'I'm moving my things. You can come in whenever you like."

Lizanne told her, "I'll be down this afternoon."

She bathed for the last time in the depressing old tub, dressed in the new cinnamon wool, severe, bracketed at the throat with the cedar clip set with what looked like diamonds. She felt better about it, seeing herself. The hotel had said that Mr. Folker was all right. No need for her to retain this nervousness because he knew Guard Croyden or because his eyes had turned yellow in rage.

It was nearing five o'clock before the transfer had carried away the new luggage and she took a cab for the hotel. No one bade her good-by. The girls were out with some of their young men; the old lady who opened cans of soup was never seen.

The door of the office was unlocked, and this time the door to Bill Folker's living room was ajar. She walked toward it. She wasn't particularly quiet but her entrance was unnoted. Bill Folker was holding Lydia's wrist, her face was wrenched with pain, certainly of that hold, for her other hand was attempting to free herself. And again his eyes were saffron. His voice: "If you think you're going to cause any trouble——"

Her almost anguished: "I wouldn't. Bill, you know I wouldn't. I won't."

Lizanne backed away. But she knew one thing then. She would walk softly with Bill Folker. She steadied herself and called out as if she'd just entered, as if she were as young and stupid as they evidently all believed, "Miss Lydia—Miss Lydia——"

Silence, and then Bill Folker, tall, charming in smile, appeared in the doorway. He looked her over from hat to toes. She didn't move. His eyes seemed to see the new satin against her body, even beneath the satin. But of course that was absurd.

"Hello, Lizanne. Lydia told me you phoned. I don't think your luggage has come yet."

He was talking on until Lydia came out, ugly pepper-and-salt coat buttoned, plain hat accenting her plain face. Her eyes looked red. Glove and coat-sleeve hid her left wrist; she favored it against her side. Lizanne wondered if he'd broken it; she remembered his fingers on the chaise arms.

The woman said, "Here are the keys, Miss Steffasson. This one locks your connecting door and this is for your corridor door." There was almost warning in the impact with which she spoke. She laid the four, tied together with a blue ribbon, in Lizanne's palm. "This is for the

office, and this"—she just glanced in Bill's direction—
"this is for Mr. Folker's suite in case he needs you to work
in there when he's away." She hesitated, spoke again, but
her voice was flat as ever. "I wish you luck."

Bill Folker shook the woman's right hand. "And I
wish you luck, Lydia." It was almost impossible to believe that there had been that glimpse.

She went away, heavily, without looking back. She
was like a hired girl, like a farm woman. There was
something sad in the way her shoulders hung.

Bill turned back to Lizanne. He was casual, just the
right employer-to-secretary voice. "You'll probably want
to look over your quarters. If there's anything doesn't
suit, let me know and I'll have it changed." He glanced
at the keys in her hand. "For obvious reasons, I prefer
that all the doors entering into the corridor be kept
locked. That includes the office, unless you are working
in the room." He moved to his own door. "I'm expecting to hear from Guard Croyden at any minute. He
planned to bring Dinky Bruce up from Washington
today. When they arrive I want you to meet Bruce."

She nodded, waited for him to leave, then used the
first key. Remembering the woman's voice, look, she
made certain that the door was fast after her.

She was surprised at the luxury. She hadn't envisioned
Lydia in anything but the plainest surroundings. This
was not bed and bath but first a sitting room, golden
wood, for contrast bright splashes of peacock, a couch
throw, glazed figurines. A tiny kitchenette opening from
it was complete, icebox well stocked, staples on the
shelves, a small dumbwaiter for disposal. The bedroom
was satin in white and gold, beyond a bath-dressing
room. Enormous closets, not a little cubbyhole hidden

by a soiled and faded curtain. There were only two doors to the outside, both in the living room, one to the corridor, one to the office.

There was no trace of a Lydia in these rooms. She must have lived on top of them. These were Alix rooms. She stopped short on that. Maybe they were Alix's originally; maybe that was the warning, against a jealous woman, not against something else. It was strange how uninhabited the suite was, as if no one had ever slept within. She walked through again, throwing open the closets, looking for a trace of someone, but there was nothing.

She looked out of the window; ten stories below lay Central Park, stripped gray, untidy snow like faded beggars at the entrance. She shivered; anything better than a park bench in this weather. And this fairyland suite, even if it weren't for long; it was worth looking into "danger's bright face."

It was almost seven o'clock before she was summoned. Guard Croyden opened the door of Bill Folker's suite. His greeting was commonplace but he spoke it as if it were mockery. "Good evening, Miss Steffasson." She didn't answer; she didn't like him and she was afraid of him.

The small bar beside Bill stood open and all three men held iced glasses. The third man was young, his legs hung over the arm of the oyster-white chair and one long hand trailed down to the rug. He was probably as tall as the other two, his too-long legs and arms showed that. His head was a little small for his length, and the bold eyes he turned on her were cobalt, the lashes darkly fringed as a girl's. His face was beautiful, too beautiful for a man. Lizanne didn't like him either.

Guard said, "Haven't you any manners, Dinky? Get

up and say how'd'do to Miss Steffasson."

He unfolded, said in a honeyed voice, "How d'ye do, Miss Steffasson," and resumed his posture. He'd had too much to drink.

Bill said, "This is Dinky Bruce whom I promised you. I didn't expect him in this shape."

The boy winked at Lizanne. She tried to keep her lip from curling. He said, "I'm your gigolo or chauffeur—somepin. My God, how about putting something in this glass, Guard? It tastes like old soup."

Guard took the glass, splashed it, and handed it back.

Bill looked at his watch. "You're supposed to take Lizanne out to dinner—if you think you can make it."

Dinky swallowed, made a gargoyle of his beautiful face, and said, "This tastes worse. What are you giving me—a Keeley?" He rose on unsteady, cranelike legs. "Sure, I can make it. Give me ten minutes, Miss Steffasson, and I'll be sober as a judge, sober enough to fool a judge anyway." He weaved to the far door, went beyond it.

Bill looked at her. "I apologize for him, Lizanne. You needn't go out with him unless you wish. But I thought you might try Jim and Jack's again."

Guard said, "Dinky can sober up quicker than any cub I ever met. He knows a trick or two."

Bill lifted his head. "Lizanne spoke with Lans Vaught last week, Guard. Also his wife. Did you know he had a wife?"

"Heard he married some little chippie out of a hash-house or honkytonk or something."

"He denies he's Viljaas, naturally."

"He doesn't look much like Lans," Guard admitted.

"A man changes in six years. He was just a college kid

then, eighteen. He isn't scrawny now and he's learned to comb his hair but he's Lans all right."

"What's Lizanne's place in the picture?"

"She's going to get acquainted with the Vaughts—if she can. At any rate, she and Dinky are going to be Jim and Jack's habitués trying. It's too bad he hasn't a job at a better spot. You say the girl invaded you, Lizanne?"

"Yes." She repeated the story. He evidently wanted Guard to know everything. Then she asked, "And after we're acquainted?"

"There's two things we want to know. Has he the cross-eyed bear——"

"He must have it," Guard stated.

"And has he heard from or of Dene in the past two years." Bill handed his glass over to Guard.

Guard said, "There are a few things Miss Steffasson should learn about the Viljaas tribe, or does she know?" He was sending out a feeler.

She answered it defiantly. "I don't know anything at all about them except what Mr. Folker told me the other day about the legacy. And except for seeing the picture in the paper of Knut Viljaas when he died."

"Then you ought to know more," Guard told her. He handed Bill's glass back refilled. "Why we're so interested in identifying Lans, for instance."

"Why are you?"

"Chiefly because we think he knows something of Dene, perhaps can even lead us to Dene. You see, Miss Steffasson, Stefan was fifteen years older than Lans while there was scarcely a year between Lans and Dene. Those two were close friends while Stefan was hardly more than a stranger to them. There were different mothers, which explains the age gap."

39

She nodded.

"Lans ran away from home when he was eighteen. He didn't return even when old Knut died, but Dene was in touch with him. We know that. It was he who gave the address where Lans's part of the check might be sent."

"If you know all this," Lizanne looked from one to the other, "why don't you know whether he was sent the cross-eyed bear?"

Bill answered, "Old Knut turned against all at the end, suspicious of everyone. Only one executor was to know who received the stamp, the steel die of the bear. This was Knut's safeguard in order that the three brothers wouldn't try to do each other out of their share of the check."

She frowned. "I don't understand."

"In plain words, lady," Guard stated, "the Old Bear expected the brothers to try to murder each other to keep from sharing the estate."

"I should think a million dollars would be enough." She spoke with real conviction.

Guard laughed without mirth. "You don't know the Viljaas tribe." His laugh came again, louder, more real.

Bill agreed softly. "What he says is true. Knut's fortune was a bloody one from scratch. The sons weren't much different from the old man."

She shivered and she said, "But Lans wouldn't kill Dene, would he? If they were dear to each other?"

"Only for money," Guard said. "Only for money, Lizanne."

Again she shivered.

Guard laughed. "You don't like that, do you, Miss? Remember the ad, you can't be afraid of danger."

Bill's voice was kind. "Lizanne admits she is afraid of

40

danger, Guard, but she doesn't run away from it."

She thanked him out of round blue eyes, and then she narrowed them. This was fronting danger and deliberately. She said, "I don't see where you two figure in this."

Guard thrust his hands into his pocket, leaned back comfortably, almost insolently. "Because, my little lady, I work for the government, the United States Government, to be exact. I'm a Fed."

She didn't believe it. If it were true, it was puzzling.

"You don't get it. Well, when anyone as important as Dene Viljaas disappears, and when anyone as important as Ambassador Tedford Bruce wants to find him, sometimes they commission a special deputy just on that job."

"Speaking of Pa?" Dinky Bruce had returned, black curly hair damp, sobriety in his dark-fringed eyes.

"Sit down and shut up, Dinky," Guard said. "We're explaining a few things to the new secretary. Now where was I?"

She spoke up. "Why does Ambassador Bruce want to find him?"

"Well, after two years, he's afraid of foul play, to tell you the truth. Besides he must close the estate by April first. That is why he's in this country now instead of on duty in Sweden. He's the senior executor, unfortunately not the one who held the secret."

Dinky giggled. "Knut knew his stuff. He told only old Jem March, president of the National, you know, and he died without leaving one sign of who might have the bear."

"No one else knew?" she queried.

"I'm the third executor," Guard stated. "I can assure you neither Teddie nor I have the least idea who got it.

It was an unwritten secret between March and Viljaas."

"And your part in this?" She turned to Bill.

He was relaxed against the back of his couch. "I represent Stefan Viljaas' interests. I could show you a little badge from the Finnish government, if I weren't too lazy to walk to my bedroom and get it. They're also interested. Viljaas mines are practically inoperative while the estate remains open as it does. And what with war needs, the government doesn't like that. You can see why Dene must be found."

If she told them where he was lying, where he had been at rest for two years—but they weren't telling the whole truth no matter how well authenticated what they had to say. These were half-truths. It wasn't Dene they wanted to find; it was the cross-eyed bear. They didn't need Dene if they had the bear. She couldn't trust them; they were Stefan's men.

She stood up from her chair. "Then all I'm to do now is try to find out if Lans is a Viljaas."

"That's easy," Dinky drawled. He walked to the bar, looked down at it, but didn't touch nor ask. "All you have to do is catch him with his pants down and give a look."

She flared, "I'm not that kind! If that's why I'm—"

Bill was beside her, calming. "He'll apologize, Lizanne. You've made a real mistake, Dink."

The boy actually looked abashed. His cheeks were like holly. "I'm sorry. I didn't know."

Guard said, "We all make mistakes. You'd better accept the apology, Lizanne. No use having a fight with your escort. You're going to be seeing too much of him."

She nodded her head. "As you say. I'll get my coat." She went across to her rooms. Someone was in the bedroom; she could hear. She opened that door.

A young hotel maid smiled, unstartled. "Mr. Folker ask that I unpack while you are out, Miss Steffasson. I am Anna." Her accent was slight. She was small and a little plump; her black hair banged. She kept her eyes held down the way a feudal servant might.

Lizanne smiled in return. "Thank you." If he were interested in her belongings, there would be nothing to report; they were as impersonal as this suite, completely without signature.

She put on beaver coat and hood, took up gloves and bag, but she didn't leave. She stood quietly there watching the maid at her work. She had to still a sudden rising of incomprehensible fear of these men before she dared return to that other room.

The night club was almost empty as before; the same headwaiter at the door. Lizanne said as she had that first night, "Near the orchestra."

He was at the piano, his back turned, but there must have been the same signal pass from him to the blonde wife at the far table. She came across the floor, tight in electric blue rayon, her behind swaying. She sat down, unmasked as before, and said, "You haven't been around lately," to Lizanne. Her eyes slid to Dinky in what was meant to be sex appeal.

His mouth was humorous. "Do I know your friend, Lizanne?"

"Sally Vaught. Mrs. Vaught, Mr. Bruce."

"You'll join us in a drink?"

She answered, "Delighted," and rolled her eyes up at him. "Scotch and ginger ale."

He looked almost nauseated as he repeated the order

to the waiter. "Lizanne?"

"Vermouth. And let's order dinner now." She didn't want him to start drinking again.

He said, "Ballantine's and soda," added: "Send someone around who knows what the chef does well with food." Then he turned his attention to Sally. "You work here?"

"My husband does." She spoke with pride. "He's the pianist."

"Will he join us for a drink?"

"He don't drink when he's working." More pride. She suggested, "Maybe after he's through. We close early Sundays—midnight."

Lizanne wondered. There must have been prearrangement. Sally Vaught hadn't thought that up alone, no matter how her eyes coveted Dinky Bruce. It would be a long wait. But this wasn't amusement; it was a job.

The girl had done her part. But she didn't leave the table. She had her drink for excuse and she was fascinated with Dinky Bruce's face. She must have been; her eyes didn't turn from it.

Lizanne made conversation; it wouldn't sound like more than that to Sally. "Do you always stay here at the club while your husband's working?"

Sally sighed into Dinky's eyes. "It's dull, but it's not so bad as sitting around a hotel room all alone."

He gave her back the look and murmured, "What hotel?"

She named a cheap one on 44th street, giggled, "Room eight fifty-seven, Mr. Bruce."

He didn't answer that, said, "Of course, you'll join us for dinner, Mrs. Vaught—Sally?"

She giggled again. "I've eaten. But that was a long time

ago, before we came over to the club. I guess I could stand some more."

He was ordering, said, "Finish your drink, Lizanne."

She shook her head, "No more for me," heard him double his own and Sally Vaught's orders.

He turned to her, "Don't look so sour, Lizanne. I won't pass out on you, not yet." He winked again at Sally Vaught and she giggled in delight.

Lizanne said no more. Of course Sally thought she was being sulky because her escort was interested in someone else. It didn't matter what the girl thought.

Dinky came to his feet, pretended unfeigned surprise and delight when Lans stood at the table.

Lans said quietly, "Hello, Dinky," and spoke to Lizanne. "You came back. I thought you would."

She stared up at him. "Not because I wanted to."

He sat in the other chair, between her and Dinky. "Who's your friend, Dink?"

"You haven't met?" Dinky was surprised. "Lizanne Steffasson—Lans Vaught."

She didn't understand anything. If Dinky and Lans were friends, why was she needed here?

Sally pouted, "Lans, I didn't know you knew Mr. Bruce."

He said nastily, "We were suckled by the same wolf," and turned his back on her. "Are you running off tonight, Miss Steffasson?"

He knew she couldn't endure him, yet that she had to play up. "Not tonight."

Sally was spattering words at Dinky, he bending his head to hers. Lans spoke under his breath, "Can you shake him?"

"Perhaps."

"I haven't time to argue. Can you?"

She retorted, "With your wife's help."

He nodded; her tone of insult didn't seem to bother him any. "Meet me at the side entrance at quarter of twelve. Sally will keep him here." He touched Dinky's shoulder, "See you," and went back to the piano.

Dinky broke in on the girl's chatter. "Were you married once to Dene?"

Sally's amazement wasn't pretense. She would never consciously allow a man to see her with her mouth flabby that way. She answered with heat, "I've never been married to no one but Lans. Never! Who is this Dene?" Her tongue was even unfamiliar on the name.

Dinky laughed. "Dene Viljaas. An old friend of mine. I think your husband knew him, too. Ask him sometime. I just thought you looked something like the girl he was supposed to have married."

Sally asked, "Why is everybody so interested in those Viljaas fellas?" Dinky ignored her question.

None of them knew if Dene really had married. None of them knew what his wife was like. They'd never seen her. But they were suspicious. Something had given them a hint.

Dinky was getting tight again. "How long you been tied up with him?" His head nodded to the pianist.

Sally wasn't quite at ease, as if she didn't know where this was leading; or was it that she didn't want questions? She answered with truculence, "I've got a license and I got a ring, see?" The cheap white-gold band was embossed with too much fancy work.

Dinky grinned. "I'm not doubting you. I'm just asking how long a cute kid like you has put up with a ball and chain?"

She liked that. "We been married two and a half years."

Time for eating. Dally over food. Dinky mustn't get bored, want to leave. But he didn't seem bored. He was annoyingly cute with the cheap little blonde. He danced with her and batted his curly eyelashes at her. Lizanne watched the time, cautiously, but if she'd stood the watch in front of her on the table those two wouldn't have noticed. They continued drinking, babbling. At eleven-thirty Lizanne said, "I'm going to the ladies' room." They still ignored her. She kept her coat around her shoulders as if she were chilly. She took ten minutes then went into the foyer again. She could see the two in the far room, their glasses in hand. Dinky's back was to the arched entrance.

Lans was already at the side door. He didn't look like a Viljaas if you ignored his eyes; he looked like a musician, navy overcoat fitted too tightly above his hips, soft black hat. He said, "Come on."

They went out into the cold night, down one step into an areaway. She walked beside him, not out to 53rd but to 54th. He said, "I can't take you to the hotel; Sally's having Dink there. I can't take you talking in a cab, costs too much. Do you have any ideas?"

She answered, "No." She didn't want this discussion conducted under the possible ears of Guard Croyden or even Bill Folker.

He said, "I want a cup of coffee." They had walked to Columbus Circle, went into the unembellished Childs on the corner. He led to the farthest rear table, away from the window. He fished out cigarettes and ordered, "Two cups coffee," then he asked, "Why did you come back?"

"I changed my mind."

He looked at her. "You or Bill?"

She didn't answer that. "I want to know everything possible about the Viljaases."

"You think I know about them?"

He had a gift of angering her.

"You boasted that you did." She said it defiantly. "You're Lans Viljaas."

"I'm Lans Vaught." His hand touched hers suddenly across the table. "Remember that. Don't ever forget it. I'm Lans Vaught."

She asked simply, "Why?"

He didn't speak right away, not until the waitress had deposited the cups of coffee, until his was creamed and sugared, stirred; the spoon held vertically. But he would have waited anyway. She knew that. He was thinking it over.

His answer startled her. "Because I don't want to be murdered as Dene was."

She tried to look as a stranger would with such a statement flung in his face. She didn't know if she succeeded. She asked, choosing words with caution, "You think Dene is dead—murdered?"

He laughed at her. "My God, what do you think?"

She said, "I don't know anything about it."

"You just work here," he jeered. "A'right. I won't argue with you. If you don't believe me, ask your boss."

She looked up quickly at him. "You do know Bill Folker."

"I told you I didn't. I don't want to. And if you came down tonight to arrange a meeting, the answer is no."

"I didn't," she reassured him. But, no matter what Lans said, he did know Bill; knew, furthermore, that he represented Stefan. He was afraid to meet Bill. She asked, "Do you have proof that Dene is dead?"

"What do you mean, proof? If your—if someone you knew as well as yourself disappeared without a word—of course, he's dead."

She looked into his eyes. "Who do you think killed him?"

The answer came without hesitation. "Stefan, of course."

"But why?"

Lans looked at her as if she were a stupid child. "To get Dene's part of the check—and the cross-eyed bear." His eyes narrowed. "But something slipped."

"What do you mean?"

He smiled now. "Maybe he got the check, maybe he got the bear. He didn't get both."

Again she asked, "How do you know?"

"Because," he spoke deliberately, "because he would have killed me before now if he had all the pieces of the jigsaw except mine. Even if he doesn't know where mine is, and that's no secret, if you're packing this information away in your pretty head to relay to Folker. It's in storage, in a good safe vault. There's a letter there, too, and a will; if anything happens to me the triangle goes to my wife, and then she'll have to be murdered." He grinned now. "Oh, there's endless possibilities for death before that little scrap of paper can get into Stefan's hands."

She listened, no more than that. When he'd finished, she asked, "Do you have the cross-eyed bear?"

His eyes revealed nothing, too black for revelation. "That's for Stefan to find out. But remember, if anyone asks, my name is Lans Vaught." He picked up the check. "I've talked too much tonight. Maybe I've been wrong, but I think it's time someone warned him. And as you're working for Bill Folker"—he emphasized the word—"what's your name again——"

"Lizanne Steffasson."

"All right, Lizanne Steffasson. Maybe you'll have a chance to tell him."

Her eyes met his; she tried to keep the fear from them. Stefan must be on his way to New York. She would meet him if she kept this job. She'd keep it; she wouldn't flee again. It was what she wanted, to face the man; she wouldn't let terror interfere.

Again they went out into the night; this time he hailed a cab, gave the West 44th street hotel address, told her, "You can pick up your date at my room. Sally should have him there by now."

He spoke again as they left the elevator on the eighth floor. "If you're as innocent as you make out, Lizanne Steffasson, you'd better get yourself a new job before it's too late." Lightly, he added, putting key in lock, "Or don't ever pretend you weren't warned."

Dinky sat in the ugly olive-colored chair. He was asleep, or near enough, his mouth open. Sally was curled on the ugly painted brass bed; she looked cross and her eyes were sagging from drinks and lack of sleep. She complained, "It took you long enough."

"We had enough to talk about," Lans answered curtly. He walked over and shook Dinky's shoulder. "Wake up. Come on, wake up. You have to take Lizanne home."

Dinky blinked his eyes. "I'm awake." His voice was thick as mush. "I'm awake."

Lans hadn't removed his coat. He said now, "If Dink can't make it——"

She spoke quickly. "He'll be all right." She didn't want

Lans to take her home. She didn't want him to know her address was The Lorenzo. Unaccountably she didn't want him to think that his insinuations were right. She coaxed, "You're all right, aren't you, Dinky?"

"Sure I am." He stood on his feet, surprisingly didn't waver. He opened his eyes now, wide and blue. "Nothing like a little nap," he said. "G'night, Mrs. Vaught. A pleasant evening. G'night, Lans."

Lizanne trailed after him out the door. He didn't speak until they were in the cab. "I wasn't asleep," he said. "Only you were so long and she was such a frightful bore, and she wanted me to make her." That was all he said until they were in The Lorenzo going up in the elevator. "How Lans could ever marry that." He sounded fastidiously annoyed. He saw her to her door, said, "Good night."

She locked the door after him, heard his steps cross to the other suite, heard him enter. She pleasured in a return to beautiful surroundings as she crossed to the satin bedroom. She undressed in almost catlike luxury, wondering again at that unaccountable moment when she knew that even if she'd had to put Dinky in a cold shower, Lans should not see her home. There was no answer to why she didn't want him to know. He was like Dene, yes, but she hadn't loved Dene. Not after that night. She shivered a little, drew the satin nightdress over her shoulders before dropping her slip to the floor.

She gathered her clothes, took her dress and coat to the closet to hang away, pulled the white satin cord of the closet light. There was no premonition to look up, to step quickly backward. There must have been a faint slissing sound. She did raise her eyes; she did move automatically, and the heavy metal box fell to the floor.

Curiously enough she felt no terror. If the box had fallen on her head, it could have killed her; if not that, a concussion. If the pointed corner had punctured her head—it was so tilted. She still felt no horror. She bent and opened it with curiosity. Nothing inside but scrap iron, junk. She knew then that it was no accident that it was placed where it would fall on her. It was too heavy to lift; she closed it, pushed it with her foot far to the back of the closet. It had not come in with her belongings; it had not been in the closet when she was there this afternoon.

She hung her dress and coat, closed the door. The sound couldn't carry to the opposite suite, that she knew. She would have been found in the morning when the soft-spoken foreign maid came to clean. An accident after a night in a club, carelessness, too much to drink. She turned on lights, went through the apartment again, still without fear. The windows were impregnable, a sheer ten-story drop to the pavement below. Both doors were securely self-locking. Bill Folker had said if she wanted any changes to let him know. She wanted bolts on her doors. It was too easy for others to retain keys.

She was really too tired to be frightened tonight. She climbed into the heavenly bed, pulled off the bed lamp. Who would want to kill her? If not kill her, at least get her out of the way. Who wanted her out of the way? Who was so determined to have her out of the way that he—she—would not stop short of murder? She didn't know. For she was certain of one thing. No one, not one person in all of New York's millions, knew who Lizanne Steffasson really was. Not one knew that she wore the mark of the cross-eyed bear on her body, even as Dene had worn it on his.

Chapter Three: THE CHALLENGE ACCEPTED

IT WAS in the center drawer, neatly clipped from a newspaper. It couldn't have been overlooked; nothing had been overlooked in arrangements for her; everything too deliberate, too suspiciously clean. The desk was a display of what the well-stocked secretary would demand, fresh paper, envelopes, stenographer's notebook, evenly sharpened pencils; nothing used.

"Divorce Granted." The picture beneath of Alix. She looked beautiful and she looked offensive. Nothing soft in that face. A woman who would have her own way: absolute monarchs must have had the same narrow arrogance of jaw.

Lizanne read the print beneath: *"Mrs. Henry Tinker granted a divorce today."* No date on the clipping. In Reno. *"The former Alix Bruce, daughter of Ambassador Tedford Bruce. The former Mrs. Guard Croyden."*

It was information but it explained nothing, not why they should all be in this together. Ambassador Bruce was a man in public service; he couldn't be mixed up in a murder. His daughter, his son, his former son-in-law—and Bill Folker.

Someone had killed Dene. He didn't jump off that sheer cliff, with a bullet in his neck. But none of these could have done it; they weren't murderers. Someone had tried to kill her last night; if not that, someone didn't care if she were killed. Someone had access to the suite.

She would get bolts today for her doors. But she would say nothing of last night's attempt at doing away with her. And she knew why. She didn't trust any one of these as yet. Government agents or no, she would wait.

It was eleven o'clock before the buzzer sounded. It startled her after the morning of silence. She took notebook and pencil, went in to Bill Folker. He was in a heavy brown lounging robe by the window. Her distrust returned. Something about the way he looked at her. But she was wearing the gray wool jersey, her hair brushed behind her ears. She knew she looked little older than a schoolgirl, seemingly nothing behind her face except a faint wonderment at her being hired for this job.

Mail was sprayed on his breakfast table. He dictated. It was business, nothing but business; war contracts, discussion of the output of certain mines, letters addressed to Washington, Moscow, Copenhagen, Buenos Aires. She was a fool to be frightened of him. He wasn't interested in her.

He asked as she closed her book, "What about the Vaughts? Dinky said you went off with Lans."

"I did. He still insists he is Lans Vaught." She didn't know why she should attempt to help the pianist. But she said, "I believe he must be. Just because his name is Lans shouldn't mean——"

Bill broke in impatiently. "That has nothing whatever to do with it. We didn't even know he used the same given name until we inquired. It's his appearance, his air—everything about him speaks for it."

"But Mr. Croyden said he didn't look like Lans Viljaas," she reminded.

"Guard forgot to notice his eyes."

She didn't move a muscle, her own eyes without expression.

"Never mind. Did he say anything about the cross-eyed bear?"

She was taking Bill Folker's money; she was in his

employ; it was a definite assignment to find out what she could from the Vaughts. Lans meant nothing to her, nor did his tawdry little wife. No reason not to give Bill an accounting, but she didn't. She only shook her head, "No." She had to think of something. Dinky had certainly reported that she was away at least an hour with Lans. "We had coffee at Childs'. He didn't even explain how he happened to know Dinky." She said blithely, "I suppose Dinky knows all the night club people."

He said, "Dinky and Dene and Lans were raised next door to each other. He knew Dinky because he is Lans. Is he interested in you?"

She knew what he meant, as a person, not as secretary to Bill Folker. She said, "No."

"Could he be?"

She met his eyes, considering it. She answered finally, honestly, "Men don't"—how to phrase it—"men don't whistle when I go past the livery stable." And she grinned at him.

He smiled back then. "I must have interviewed at least fifty, nearer a hundred beautiful women in answer to that ad. Not one met the requirements. It was essential that the person for the job have some semblance of a brain. She had to be able to act a secretary's part and"— he gestured to the mail—"and at least help me out, along with her other duties."

She didn't know where this was leading.

He went on easily, "Most of the applicants, I believe, thought I was a white slaver, and were willing. Not one fitted the picture I had, until you came along." He poured more coffee for himself. "You needn't tell me again nor will I tell you that you're no beauty. But even looking like a damp rabbit as you did that day," he smiled and she bridled, "you did, you know, just exactly—there was something to pique the interest of a man, in particular of a man surfeited on mere beauty. And the café crowd is just that, Lizanne. Even Guard, old cynic that he is, agrees with me on you where that is concerned. That's why I told you to get yourself dressed up. The right clothes and you can walk into a room with your hair and eyes and innocent look—and have every man in the place start sniffing around."

She went on listening, a flush on her cheeks. She wasn't used to being discussed by a strange man point by point as if she were a colt. But she said nothing, tried not to be afraid. She wasn't used to eyes looking through her to her very skin.

"Your body's good, a little thin, although you don't play it up. You're probably too honest a person to have anything but scorn for that, the stock in trade of every beautiful girl in New York, whether she lives on Park or Seventh Avenue or at the Barbizon. You may not have a damn bit of personal experience in getting a man, but you've seen other girls in action. At least in the pictures. You know how it's done. And doing it clear-headed that way you'll probably get a lot farther than those pretty ones that came walking in here who could do it in their sleep." He took a breath. "Now. Could Lans Vaught be interested in you?"

Again she didn't answer immediately. She was relieved. He hadn't been speaking personally; he was thinking only of the search. She thought it over. "He has a wife."

"I'm not interested in his morals. Could he be?"

She said, "I can try it." She thought out loud. "Right now I'm a cross between anathema to him and something non-existent." She looked up at Bill. "I mean I'm no more than a symbol of you, of someone insisting that a man isn't what he says he is."

"You can be more than that? You can make him see you as a person?"

"I can. Of course, I can." Her chin tilted. She was surprised at herself. She liked this assignment; she was actually eager to try it, to make Lans realize her.

Bill's eyes approved. "You can do it," he repeated softly. "Never mind about the wife." He was matter-of-fact now, lighting a cigarette. "Dink will keep her amused. You concentrate on Lans."

She looked aslant at him. "And after he is interested?"

"Maybe he'll talk." Bill moved to the window, looking through the gray pane. "Maybe he'll tell you about the cross-eyed bear. Maybe he'll tell you why Dene disappeared."

"You think he knows that?"

He turned back to her. "He knows something. What, I don't know. But you can find out." Abruptly he ended the conversation. "Just leave the letters in the basket on your desk for my signature. There's nothing else for you today until about five. Dinky will pick you up then and take you to Alix's for cocktails."

"No!" It came out without meaning to.

He raised his eyebrows. "I don't blame you. But I can't go. And there will be people there who know the Viljaas tribe. The affair is for Tedford, the Ambassador; he's in town for a few days. I want a blow by blow account of what's said when the Viljaas name is brought into it. Don't worry, it will be. You needn't talk, just listen."

She didn't want to go to Alix Bruce Croyden Tinker's, to be insulted again by a drunken strumpet. Bill Folker could go; at least he could when he wanted to, at night, alone. She couldn't argue. This was a definite order. She said, "I'll go but some day I'll lose my temper with her."

He laughed. "I want a ringside table." And then he said, "Be careful when you do."

She remembered Alix's glass-cold eyes.

She went out into the office. At least she knew what was wanted of her. Definite now. Everything was pointed at Lans. It was he they suspected of having the bear. And they didn't have his triangle of the check. Doubtless they had Dene's. It had been gone when she and Uncle Will came upon the body in the snow. Lans was the only unknown quantity in their picture. And the real and only reason they wanted a girl, an unknown girl, was to get Lans.

Again she felt that faint unsureness of herself, thinking of him. He had a wife, and Lizanne was no divorce addict like Alix. He didn't mean anything to her, nor could he. The fact that his eyes were Dene's meant less to her. She hated even the memory of Dene Viljaas.

She dressed for Lans rather than for cocktails. The new rich black dinner dress, military jacket braided in silver, buttoning to her throat. A ridiculous black hat she wouldn't have dared wear a week ago. Teetering heels on her dull silk pumps. She carried the silky black caracul over her arm as she crossed the semi-dark of the office. She must remember always to light that room before twilight. Anyone could come in—locked doors were of no avail here—who, she didn't know, but she didn't linger, and she scarcely waited to be summoned in once she tapped on Bill Folker's door.

He seemed surprised at her appearance. The damp

rabbit impression must be firmly rooted in him.

Dinky was linked over the chair. He asked, "Are we going somewhere?"

She said, "I thought we'd go back to Jim and Jack's for dinner."

He shuddered. "Vile food. Can't we get Lans a better job, Bill?" The idea appealed to him. "Even waiting tables, say at Longchamps, would be an improvement—at least for my stomach."

He annoyed Lizanne. It was like having a smart-aleck child in the house. "Your stomach would be better off if you'd put food in it more often."

"Food is poisonous." He tilted his glass, drained it. "I suppose we might as well start. Bill insists we go to Alix's foul levee."

Bill told him, "Go on and stop grousing about it. You'll have a great time when you get there. You always do, y'know." He came to Lizanne, put his fingers on her arm. She was afraid of them, knowing they could be steel as well as blood and bone.

"I'd have a better time somewhere else, y'know." Dinky winked at her with his great fringed blue eyes.

She saw no real reason for his existence save perhaps to be her temporary escort. This time she recalled, "Mr. Folker, would you call the desk and ask them to have bolts put on both my doors? I meant to ask you this morning. I know I'm silly but I just get scary at nights and I'd feel much safer."

He accepted her reason. "I'll see to it right away."

Waiting the elevator, in the cab, Dinky was silent, without lightness. Alix's apartment was like her, brittlely modern in chromium and glass. She came to greet them, trailing green and silver, her nails a mandarin's in smoky red. Her shoulder turned on Lizanne but it wasn't with the intentional rudeness of that other day. She was appealing to Dinky. "Try and act half-way decent, won't you? You know how Father feels."

Dinky was blithe. "I'll do as well as you."

She said, "I've only had a thimble of brandy. You reek already. Is Bill coming?"

"No. Regrets and all that."

Her smoky red lips thinned.

"Guard'll be here."

"I know. I sent word because of Father."

Dinky took her on one arm, Lizanne on the other. "Why don't you slip me just a small glass of brandy before the locusts descend?"

She said brutally, "You don't need it. I hate to waste it on you," but she spoke to the manservant passing from dining room to the living room. "Bring a small brandy to Mr. Bruce."

"Not too small," Dinky amended.

No one introduced Lizanne to anyone. The man with blue-gray hair, the man who looked as if he alone were real among all these narrow, paper-doll people, was Ambassador Bruce. Alix had his height, Dinky his smile, although the son's was impudent where the father's was kind. No one cared where you stood, what you did. Lizanne was on the outskirts of the group surrounding the Ambassador. Nothing was said of the Viljaases. Guard Croyden arrived, big and ugly and harsh, and the fanciest women, all but Alix, circled him. Lizanne didn't know why. He was brutish, not a man you would expect women to circle. And then Guard was in the Ambassador's group, and Dinky and Alix came nearer.

The Ambassador said, "We miss you in Washington,

Guard. Coming back soon?"

"It doesn't look that way. It goes slowly."

Dinky blurred, "You don't miss me and I'm working twice as hard as he is trying to trace Dene Viljaas."

There was a little stir in the room, as if a wind had come up. An unaccountable silence. Alix's mouth was thin again and her fingers fidgeted with the trailing silver sleeve.

The woman with the salmon birds on her hair looked at Alix and laughed. "Are you still expecting to find Dene? Better leave well enough alone."

Dinky raised his eyelashes. "Hetty, how you talk! Just what do you mean?"

She laughed again to Alix. "Don't you agree, darling?"

Alix touched her lips as if they were dried. "Father must close the estate, Hetty. He's senior executor, you know." She came through the circle. "Let me freshen yours, Father. And you, Hetty, haven't had a thing yet." She'd broken it off concisely. The Viljaas case was out of conversation, if not out of mind. But why had she been nervous in its discussion? There was no reason for her to have killed Dene.

Lizanne waited in a corner for Dinky to come to her. There were fewer people in the room when he did. Alix stopped them in front of the Ambassador and Guard. "Dinky, you're dining with Father, you know."

He drawled, "Oh, no, I'm not. I have a date." He put his hand under Lizanne's arm.

Alix said rudely, "You can get rid of her. Father expects it."

Dinky bent past her to the Ambassador, turned on his dazzling smile. "So sorry I can't join you. I'm tied up, y'see. But I know you won't mind."

61

"I don't mind." His father barely glanced at him.

He flashed triumph at his sister. She followed them into the foyer. There was fury now in her eyes, in the colorless gray of them.

Dinky laughed maliciously. "You can postpone Bill a few hours. He'll keep."

She said, "You did it on purpose."

He angered suddenly. "It won't hurt you to be human to Father for once. You never see him. After all, living with him I get my share." He held Lizanne's coat.

Alix's hands were shaking against the silver of her sleeves. "You know I can't stand to be near Guard."

Dinky had regained control. "He won't hurt you. He doesn't want you"—his voice was contemptuous—"now." He looked her over as if she were diseased.

She didn't say anything, turned abruptly, and left them there.

Lizanne followed Dinky in the customary silence, out into the night, into the summoned cab. She said, "We'll go to the club. I want to see Lans again."

He gave directions and was silent.

There was too much that Lizanne wanted to know. She had to ask, "Who was that woman, that Hetty one?"

"Alix's best friend. When Alix was married to Guard, Hetty was trying to take him away from her."

"Didn't Alix mind?" She wouldn't try to take an old penny away from Alix Bruce.

"Not really. But she's possessive as hell. As a matter of fact, it gave her more time for Bill."

"She knew Bill at that time?"

He looked at her from the slant of his eyes as if she were a backward child. "She's been nuts about Bill since she was in rompers." His voice implied that anyone would know that.

They had arrived at the club, at the same table. Lans saw them enter but his back was immovable. Sally's eyes were fixed on Lans; she did not move until something passed between them, then came avidly to the table.

Dinky muttered under his breath as she started. "Oh, God, why couldn't he have picked a semi-lady? You'll have to make it snappier tonight, Lizanne. Or I will get drunk. I simply refuse to make her and she's unbearably persistent."

The girl was bright-eyed and she didn't hear what he'd said. His smile and voice were cooing. "And how is our little Sally?"

Lans came during first intermission. He didn't even speak to Dinky or Sally. All he said to Lizanne was, "Back for more dope for the Boss?"

She spoke defensively, "I didn't tell him anything you said."

"Why not?" She didn't answer.

"You're getting paid for it, aren't you?"

She was still silent.

"Maybe I didn't tell you what you wanted to know?" He waited. "Well, you can't see me till midnight."

She swallowed anger at his rudeness.

He asked, "Where do you live?"

She kept silence. She didn't want him to know; moreover, she didn't want him coming there. The others were waiting for just that. Dinky was still engrossed in Sally; he couldn't have heard their quiet words.

Lans touched her wrist. "Are you living with Bill Folker?" His smile was taunting. ·

She blazed, "No, I'm not!" She knew he didn't believe it. Her voice was hushed, for his ears alone when she explained, "I am living at The Lorenzo—but only as a convenience." She was embarrassed, realizing that any explanation must sound false. She wasn't paying for a room; she was living in Bill Folker's suite. She could have explained easily enough to anyone without preconceptions but not to Lans Vaught's black eyes. They would refuse to believe the truth. She asked abruptly, "Will you meet me tomorrow?"

"Yes, I'll meet you." He looked at the table. "But I won't walk into your parlor."

"I'm not asking you to do that. Any place you say."

"My room?" He was taunting her.

She held to her temper. "No. I want to see you alone. Meet me where we went the other night. At two o'clock."

He nodded and rose from his chair.

Dinky spoke then. "Pa's in town. You don't want to join us later?"

Lans said rudely, "I don't," and went on.

"Charming person," Dinky confided.

Sally defended him quickly. "He's not always like that. He can be as good fun as the next, especially with a drink or two. But he's been worrying a lot lately. Ever since we come back to New York. He don't say nothing but he tosses around after we go to bed, and half the time he'll get up and sit by the window and smoke till the sun's up."

"What's the trouble?" Dinky's crocodile sympathy was hard to listen to.

"I don't know. He won't tell me nothing. If I ask him he just says it's something he ate or he's working out a new arrangement or something. But I know better. He's not eating anything these days. And he don't act this way making arrangements. He needn't think I'm fooled."

Lizanne just watched Sally as she talked. Incredible that Lans could be married to this girl. Despite his careful Seventh Avenue disguise, anyone would know that he was not of such a neighborhood; he had known better. And Sally—it might well be a step up in her life. Lizanne broke off her thoughts, suddenly realizing that there was only one reason to be thinking as she was. And that was too much interest in Lans Vaught. She would never allow herself heart interest again, not after Dene.

She spoke suddenly, "Finish your drink, Dinky, and take me home."

"We haven't eaten." He seemed surprised.

"I'm too tired to stay out. I'm not used to all these late nights." She didn't want to stay here now, watching his sleek black head bent to the piano keys. She didn't want to see Sally's flat painted face, alive because Dinky Bruce had eyelashes.

In one raised eyebrow Dinky let Sally know he was loath to leave. And outside he said, "Lizanne, you have a heart after all! I couldn't have endured her tonight, not after an afternoon of Alix. I'd have throttled her with my bare hands." He turned his head. "Do you really want to go home or was it to get out of that dismal place?"

"I really want to go home." ·

He dropped her at the hotel. "I won't take you up. Maybe I'll find the others. It might be amusing by now." He giggled like a woman.

Chapter Four: STRANGLED

THE thumping, insistently rhythmic over and again, penetrated sleep. Someone pounding at the door. Quickly

Lizanne pulled on the lamp. Her clock said two in the morning. She wrapped the golden satin of her gown within the heavy coppery robe, slid into the copper scuffs. Bill Folker, dressing gown enfolding his length, opened his door even as she did hers.

She said stupidly, "I heard knocking. It woke me."

The pounding was continuing. Without answering her he flung open the corridor door. She was at his elbow. She stepped back and her mouth rounded O. He, too, stepped back, amazement in his motion. The uniform of a policeman, behind him another man, narrow-faced, hat remaining on his head, doubtless a plain-clothes man. He came in first, the officer following.

"William Folker?"

Bill nodded his head, puzzlement between his eyebrows.

"I'm Inspector Tobin, Homicide Squad. Sergeant Moore." He flung out his elbow introducing the officer.

She just stood there looking at them, at Bill. She couldn't try to figure it out. And then there was a sudden little chill in her. Lans! Lans was in danger. Bill had said it. She clenched her hands waiting for the word.

The Sergeant was memorizing the office.

Inspector Tobin said, "Sorry to disturb you at this hour, Mr. Folker, but I'm afraid I've got to ask you a few questions." He yawned, a real yawn.

Bill said, his voice puzzled as his face, "I don't understand. But certainly." He began to lead to his suite.

Lizanne just stood there. She didn't know what was expected of her.

Tobin nodded his head back. "The girl'd better come, too." Something in the way he said it was as if he thought they had been bedded together. She felt a flush in her cheeks.

Bill Folker said, "My secretary, Lizanne Steffasson."

She couldn't understand why both the police suddenly focused their eyes on her. It was almost as if they were suspicious. It had nothing to do with what might have been suspicion of her morals.

Tobin repeated, "Come along."

She obeyed, still wondering.

Bill lighted lamps. There were three unwashed glasses on the opened bar; the room looked as rooms do when several have been drinking through an evening and retired without setting things right. A black velvet opera bag, mounted in brilliants and gold, was on the circular glass table. She knew to whom that belonged.

Tobin took the chair opposite Bill on the chaise. He motioned to Lizanne and she drew another chair uncertainly into the circle. Sergeant Moore wandered about before coming to rest behind the Inspector. He was awkward as a St. Bernard but he saw that bag; he saw everything.

Bill offered, "A drink?"

"Not on duty," Tobin refused. He looked a little longingly at the bottled array.

"You are on duty then?"

"Wouldn't disturb you at this time of the morning otherwise." The Inspector crossed his knees.

Each one seemed waiting for someone else to say something. Lizanne folded her hands tightly together and then loosened them. His eyes out of the corners might notice, might wonder. She felt she would scream if the police didn't speak, explain. She couldn't ask if Lans were . . . like Dene, his black eyes seeing nothing.

Bill spoke first. "May I ask why you are here—on

duty?"

Tobin nodded. "Do you know Lydia Thorp?" The flick of his eyes included Lizanne as well as Bill.

She was bewildered. It couldn't be that anything had happened to the plain woman, and yet—as if printed with ice—that fragment of scene she had almost blundered against on Monday night.

Bill was answering, "Certainly. She was my secretary."

"Not now?"

"No. She gave notice about a month ago. Miss Steffasson took her place."

Tobin turned the edge of his eyes again on Lizanne, then away. She kept wondering.

"Miss Thorp was living at four hundred and five West One Hundred Eighteenth street?".

It sprang out of her mouth. "But——." That had been her address.

Each of the three men was eyeing her. It was Bill's eyes that closed her lips. They warned. And she was frightened, suddenly frightened. She hadn't been before: she'd thought she'd known fear but not like this. She stammered, "But why—why are you asking this?"

Tobin said, "Lydia Thorp was murdered tonight."

Lizanne didn't, couldn't believe it.

Bill Folker sounded a gasp and his voice came quietly, unbelieving. "Lydia Thorp murdered?" and then he shook his head. "I don't understand."

"Don't understand what?" Tobin asked mildly.

"I don't understand why Lydia should be murdered nor why you are here."

"The last's easy, Mr. Folker. She had an identification card in her purse to notify you in case of accident. We thought maybe you could help us out on the first one."

Bill shook his head. "This is unbelievable to me. Do you mind if I have a drink even if you don't?"

The Inspector shook his head to that.

Bill took a fresh glass from a lower tray, put a splash above the Scotch. "Lizanne?"

She said, "No, thank you."

"It is unbelievable," he continued. "She couldn't have had any enemies. I don't believe she knew half a dozen persons in New York. I don't know, of course. She never spoke of her private affairs. She was a quiet woman. But I do know she seldom, if ever, went out. She had the secretarial suite across the way that Miss Steffasson is occupying now. And to my knowledge no one called on her."

Tobin asked, "When you hired her, did she give references?"

"I didn't ask for them. She was doing secretarial work at the Claridge in London. I was stopping there at the time. Her efficiency impressed me and I asked her to work for me. That was all."

"Don't know anything about her folks? Family ties?"

"I doubt if she had any. It would seem that if she had, the years she was with me I would have heard her mention them. Although really, Inspector, she didn't ever speak of herself that I can remember."

Lizanne was certain he was lying even if his words, his presentation of them, were deliberately weighted with truth.

"She was English?" Tobin asked.

"American, she told me. I don't even know that for certain. She took care of her own passport when we came over last year, a little over a year ago, in fact. Poor soul." He shook his head as if in pity for the plain woman.

Lizanne couldn't help asking although her voice wouldn't come for the moment and when it did, it was almost a whisper. "Wha-what happened to her?"

Tobin looked over at her hands, and quickly she relaxed them. Then he raised his eyes to meet her blue ones. She would do as well as Bill Folker, keep hers blank, without guile.

Tobin said, "She was strangled."

Pretense went away. Horror scrawled over her face. Even Folker put aside his glass with a quick gesture.

He asked, "Could you tell me—is it permitted—exactly what happened?"

"Sure. It'll be in the morning editions, probably on the street by now. The girl that discovered her called the station right off so the newsboys were in early on it. In fact, they'd have beaten me there if I just hadn't happened to drop in the station on my way home and saw Moore here starting out."

Moore said, "The captain was buzzing your place and sending the cruise car after you."

They were conversational as if nothing had happened. But Lizanne held breath waiting and Bill Folker was handling his glass again. He prompted, "She was living with someone? The girl who called?"

"One of those apartments, rooms rented out to working girls or students the way we got it. Just off the Columbia campus," Tobin explained. "Apartment five."

Lizanne said nothing. That was the apartment. There wouldn't be another vacant room. Lydia had taken hers. But why?

"She'd only been there a day. None of them knew anything about her. Kind of funny how she happened to be found so soon."

"It was Fate," Moore pronounced, and then looked more embarrassed than ever.

"Moore's right," Tobin agreed. "The girl in Room Number Three came home, sick, too, much celebrating it looked like. Called on girl in Number Two—Janet—"

"Leeds," Moore supplied.

"—for assistance. This Janet had felt kind of under the weather that very morning and Lydia Thorp had given her some bicarbonate. And then she'd said, according to this Janet, 'If you need more, help yourself.' She set the bottle back on her bureau. So"—he moved his hat—"when Number Three——"

"Eva Jean Schumacher." Again Moore looked in his book.

"When Eva Jean was groaning around, Janet went and tapped on Lydia's door, Room Number Four. She says she knocked enough to wake the dead——"

Lizanne swallowed.

Tobin missed nothing. "She felt the same way, Miss Steffasson, after she'd said it. Anyhow she was about to give up when she remembered the woman had had a phone call about eight. So she figured Miss Thorp might have gone out, and she'd just step inside and get the bicarb, little Eva Jean being worse off than ever. She went in, turned on the light—and then she called us."

"And that's all you know of it?"

"That's all. The two girls were scared out of their wits. It even sobered up Eva Jean. And Number One, an old dame with her hair on the bedpost and a boudoir cap with blue ribbons on her pate, had slept through all the dingus. Heard nothing."

Lizanne held her breath. Of course, they'd asked who had formerly occupied that drab little room.

71

There was interruption. Alix, standing in the doorway to what must have been bedrooms, saying, "My God, Bill, why don't you come to bed? Send your friends home." She was swathed in red velvet, her breasts pricking above where she caught the robe at the waist. At least she would let the police know that there was nothing personal between Lizanne and Bill.

He said, "Go back to bed. This is business."

Her eyes were glazed but she saw Lizanne. "Business!"

Bill had crossed to her, stood before her, his back to the room. "Go back to bed." And he added, "Lydia Thorp was murdered tonight."

She just looked at him for a moment and then she believed. She scuttled back from where she had come. Bill Folker closed the door tightly behind her.

Tobin was half out of his chair. "Wait a minute."

Bill Folker stood in front of that door. He was pleasant but he was firm. "Alix Bruce and her brother, young Tedford, are my house guests, Inspector. If you wish to question them, I will produce them at any time you say. But I fear you must excuse them right now. They have retired." He had come over to his couch as he went on speaking, still with gentleness, at ease, but brooking no argument.

Moore asked, "*Ambassador* Tedford Bruce?" He was writing in his little book.

"His offspring," Tobin supplied.

"Of course, they can hardly be expected to know anything about my former secretary," Bill continued. "They are social, not business friends."

Tobin nodded, yawned. "We can see them tomorrow."

"If need be."

"Better talk to them." And he asked, "When did you

last see her, Mr. Folker?"

"You mean Miss Thorp?"

"Yes."

Bill said, "Not since the day she left—Sunday." He seemed to remember. "I asked her to let me know when she was located, but I hadn't heard from her."

Again Lizanne knew that he was lying. She knew, without knowledge, that he had heard from Lydia Thorp, that he knew she had been living on West 118th street. Perhaps he had even sent her there. Why, she didn't know. She kept her eyes on her hands. The question came so suddenly, she started.

"Did you know she'd taken your room, Miss Steffasson?"

She shook her head. She couldn't make words as easily as Bill Folker did. She said, "I didn't. Of course, I didn't. I only saw her twice, the day I came here to apply for work"—the day Lydia Thorp had warned her, against what?—"and the day I moved here, the day she left." She added, hoping it would ring with truth and knowing it didn't although Bill's lies had, "I didn't have half a dozen words with her."

Moore pondered. "Funny she took your room."

"I can't understand it."

"She knew it was yours?"

Lizanne said, "I left my address the day I came here. She may have remembered it."

"I can see a rather natural explanation." Bill spoke easily. "She didn't know New York well. As I told you, she'd hardly been out of these rooms since we came over. It seems rather natural that knowing there would be a room vacant there, and knowing it must be a good clean place or else Miss Steffasson wouldn't have lived there, she looked into it."

"Makes sense," Moore allowed.

Lizanne wasn't sure. She wasn't even certain that Lydia Thorp had really broken off connection with Bill Folker. Could she have gone there to investigate? It was absurd. They couldn't suspect Lizanne of any Viljaas connection. Yet Guard Croyden hadn't trusted her, the night he took her home.

Tobin said, "Well, it's getting late. No use keeping you up all night. Thanks for the information." He and Moore stood together. But he had another question. "Why did she leave the job?"

Bill Folker spread his fingers. "I don't even know that. Perhaps if I knew——"

"Yeah. That might answer it."

He led toward the corridor door. "Come to me for any arrangements to be made for her. I feel responsible in a way that I didn't know more of her life."

Lizanne didn't want to be alone there with him but she couldn't leave now. She had to wait in the chair, pressing her bedroom slippers on the carpet. He returned looking only disturbed, not dangerous.

He said, "She must have found out something."

Lizanne's eyes widened. "You mean——"

He smiled gently down at her. "I told you there might be danger." He sat down again. "Are you afraid now?"

"I'm scared silly," she admitted.

They laughed together but it was no more real with him than with her. And he asked, "Too afraid to go on with the job?"

She shook her head. "I told you I needed it. I do. But I do want bolts for my doors."

"You shall have them tomorrow. I may get some, too."

She hadn't heard the door open; she hadn't heard Alix move across the rug, but she was standing there turning her eyes from Lizanne to Bill and from Bill to Lizanne.

Alix said, "So Lydia got hers tonight?"

Bill seemed weary. "Why don't you go to bed, Alix?"

She spoke furiously. "Send this little slut to bed first!"

Lizanne was white. Bill said, "Alix often speaks like a fishwife. You will excuse her?"

It quieted Lizanne's temper but she wished he wouldn't sponsor her, not before Alix. It could only make things worse. She said, "I am going to bed right now."

She went in silence. She turned on all the lights in her apartment, looked even in the closets, before returning to bed. She didn't know who or what she was expecting to find but she didn't want to take any chances. Lydia's death was no accident, nor was that leaded box placed to fall on Lizanne's head.

When the Inspector returned, he would ask more questions, too many questions. You couldn't lie to him; every item would be checked. All you could do was refuse to answer. She must refuse if he asked where she lived before she came to New York. She couldn't tell anyone that, not even the police. One of this group was a murderer; with no proof, that was certain. She wouldn't be alive now if they knew the mark on her; if they knew who Lizanne Steffasson was.

Chapter Five: FRIGHTENED GIRLS AREN'T SAFE

JANET LEEDS asked, "Do you live here?" She was impressed. But she hadn't come to the apartment this morning for that, not to see what Lizanne had fallen heir to. She had come with her own startling news. Even so it was strange that the music student had come. They had known each other so slightly.

"Did you hear what happened at the apartment last night?"

Lizanne answered, "Yes. The police came here."

"I found her. My picture's in all the papers this morning. I'll bet my family makes me come home now." She asked a little hesitantly, "You live here alone?"

Lizanne said, "Yes. This is the secretary's suite."

"Where she lived?"

"Yes." She didn't want to think about that. If Lydia Thorp had stayed, would she have been safe? Or did she move because the place wasn't safe: was she trying to outrun danger?

"Did you know her?"

Lizanne shook her head. "I only saw her twice." She said, "Just a minute, Janet," and went into the kitchenette, brought back coffee and orange juice for both of them.

The student demurred, "I've eaten."

"It won't hurt you to have a second breakfast while we talk."

The girl took the cup and glass. "It was simply awful. I've never seen anything so dreadful." Her whole face was sick again remembering. Then she asked, "What did the police want?"

"Routine. Mr. Folker's name was given for identification. I only happened in because I heard them knocking at the office and went to see who was there.'

Janet put down her coffee. She looked around nervously. "You're alone?" she asked again.

"All by myself." Lizanne gave reassurance but she didn't understand the girl's unease.

She was fumbling with the clasp of her bag now, had it opened and took out an envelope. She handed it to Lizanne, looked over her shoulders and spoke in almost a whisper. "I didn't tell the police about this." It was a plain envelope, unaddressed save for Lizanne's name printed upon the whiteness. "I don't know why only I just didn't want to. It seemed as if enough had happened to the poor thing without having her last wish almost not get carried out."

"I don't understand."

"Lydia Thorp gave me this last night and asked me to see that you got it today."

Lizanne held it but she couldn't believe it. "When did she give it to you? I mean, what time?"

"It was after she had that phone call. About eight it was, I guess. She went back to her room, you know how every footstep in that place tells you where everybody is at any time, and she walked kind of heavy. I thought she was getting dressed for a date, of course. And then a little later she came to my room and she still had on her old black dress and she wasn't fixed up at all but she had this letter."

Lizanne still held it, just looking at it. She knew Janet was avid with curiosity but she couldn't read it while the girl was here; it might even draw her into the web. She said, "I'm glad you didn't give it to the police." She was seeing the woman move off heavily, sadly, as she had that day. "Did you see her visitor?"

"No one came. Not while I was there." She looked up. "Do you know what I wonder? Maybe she had a premonition something was going to happen to her and that's why she wrote it. Maybe it even tells . . ." She broke off, looked nervously around again.

77

"She gave me this, too." She took another envelope from her bag. It was long, heavier. Lizanne read the address without understanding. It was to Lydia Thorp herself, in care of general delivery, Washington, D.C.

Janet was saying, "She said it was important it be mailed today and she might not have the time or the opportunity to mail it. I didn't tell the police. I don't know why exactly but I was scared." She looked as if she might cry. "I didn't want them to think I was mixed up in any way with what happened. I didn't want them to think I knew her. I didn't." Her lip quavered. "I don't know what to do with it now."

Lizanne held it fast. "I'll take care of it, Janet. I won't mention you." She stood up, still clutching the two envelopes. She said, "I have to dress now. I have some letters to do. Thanks for bringing the note and for saying nothing." She promised as a sop, "If there's anything important in it, I'll let you know. And of course I'll let the police know if there's anything."

Janet said almost apologetically, "I am interested. Finding her that way."

Lizanne said good-by at the door, wished again silently for bolts, and for additional precaution locked herself in her bathroom before opening her envelope. Her fingers were trembling. Yesterday at this time Lydia Thorp was alive, this had not been written:

I am afraid to stay here longer. I think I will get away in time. Before I go, I must warn you again. If it is true what you said, that you need a job, you can find another one. If you are in this for some other reason, you had better get out while you can. You do not wish to die.

It was not signed. She read it again; it was stippled on her memory. "*You do not wish to die.*" Dene had not wished to die. Lydia didn't want to die. Death always came too soon. Did Lydia know that Lizanne was already marked for death? Stubbornly she refused that thought. Not yet. She was too alive. She would come out of this unscathed. Lydia was frightened. Perhaps when you had outgrown usefulness to Stefan Viljaas' interests, you would die. But it wasn't just being connected with the cross-eyed bear that brought death. Too many lived. Ambassador Bruce, Guard Croyden, Bill, Alix, Dinky, Lans——

She turned the second envelope in her hands. She didn't know what to do about it. Lydia hadn't escaped. Without apology she suddenly tore it open, drew out the two enclosures. A passport, *Lydia Thorp Viljaas*. A marriage license, *London, Lydia Thorp, Stefan Viljaas*.

She stared at them until she couldn't see them. Had Stefan Viljaas arrived in New York?

She must leave the apartment. The police would return. It was in their faces last night. She might not get away to meet Lans, and if she didn't meet him—— He wouldn't ever meet her again. He would be angry, wouldn't believe what she told.

She dressed in the innocent gray jersey; better if the police believed her young and simple. She couldn't tell them about Lydia's letter; it would mean they would be suspicious of her, insist on knowing about her. It wasn't as if she were withholding any real information. If she sent them the documents, could she be certain no one would know from whom they came? She couldn't be. Janet might talk.

She had seen Bill Folker and Guard Croyden in anger. They could find out; maybe it was for these papers that Lydia had been killed. If so, she had thwarted her murderer, but she hadn't thwarted murder.

For the present she would put them away; she wouldn't risk giving them even to the police. She put on the gray hat, took her coat across her arm. The envelopes were in the depths of her bag, zipper tight, bag close under her arm. There was yet another reason why she musn't suggest any of this group to the police, and it was the important one. Inspector Tobin wasn't interested in what happened to Dene Viljaas two years ago, what might happen to Lans Viljaas at any moment, what would happen to Lizanne if it were known who she was. He wouldn't believe such fantasy. She must have proof, definite proof. There was nothing to connect any of them with Lydia's murder. And it would end her connection with the Viljaases, even if it didn't end her very existence, if she pointed to them. She must keep quiet. If Janet should talk, Lizanne knew it would make her suspect. Despite this additional danger, she must keep sinking deeper into the Viljaas whirlpool. Only when Dene's murderer was caught would she ever be safe again.

Too cold to walk downtown; the sun was out but the air more bitter than it had been in snow. She went swiftly the block and half to Fifth, just caught a Fifth bus, lumbered slowly to 42nd street. No one could have followed her; she entered the bus alone; she was lost in those eastward crowded blocks before entering the bank.

No matter how hard it had been these eight months, no matter how foolish it had seemed, she had paid her monthly fee for the deposit vault, a tiny one but large enough for her needs. She opened it now, added Lydia's license to the similar license there. *Mary Elizabeth Porter—Dene Viljaas*. She added Lydia's letter to the letter that lay there, the letter dated over eight months ago, to Mary Elizabeth Porter, signed *Stefan Viljaas*. She knew well what was written therein. That strange request coming after a year's lapse, to see her, to talk to her concerning Dene Viljaas's disappearance. That letter had set her fleeing away from Vermont into the anonymity of the city. She had known then that even this crowded city wasn't safe; no place would be for her until she had found the murderer of Dene. Nor would Uncle Will ever be safe until the murderer was turned over to justice; he, too, knew too much. She hadn't known that Uncle Will would be dead before she could even begin to succeed. Her eyes filled, here in the dim vault, remembering gentle Uncle Will, who had never in his life harmed anyone. Dene's murderer had killed him as truly as if he had put a bullet into him, too. If Uncle Will had not gone into the snow that night, there would have been no pneumonia and its aftermath of the lung disease.

It was Uncle Will's death which had strengthened her in her resolve to find that murderer, before he killed her, too, that had added anger to her fear. It was that which had made her adopt a new personality, dye her hair the horrific orange shade that she might better be disguised for her search; take a new name, deliberately choosing a Scandinavian one, that she might possibly be led to the Viljaas circle.

Trembling even in the security of the private vault, she removed the worn rubber bands from the tiny brown-paper packet. It was safe. That cruel little die, the cross-eyed bear. .

She rewrapped it quickly. She was thankful she had saved it; she knew now its value, knew that eventually the murderer in seeking for it must reveal his identity. It wouldn't be found until he did.

The lunchers had been fed and gone their ways; she had dawdled interminably over extra coffee. Yet he came before two. Her heart gave a little thump as she saw him walking down the aisle to the small table at the rear. There must be none of that. Heart must not enter into this business. She wouldn't allow it.

He sat down, said, "I haven't eaten. I hardly woke in time to meet you." He ordered coffee and a cinnamon roll. They were silent until the waitress brought his order and departed. He said then, "Well, we're alone. What do you want to find out today?"

So many things but she wasn't supposed to know much. She asked abruptly, "Did you know Lydia Thorp?"

"Bill's secretary?"

"Yes."

"No, I didn't." He made it clear by his intonation that that tangent was dead end as far as he was concerned.

She asked, "Did you know that Lydia Thorp was murdered last night?"

It shocked him out of his deliberate shell. She had hoped it would. His voice was husky. "No, I didn't know that."

"I didn't think so." She didn't think he would have read the papers after the club closed even if the news had been on the street then. She had seen how wearied he was at that hour.

He asked quietly, "Why?"

She said, "What do you mean?"

"Why was she killed?" He was asking it as if she knew, as if she had been there observing it.

And it angered her again, as his suspicions must always anger her. "How should I know?"

"I just thought you might. You stepped into her shoes,

didn't you?"

She shivered just a little as he said it. It wasn't true, not that way. She hadn't taken anything away from the dead woman.

She defended herself although she knew to no avail; Lans had made up his mind about her on first meeting.

"No. That isn't quite true. She had already given notice weeks before." Bill had said so. "I only answered the ad and was hired."

"You mean that darb about the beautiful girl?" He had seen it then, connected it, or someone had told him. He stared at her mockingly. "How did he happen to pick you?"

She felt her cheeks redden. She wasn't beautiful but she wished he would think so. There must be none of that. She lifted her head. "I know I'm not beautiful. Maybe I was smart enough."

"You didn't know Bill before?"

"I never even heard of him." She was definite.

He had finished his breakfast and lighted a cigarette. "You know why he wanted a beautiful girl?"

Yes, she knew. But her eyes met his questioningly.

"He hasn't told you that yet?" He laughed again, put his elbows on the table. "The better to catch me with, my dear. That's why. It's so simple, you see, just the sort of thing Bill would think up. I fall for the beauty and she leads me right into the ogre's den."

Her cheeks were scarlet at the scorn on his face.

"But you needn't worry. I'm not going to fall for you. I played that game once with Bill, and I found out in time." His voice had gone harsh, his eyes blind in remembering, and then he smiled. "He must be losing his grip to think I'd be caught a second time." And by such as you, that smile said.

Again on the defense, she didn't want to lie to him but it was necessary. If she admitted it, he wouldn't see her again. "I don't know anything about that. He hasn't even suggested it." And she bit her lip. "I think you're just making it up to insult me. That's all you've ever done, insult me."

"What do you want me to do, kiss you?" His voice was hard. "Gum-shoeing around for Bill Folker and you expect me to like it." He leaned back in the chair and looked his scorn again. "All right. Go ahead. Earn your keep. Find out what you can. Still trying to pry the cross-eyed bear out of me?"

He was trying to make her lose hold on herself. She wouldn't let him succeed; she hated him. He could never mean anything to her. She loathed him and his Dene eyes.

She should have had more pride than to continue defense now. She despised herself for trying it. But she said, "I told you once I haven't repeated anything to Bill Folker that you have said. That is the truth. I haven't because—because maybe it would be dangerous to you if I did."

Their eyes met silently and then hers dropped.

"Maybe that isn't the reason at all," she bit out. "Maybe it's because you haven't said anything worth repeating yet." She turned the napkin over her finger, not wanting to look at him, waiting for him to speak.

He finally did. "I suppose you know you're mixed up in a pretty dangerous business?"

She said, "You told me that before. Everyone's told me that. Even Bill Folker warned me." That again deflated him. She didn't mention Lydia. He'd denied knowing her. Besides it was better now not to know much about Lydia Thorp.

"But you're sticking. Why?"

She tossed her head. "I took the job. I needed it. I knew there'd be danger; the ad said so, you remember."

He said impatiently, "All right, all right. Well, let's get on with it. What do you want to know today?"

She began slowly, "You won't believe me but what I want to know is for myself alone. It has nothing to do with Bill Folker." It was dangerous to let him know of her own interest in Viljaas; he might not accept it as idle curiosity. She knew that even as she spoke. But she could ask no one at The Lorenzo, not Bill, certainly not Guard Croyden, not the drunken Dinky Bruce. And if it were Lans, not Stefan's men, who had taken Dene's triangle, he still didn't know that she belonged in the Viljaas circle. She asked, "You know Alix Bruce?"

He nodded. "I did once."

"Why should she be afraid to talk of Dene?"

He looked at her.

"She was afraid, nervous. Her hands—fiddled."

He said, "I've always thought she knew something. I've always thought that was why she divorced Guard."

"What would that have to do with it?"

"Elementary. If she had something on Bill, she'd think she could snare him sure. But he fooled her. You don't catch Bill that easy. He skipped out, and after a while she married Hen Tinker's wad." He said slowly, "Maybe I ought to see the darling Alix. If I wouldn't have to run into Bill. Are they sleeping together again?"

She nodded. But she had another question. "Do you know a woman named Hetty?"

"Hetty Creighton? That ass."

"Why should she suggest it better to leave well enough

alone in Dene's case? She said it to Alix. And she laughed."

He was alert. "Alix does know something. I'll have to see her. Can you fix it?" And then without warning he laughed and laughed, and when he stopped his mouth was small and wry. "I nearly bit on that one, didn't I? Nearly walked right into it. My God, Bill can pick 'em, can't he? I thought he'd slipped when he chose you. My apologies, Madame. That big-eyed innocent truth stuff just about had me."

"Lans! Lans, what are you saying?"

He'd stood up, started putting on his overcoat. "Go back and tell your boss it didn't work. He'll have to think up a new one." His mouth and eyes were hard. "The Bill-Alix combine took me once but not again."

"Lans, it isn't true what you're thinking!"

He set his hat carefully on his polished hair. "You, my pretty little whited sepulcher, can go straight to hell." He bowed mockingly. "So sorry to leave you, Miss Steffasson. but I must go to a rehearsal." His voice was violent again. "And you needn't come around another time."

He had gone, without looking back, his hands in his pockets, his shoulders set. She began to cry just a little. The waitress looked sorry for her, sniffing romance, not knowing how far she was from truth, how near. Lizanne took up her napkin and rubbed her eyes roughly.

She forgot New England thrift; she was too miserable to walk in the cold back to the hotel, or even the intervening blocks for a bus. She took a cab. She should have known before she came to New York that this would be too big for her. She should have left it to someone who knew how to do these things; she was amateur; she didn't even know how to start. She rubbed her eyes again hard.

She couldn't give up now, not after eight months of blankness, now that through some miraculous providence she at last had been thrust into the inner machinations. At the moment, however, nothing mattered. She only wanted to be alone.

Her feet stopped on the threshold of her living room. She didn't believe what she saw. Alix, at home on her white couch, cigarette in hand. Lizanne didn't have words. Surprisingly, she wasn't frightened; she was furious.

Alix looked up at her with oblique brows. "You don't mind? They're conferring and so stupid."

Lizanne asked with tight throat, "How did you get in here?"

"Bill let me in, of course."

She didn't know if Alix were lying or not. Her anger bubbled to the open. "I hardly expect to find unwanted people in my room."

Alix smiled. "You can expect anything with Bill. But you don't know that yet, do you, darling?" She put the cigarette out, slowly, insolently. She was tall, and beautiful under the sinuous black of her dress. She gathered her silver fox wrap, tiny black jeweled bag. Her eyes were again like to glass. "I've been wanting to see you alone to warn you. Keep your hands off Bill." She went to the corridor door, turned to command, "Don't mention this to him."

Lizanne sat down where Alix had been. Suddenly she was weak. She didn't understand any of them. But one thing certain, Alix wasn't going to appear in these rooms another time unannounced. She marched straight across to Bill's door. A voice within halted her, Guard's voice. "You've got to get this thing moving, Bill. I can't stay away from Washington for so long. Garth doesn't like it."

"You're not working for him now. You're working for me."

"He doesn't know that."

Bill continued, "The Ambassador does, and he says it's all right."

"But I'm not getting anywhere and, God knows, neither are you. You're going backward. When Dinky barged in this morning with the news about Lydia—well, I didn't expect that."

"Neither did I. I didn't plan that, Guard."

"I didn't think you did."

Guard asked, "Was she really giving out information?"

"Yes." Bill's voice was flat.

"The Three might have found out?"

"Possible."

She crept back to her rooms. But she was still determined to strengthen her own safety. She took up the phone. "I've asked three times for bolts for my doors and all I get is promises. What is the matter?"

The clerk was apologetic, not at all as he had been when she was shabby tweed. He knew nothing of it. It would be attended to at once.

But she didn't tell him that her room was being entered. Again, for some reason she was afraid to mention that. It might bring investigation and she didn't want it. She knew Bill didn't want it. She might lose the job if she brought additional trouble on him. She mustn't be dismissed now. She'd take her chances with the bolts; she'd be safe when in the apartment; when out—there was nothing for anyone to find in searching. She was without laundry marks.

The knock came at her corridor door. She opened it to Inspector Tobin. She must have peered because he said, "No, Moore's not along. The Lorenzo doesn't like uniforms. Might shock their paying patients." He sat down unasked. "Nice place here, Miss Steffasson. Not much like One Hundred Eighteenth West, is it?"

"No, it isn't." She wasn't nervous now. She could sit quietly, hands in lap. If you always took your time, nothing would startle you into too quick an answer.

"Wonder why Lydia Thorp gave this up."

She said truthfully, "I don't know."

He scratched his head under his hat. "Funny how she took your room." He crossed his legs, leaned comfortably in the chair as if he were prepared to stay a long time. She didn't care. There was nothing he could find out, for there was nothing she could tell. The letter had no bearing, not as yet.

"We run into some funny things sometimes on cases."

She sounded as innocent as she could, made her eyes wide. "I'm sure you must, Inspector."

"Coincidence and chance. They always seem a little phony, don't you think?"

"Sometimes they do happen."

"Yeah, sometimes they do. But that doesn't make them seem less phony." He seemingly changed the subject abruptly. "Strangling's the safest way of murder. No fingerprints. If you just aren't caught on the scene you're pretty safe. Mind if I smoke?" He lit from a pack of Luckies, Lans's brand. "Whoever murdered Lydia Thorp took a long chance on being seen, but he, or she, wasn't. Nobody saw him go into the apartment. Elevator boy didn't see him. None of the women in the place saw him come or go. It's almost as if he didn't plan on killing her, as if it just happened."

In her ears: *I didn't plan that, Guard.* She held her hands tightly, remembered to loosen them.

"Nobody knew her. It's almost as if she moved in there just to give the murderer a chance to get rid of her, isn't it?"

She nodded. She didn't know why he must talk to her this way. Surely he could find another, a better confidante.

The question she had been fearing came. "Where are you from, Miss Steffasson?" He was just waiting to investigate her.

She was silent. But she knew she must speak. "I can't tell you where I'm from or anything about me."

"You won't?"

"I can't. Believe me. It's absolute truth that I know nothing about Lydia Thorp. I didn't have anything to do with her murder." He had to believe that; it was true.

He had moved to the grilled window, stood looking out. "Where were you?"

She had no alibi, she realized with a sinking feeling in her stomach. He couldn't arrest her for murdering Lydia Thorp! She didn't even know about it until he came here last night with the news. She didn't want to be arrested; she couldn't do anything behind bars. Yet the police did get the wrong person; over and again you read of cases just like that. She almost cried out, "I don't know what time she was killed! I haven't seen the papers. I can tell you what I did yesterday. Dinky Bruce and I went to a cocktail party at his sister's and afterward we stopped at a night club." She might as well name it; he would ask. "Jim and Jack's." His expression embarrassed her, for no reason at all. He needn't think she was interested in Lans. "I was at home before eight and asleep by nine. I didn't wake until you came."

She didn't think he was satisfied with anything she had told him but there was nothing more to tell. Not now. She couldn't ask him to find Dene's murderer. That was too long ago and far away. That had to be up to her.

He said, "I'll be seeing you," and went over to the outer door. If she could talk to him; if she could talk to anybody. She was so futile. And she couldn't tell anyone. She could only walk carefully, pick up a fragment here or there, and try to piece it all together. He left.

Again there came knocking on the door. He hadn't gone. He was returning to begin again. She was without strength to go on forever refusing information; he knew it. She steeled herself to re-admit him.

It wasn't he. It was an overalled man who might have belonged to Ned Smithson's shop in a Vermont village. She sat listening as he pounded away, as if the sound were lullaby. The bolts worked, were solid, imbedded in the door, not the sort an inserted tool might pry away.

The carpenter twanged, "You'll feel safe with these, Miss. Can't say as how I'd of felt safe myself living in her rooms." His tongue clucked. "Imagine a murder almost happening right here on top of us in The Lorenzo. The management wouldn't of liked that, I can tell you. She didn't look the sort of woman would be murdered, leastways from what I've heard down below. It just shows you never can tell, can you? It's the play girls, the butterflies, you expect to get murdered. Not a woman like Miss Thorp was."

He was wrong. The play girls knew how to take care

of themselves well. It was plain women like Lydia Thorp, frightened girls like herself, that weren't safe. They didn't know how to protect themselves as the Alixes did.

Chapter Six: To Go on in Danger

THE THREE men were in the lamplit twilight over highballs, relaxed in their customary places, but their faces weren't relaxed. Automatically the tension was wiped away as she came in, just as if she weren't in this as deeply, more deeply, than they.

Bill said, "Inspector Tobin asked us all to be together this afternoon. He wants to ask some more questions."

She nodded.

Dinky said, "My God, what does he expect me to tell him? I only saw the old hag once."

Guard stated, "Not good word choice, Dink. Not to a police officer."

"You're not investigating this too, are you?" He draped his legs more comfortably.

"I'm just warning you in advance. You don't have to act like an utter idiot before Tobin. He'll catch on to you without that."

"Oh—fudge." Dinky winked at Lizanne, passed his glass.

The knock sounded. Lizanne rose and Bill nodded to her. She went over, opened the corridor door. Alix swept past her as if she were a doorstop. Alix, tawny fox on her thin blackness, scented with a beauty parlor and white glacé gloves, a great swirl of violets at her breast. She walked directly to Bill. "What is this conference about, after disappearing all day and breaking your

92

luncheon date, with me waiting hours?".

He said, "Sit down and keep quiet. It's about Lydia Thorp."

She sat down, as nearly out of Guard's vision as possible, flung her coat from her shoulders and began to smooth off the gloves. "She should be buried with full honors by now, the time you've taken about it."

Guard said with deliberate brutality, "She's in the morgue. That's where they take murdered women."

Lizanne sat down again very quietly. She had icy hands and feet.

And Alix shrilled, "You don't have to say things like that! Give me a drink, Bill."

He began to mix it. "This conference is at the request of Inspector Tobin. He's on his way now."

"Do we have to talk to him?" She dropped her gloves, picked them up nervously, and her red-taloned fingers twisted at the clasp.

"He'll talk. We'll listen." It was almost command. Bill passed her the glass.

Dinky drawled, "My God, you can't expect Alix to keep her mouth shut. You ought to know that by now."

Alix glared at him. "Dinky will be a help. Drunks always are when the police come into it."

"Smart girl. Knows her investigations." He grinned wickedly, and she drank without a word.

Guard spoke, again not looking at anyone. "The police are strangely psychic about undercurrents. You'd better stop hating under your breaths. They can sense a scene."

"I hate you," Alix said. She stated it as a fact.

He pushed his chair now where he could look straight into her empty eyes. "And I hate you. And Bill hates you. And Dinky hates all of us because we let Dene die."

Alix's mouth twisted. "You forgot we have company." Her eyelashes lifted at Lizanne.

Guard said, "She's in this too whether she likes it or not."

Alix interrupted him, "And we don't know Dene is dead."

Dinky said, "You know he's dead."

"I don't." She was frightened, as she had been at her cocktail party. "You may know but I don't."

Bill's voice was calm. "Guard suggested we simmer down. He's right. Tobin is considered the smartest cop on homicide."

Dinky flung an arm. "Maybe we should try loving thoughts! My God, give me a drink!" He shoved his glass across. "What's Lydia Thorp's death to do with Dene?"

"Don't be a fool." Guard took the glass again. "You know it's all linked. It's all the cross-eyed bear."

Dinky said, "Someone should have potted the Old Bear before he made such a screwy will. Nobody but Jem March would have let him ball things up this way."

"And Father," Alix supplied. "Father helped."

Bill's voice was calming anew. "If they hadn't all been directors in National, he wouldn't have got away with all that business of a mutilated check and a stamp for a signature."

"There's plenty he wouldn't have got away with if he hadn't been the richest man in the world," Dinky said. "He was nuts. Plain nuts. And we all know it. There was a streak of insanity a yard wide and all wool in Old Viljaas. We all know it." He was beginning to show the liquor he'd been gulping. "If he hadn't been the richest man in the world, with Jem March and Ted Bruce as his cohorts, that will could have been thrown down the drain the day it was filed, and you know it." He waggled his finger under Guard's nose. "It wouldn't have held up in any court if the Ambassador hadn't been his lawyer. And Jem his banker!" His voice was rising hysterically. "And if you'd torn up the god-damned will and given the Viljaas brats their bloody money that day, Dene wouldn't have been murdered!" He screamed the last word and then collapsed like an old balloon into his chair, sobbing, his head in his arms.

Alix said maliciously, "He still carries the torch."

Guard thundered, "Keep your mouth shut." He took Dinky's glass and set it into the drooping fingers.

Bill said, "Of course, Dinky's right. Knut was insane. He hated all three sons as only an insane man could hate. Otherwise he'd have left the money straight out to his fool charities and his prevention-of-criminals hobby. He meant for it to go there." He leaned forward, his voice softer than before, but his eyes were beginning to turn yellow as lamps. "He wanted his sons to suffer first. He planned it, two to be murdered and one to be hanged."

The corridor door was rapped upon. Lizanne went on padded feet toward it.

Sergeant Moore was with Inspector Tobin now but not in uniform. His blue suit didn't fit very well, and his face and shoes were still those of a policeman, but he wouldn't shock the marble-and-silver-brocade lobby, passing through.

Bill came forward, hand outstretched, again the perfect host, again with blue gray eyes. He took Tobin's hat; Moore clung to his. "We've been waiting for you, Inspector. You know Guard Croyden, of course; and Miss Steffasson. I don't believe you've met the Bruces. Mrs. Tinker"—Alix's eyes didn't move—"and Mr. Bruce."

Dinky lurched up his head. He was decidedly drunk now. " 'Salways nice to meet friends of Alix," he bubbled.

Guard and Bill both turned warning eyes on her and she said nothing, but her look was murderous.

Bill spoke quickly, easily, "I suppose it's still 'no' on joining us in a drink?"

"Sorry," Tobin said.

There was a circle of them now. Moore, as before, rambled the room before seating himself on the outskirts. He looked at Dinky as if he were of a distinctly different species.

Tobin felt for his hat, seemed to notice it was gone, and dug his hands into his pants pockets. "No use hedging on this. A woman's been murdered. There isn't anything like a clue to go by. Usually isn't in this type of murder. But one thing seems to stand out. No one in New York knew this woman except a certain group of you."

"In'imates," Dinky beamed. "Absolute in'imates." Then he muttered, "Never could see why ol' Bill kept ol' sourpuss so long for his sec'tary. Could 'a' had his pick."

"You can see he won't help." Alix played with her wide diamond-and-sapphire bracelet. "Before you came he mentioned that he only saw Miss Thorp once. But when drunk, he fancies himself a comedian. You can't trust a word he says."

Bill cut her off. "I'm certain, Alix, that Inspector Tobin has had plenty of experience in dealing with those who have had a bit too much."

"A bit," Alix scorned.

This knock on the door surprised Lizanne. Everyone was there already. But Tobin said, "That will be the others." Moore was on his feet. "I hope you don't mind my asking them to join us. I'm certain they belong with those connected with Lydia Thorp. No matter what they say."

All eyes were on the door Moore was opening. And Lans and Sally Vaught walked in. Lizanne started out of the chair and then she sank back. It was foolish to think of protecting him now. He was safe with the Inspector of New York's homicide squad and his chief aide present.

Bill wasn't even prepared for his coming. That was on his face, on the faces of all of the others in their first unmasked surprise, although Guard was always unrevealing, and Dinky in his haze recovered quickly.

"It's Sally, my pal Sally." Dinky sounded delighted.

Sally was ill at ease; it wasn't the police; it wasn't anyone. It was the room, for her eyes skittled it, the oyster-white and maroon and modern molded glass; it was violets and carelessly flung fox. Her cheap tan fur coat, the cheap black hat—too extreme in style, the cheap scrap of black veil too short for her nose—everything she wore, even her face, didn't belong. She was conscious of it.

Lans was ill at ease but it wasn't that he didn't belong. He did. He was only pretending in his Seventh Avenue costume that he didn't. He didn't want to see these people, especially for them to see him.

Alix's eyes were wide. "Lans!" She cried it.

He barely said, "Hello," and to Bill's, "We are honored, Lans," he didn't answer.

Tobin said, "Mr. and Mrs. Vaught, but I guess you all know each other."

Guard gave his chair to Sally. Lans was taking off his form-fitting overcoat, flinging it as if the beautiful table were no more than a boarding-house hall-tree. He caught at a chair, dragging it over the thick rug to Lizanne's.

She didn't glance at him.

"Drink, Lans?" Bill asked.

"If it isn't poisoned."

"If it is, I'm dead," Dinky said gaily. "My pal Sal wants a drink, don't you, baby?"

She answered, "No," and "Yes," and wasn't comfortable.

He insisted, "Sure you do. Everybody wants a drink. Everybody but Alix's pals." He bleared at the police.

Guard said, "Sit down, Dinky. I'll take care of Mrs. Vaught."

Bill held out to Lans the glass he had fixed. Lans took it but their eyes stared unwaveringly at each other as their fingers almost touched. Lizanne stopped looking at them.

Tobin said, "If you're all comfortable, I'll go on. No clues, no acquaintances except you that are here. I don't know why Lydia Thorp was murdered. I'm pretty sure one of you"—he leaned back and looked out from under his half-shut eyes—"if not every one of you, knows that answer. Motive."

"Incredible," Alix murmured.

Sally bit out, "I never even heard of her! You can't count me in this."

"T-t-! Mustn't interrupt," Dinky warned playfully.

"On the face of it, there isn't any motive. Spinster, age about forty, no money, no valuables, no reason for killing her." He hesitated. "And she was killed. I don't know why. Somebody does. Somebody did it."

"You don't think one of us." Alix's voice was amused. Her mouth wasn't.

Dinky leered, "It was the Phantom Shadow." He tittered gleefully.

Alix turned thin lips to Bill. "Make him keep quiet."

Bill told her gently, but there was a tension in the lines about his mouth, "Dinky's all right. He is just a little difficult."

Guard turned to Tobin. "What did you hear from London?"

"No more known of her there. Worked two years at the Claridge. No previous references. Left to become secretary to Mr. Folker. She lived at the hotel; didn't seem to have any more friends than she did here. Never did anything nor went any place to anyone's knowledge."

Bill asked, "What did her passport tell, Inspector?"

"We've been through all her things. No passport, Mr. Folker. No papers of any kind, except a few receipted bills, for milk and dentist, ordinary things. The dentist, by the way, doesn't even remember her."

Bill said, "She wasn't a woman that would be remembered by someone meeting her casually."

Tobin nodded. "So I'd gather. Well, that leaves me right where I am. With you who did know her."

A slight something, maybe a stiffening, a wariness, crawled about the circle.

"I might as well say that if you were less well-known persons, if this were under the El tracks, if Captain Croyden weren't vouching for you—well, men and women have been pulled in on less suspicion."

Evident Tobin didn't suspect Guard. But a government man could kill as well as anyone else. It didn't make you infallible just because you had a job that your ex-wife's father had given you.

Alix touched her violets. "You mean we are suspected——"

"That's what I mean," he stated distinctly. "Now

we're going to talk about Lydia Thorp."

Moore hauled out his little book and a brand-new yellow pencil. He did it with gesture, calling attention to what he was about to do.

Guard had taken Sally's glass, refilled it, placed it in her hand. Lans shook his head but she wasn't watching him. Her eyes were on Bill Folker.

Bill was prating glibly, "I told you last night all I know of Lydia Thorp. If you want my alibi, I fear it's not much good. I spent the evening here in my room working until Mrs. Tinker phoned me, sometime after ten, I presume." He turned his eyes on Alix. She nodded briefly but Lizanne felt certain this was surprise to her. "She asked me to call for her at the Waldorf, which I did. We came here, had a drink while we waited for her brother." He shrugged. "That's all. I wasn't out for more than an hour at the most all evening. Unfortunately, there's no one to vouch for that."

It was possible that he had been there in an inner room. But there had been that indefinable sense of being alone when Lizanne came in, for once of there being no one save herself in the suite.

"Did she ever appear menaced by anything fearful?" Tobin asked.

Bill's whole expression bespoke the absurdity of the idea. But Lizanne knew, knew the woman was afraid. And she realized something else: Lydia Thorp had gone away because she dared not stay, because it had been ordered that she go and she was afraid not to obey. But why had she been killed? She had obeyed. Surely, in those few brief hours away, she couldn't have suddenly become a menace to Stefan. And then Lizanne knew with a certainty that left her with stone in her breast,

Lydia Thorp had been marked for death that day when she went out with sagging shoulders and her left hand limp in her coat pocket. But there was nothing she could do, no one the plain woman could trust. A shudder she could not control trembled Lizanne from shoulders to knees. She was amazed to feel Lans's hand cover hers but when she looked at him, he took it away quickly and muttered under his breath, "Getting cold feet?"

Tobin tackled Dinky. "Mr. Bruce."

"I like questions," Dinky declaimed grandiloquently. "I like questions and answers both." He hadn't sobered, though the quick lifting of his head made him seem aware. "I welcome 'em!" he confided.

"Good," Tobin said patiently, and prodded, "What about Miss Thorp?"

Dinky truly seemed to welcome questions. He wanted to talk. He felt talkative. It was written all over his face in triumph. They couldn't shut him up now. "Minute I laid eyes on her I said, 'Why's Bill got that ol' sourpass sitting out there?' I said, 'Bill, why you got that old hag out there? Whyn't you get one of your little beauties to welcome the long-lost friends?' Tha's just what I said." He rambled on.

Tobin recalled him. "You knew her then?"

"Only laid eyes on her once in my life. Came up from Washington and laid eyes on her and said——"

He was off again. Alix's hands were clenched and Bill was only pretending boredom. Guard was watching carefully.

Alix broke in, "You can see you won't get anywhere with him!"

Dinky said, "Sssst!" to her and to Tobin, "Now what you want to know?"

"Can you remember where you were last night?" Even Tobin seemed to have given up.

Dinky was concentrating hard. "Last night. What was last night?" He screwed his face into thought.

Lizanne spoke, reminding him rather than the Inspector. "He was with me early."

"That's it!" Dinky was triumphant. "And I brought Lizanne home because she wasn't hungry at all after we got to Jim and Jack's. Tha's a woman for you. Starving one minute and the next minute not hungry. Can't say I blame her." He swung around accusingly to Lans. "The food at that dump is *terrible*, simply *terrible!* Don't see how you can stand it."

Lans muttered, "I don't have to eat there."

"And after you left Miss Steffasson?" Tobin suggested.

"Then I went down to see the old man, the Ambassador, my father."

"How did you know where he was having dinner?"

"Called Alix's apartment. Sure." He was tremendously pleased with himself over that. "Told me they were heading for the Crillon. So I went, too. But they weren't very friendly."

"I should think you would have been there before the others." Tobin was checking. "They didn't leave until about nine, Mr. Croyden told me. And Miss Steffasson was in bed by that time, she says."

"Maybe I stopped a place or two on the way," Dinky said slyly. "A bar here, a bar there. They were eating dinner and they weren't friendly so I didn't stay very long. And then——"

"Yes?" Tobin was waiting now.

"I went lots of places!" Dinky was triumphant.

"Can't you mention a few?" Guard asked coldly.

102

"Oh, just every place." Dinky waved a vague hand. "I don't know their names. They all looked and smelled just the same. Music and long bars. You know they're all just alike, Guard. You couldn't tell 'em apart yourself." He smiled seraphically, well pleased with his recital, and passed his glass across. "Give us a drink, Guard, and make it taste like something better than old soup."

Alix said acidly to Tobin, "I trust you found that helpful."

He smiled at her, eliminated the smile, and turned to Lans. "Mr. Vaught?"

Guard handed Dinky the refilled glass and took Sally's from her unprotesting fingers.

Lans was playing a part, one that might have been real to Jim and Jack's but wasn't here. "I told you I never saw the dame. I told you there wasn't any reason to drag me and Sally up here."

"I suppose you don't know these people," Tobin insisted.

"Maybe I did know them once. I haven't laid eyes on any of them in years and what's more——"

Sally helped out. Her two drinks had evidently been heavy. "We don't know any of them. Except that redhead and her fellow." She pointed out Dinky. "They've been coming to the club a couple of times. We didn't know the woman that got killed, never even heard of her."

Guard handed her refilled glass and he said, "Here's your drink. Don't spill it." Something like that. No more than that, but a light blazed in her face. Wonderment and knowledge, wonderment at the sudden knowledge. "Wait a minute," she cried.

Lans was trying to catch her eye but he couldn't signal. Not in the silence that dared Sally Vaught to continue.

"Wait a minute. Was she the dame that came to see you? She was!" She was triumphant. "Of course she was, hon. Kind of old and faded out. Used to come early and talk to you before the music started." She faced Guard. "You were there once, too. Remember? And you said to the busboy, 'Don't spill it,' just like you did now. You looked just the same." She went on babbling in excitement over her discovery.

There was black cloud over her husband.

"Well, now what do you say?" Tobin asked.

Lans muttered, "All right, she was. I still didn't know her."

"What did she want with you?"

Lans hesitated. He said finally and with finality, "You wouldn't believe me if I told you."

"What did she want?" Tobin repeated.

Lans laughed shortly. "She wanted to steal something of mine." He repeated the laugh. "I told you, you wouldn't believe it."

Tobin didn't. That was obvious. Neither did Sally.

"Why, hon," she began, "you told me she was an old friend looking for a job."

"I lied to you," Lans said flatly. He turned on Tobin again. "I'm telling you the truth. She came to steal something for her boss—but I don't keep things where they get stolen." He was grinning now. "I've got more sense than that. And no matter how much any of you think you're going to hang on me, I've got a castiron alibi at the club. I couldn't have killed this Thorp dame even if I'd wanted to, and I didn't. She couldn't help what she was doing. She was just trying to earn a living." Finished, he settled himself as if at ease, but his hands trembled on his pack of cigarettes.

Tobin wasn't through with him. "And what did Miss Steffasson and Mr. Bruce want with you?"

Lizanne opened her mouth and then she shut it again quickly. She couldn't speak now with Bill Folker sitting over there; it was his business, not hers. Bill was silent.

Dinky said thickly, sleepily, "I didn't want nothing, want a drink," then dropped his head again.

Lans began pleasantly, "I don't know what they wanted. Why do people come to night clubs——"

But Sally interrupted with a glare, "She came in asking if he was Lans Viljaas and I told her——"

Tobin didn't let her finish. He said, "Viljaas," repeated it, savored it, "Viljaas. The Old Bear." He had a smile of contentment now as if suddenly everything was clear. He looked around the circle with the smile still on his lean face. He didn't even appear to notice the crackling in the atmosphere that came with Sally's blurting of the name, the thunder-burst of silence that now covered all, save Sally with her nose in her glass, and Dinky's drooped head.

"Well," he took a deep breath and his smile broadened, "the Viljaas estate is to be closed April first, I believe. So that's it." His eyes turned hard. "So you're Lans Viljaas?"

Sally came out of the glass. "No, he's Lans Vaught. She thought he was Lans Viljaas."

"Keep quiet," Lans warned her harshly. "You've said enough."

She pouted out her lip as she looked at him and then suddenly she was awake; she wiggled, frightened, back into her chair.

Lans continued, "None of the sons use the Viljaas name, Inspector. It was too well known after the Old

Bear's will was published, if not before. It left them open to too many inconveniences."

"And you thought he was Lans Viljaas?" Tobin asked Lizanne softly. "I wonder what made you think that."

Lans answered for her. "Why don't you ask Bill Folker that one?" He relished his question, his mouth mocking Bill there on the chaise longue. He wasn't nervous now, not even when Bill's eyes lifted to meet his, lifted flaunting the danger color. His was wickedly enjoying it.

Tobin's brows were together. "The Viljaas case. You're interested in that, Mr. Folker?"

"I represent Stefan Viljaas."

Tobin continued, "There was a third brother, if I remember."

Dinky lifted the groggy head. "They killed him."

Tobin was alert. "They——" His eyes went around the group.

No one spoke. It was as if each waited for the other. Alix, turning her bracelet round and round, couldn't endure the silence. "He doesn't mean us." It would have been better if she hadn't said it and she knew it at once. And then she had to go on, the bracelet whirling more and more nervously. Again everyone was waiting. "Dene disappeared. Dinky's always thought he was killed. He gets ideas, you know."

"Disappeared. I remember the case. Headlines. And then it was dropped. Never found him, alive or dead."

"That's right." Dinky nodded heavily.

Alix didn't control nerves. "If he'd been killed his body would have been found, of course—in two years."

Guard leaned forward. "We—Bill and I—are trying to find him, Inspector. According to the terms of the will, he must be found before the first of April."

"What for?" Lans was insolent. "You don't need him. You only need his part of the check. And you've probably got it, one of you."

"Are you accusing me——" Guard began. His face was uglier.

Lizanne's hand without her own volition was on Lans's coat sleeve.

"Have it any way you like," Lans swaggered.

Tobin took over again. "Motive. That's what was missing, but not now. Not when it overlaps with the Viljaas business. Almost too many motives you can think of. Maybe she knew too much. Maybe she was working for the wrong government. Maybe lots of things." He pulled out his watch. "Better get on with this. You'll be wanting your dinner." He looked at Alix.

She was armored. "I didn't know Lydia Thorp. I certainly didn't kill her." She wasn't nervous in speaking of this. It was mention of Dene that upset her. Yet she couldn't have been there when Dene was killed. Everyone would have been talking about her if she'd been at the Lodge. She wasn't someone that could be hidden underground.

Lizanne didn't listen to the perfunctory questions the Inspector was asking. Of them all her story was weakest and she knew it. But no one could think she killed Lydia Thorp. Tobin was looking for motive; she had none. And she wasn't afraid even if he did go far astray and select her as guilty. She alone could be cleared completely. Lydia's own message made her safe where this was concerned.

Tobin leaned to them. "This is all for now. I'm counting on each of you to let me know if anything turns up that might help me find the murderer of Miss Thorp.

Just remember, none of you is in the clear yet about this." The men were standing now, moving about. "Where's my hat?"

Lans said loudly, "Don't go until Sally gathers herself together. You promised me safe passage out of here, remember." He looked around him insolently.

It was past seven by Lizanne's wristwatch. He must have a substitute, someone who could fill in if he were away, delayed. The import struck her with a little chill. He could have been out of the club last night. She looked up at him but he ignored her, walking over to stand safely beside Tobin and Moore.

Dinky whispered to Sally and her eyes brightened. She teetered to Lans and the police. They went out.

It was as if everyone remaining drew breath again.

Alix said, "A drink, Bill. My God, why did you let Dinky stay when you knew how drunk he was?"

"I'm not drunk," Dinky protested gayly.

"You were," she retorted. "At the wrong time. As usual." She took the glass Bill passed to her, drank one-third of it without stopping.

Lizanne asked, "Do you need me?"

Bill smiled at her. "I'd rather you'd be here. Take a comfortable chair."

He rearranged the one Sally had had. It was beside Guard's, and she was afraid of Guard. She half-turned where she wouldn't have to face him. She couldn't relax. Not in a circle where a murderer might be sitting, where hate was only momentarily leashed.

Bill continued, "We must get this thing lined up. We haven't any time to waste. Isn't that what the Ambassador told you last night, Guard?"

"Emphatically." Guard went on, "He's worried about

these other governments. It will be suicidal for the civilized allies if the combine of Three get the mines, yet they can outbid any other government and we know it. We also know they won't stop at anything, to throw the mines on the market."

Lizanne started up. "But Lans isn't careful."

Guard looked at her. "He doesn't admit he's a Viljaas. These agents wouldn't know him. He's been away so many years he's almost lost identity."

Bill explained, "I've been attending to the foreign end of things for Stefan, Lizanne, and they all know me. That's why I'm under lock and key here, most of the time. Of course, they could trace Lans down."

"He should be warned!" she cried. "I know he doesn't realize. Surely, he wouldn't just go anywhere if he knew, and live in that dreadful hotel, and——"

Bill said, "If he'd listen to reason, if he weren't so certain that we were trying to get his triangle—but you can't talk sense to him. Lydia tried. She told him in what danger he stood, and if he'd only come in with us, turn over his papers to Guard or the Ambassador——"

"And the bear," Guard added.

"You've still Dene to count in," Alix reminded.

Bill told her impatiently, "If Lans would get together with us on this, I think we'd find him in a hurry. But, of course, Dene's afraid to come into it when we're standing apart like stray bulldogs."

"If he's alive." Dinky was sober enough now.

"Dead or alive, he has to be counted on," Guard amended. "The three sections of the check must be put together on April first."

"With the bear," Alix repeated. She added, "You'll have to count me out where Lans is concerned."

"We're all counted out there," Bill said. "That's why I have Lizanne here. She only has any chance of getting to him. Because she's new, not one of us."

Lizanne wasn't enjoying this. It was senseless to feel that Lans's name belonged on her tongue alone, yet she did. She wished they would talk of something else.

They might have been idling with gossip, rather than making every word count in a fabulous plan. She knew this combination wasn't newly formed. Bill, Alix, Guard, and Dinky, without need of words, understood each other. Admittedly, they stood for the dreaded Stefan Viljaas, and she knew that his work had already included two murders. Nor would he hesitate at others, if it were to his advantage.

Alix said, "What about the wife? I'm not saying she could do anything with Lans. No one ever could. But a husband and wife share intimacy no matter how much they hate, especially if they're cooped up in one little hotel room the way he and Sally are. She should know where to lay hands on his triangle, and the bear. If Lans continues stubborn despite your secretary, Bill"—her lips were narrow—"I think you should set Sally to work."

Dinky said, "Sally doesn't know a thing, not even his right name. But don't worry about her. I'm taking care of that. Of course, I'm not pretending, darling sister, that I have the fascination of Bill. But I'm young. Maybe I'll learn." He swished over to the oval hanging mirror. "I'm really a handsome devil." He examined himself with more than approval, with fondness. "Much better looking than Bill."

Alix said, "You nauseate me, Dinky," and turned her head.

"The wife is an idea." Bill might have been thinking

aloud. "I wonder about her loyalty. Women of that class are generally too loyal to their husbands. You noticed she sprang to his defense every time she opened her mouth today."

"But, God, how stupid." Dinky pushed back his chair. "Letting it out that Lydia had gone to him. After he'd denied it."

"She will always act on impulse, that type does," Guard said. "And a little liquor helps."

Bill said, "Maybe it could get her to remember where Lans has hidden the bear."

"How do you know he has it?" Lizanne asked quickly, not as if she cared, as if from idle curiosity.

"He must have it," Alix cried. But warning had passed to her from Bill and she was quiet. Nor did anyone else speak.

Lizanne looked around at them and apologized. "I didn't mean to be curious." She hesitated. "I wish I could see what I'm supposed to get from Lans."

Bill said, "I have Stefan's section of the check here. The imprint of the bear is on it." He took from his inner pocket a billfold.

Guard said angrily, "You know you're a fool to carry it about with you, Bill."

"So you tell me. But I feel safer with it under my hand, and I don't always carry it, Guard. I change my purloined letter frequently." He smiled. He had taken the bit of paper from the fold, passed it now across to Lizanne. It was the equilateral triangle. It was Dene's. Stefan's must be the scalene and Lans's the same. There was no other way to triangle the check. This one she had seen before, held in her hands before.

Her fingers would have quivered, but she rested her

wrist on her knee before handing the tiny piece back, saying, "That is the cross-eyed bear?"

"Yes." Bill replaced it in the billfold. "It isn't large, you see; it's something a man could hide away easily, or carry about with him. If you could find out where he keeps it, it would help." Not his final words, but the softness of the way he spoke them, put the taste of fear again into her mouth.

Lans wouldn't die until they did find out. Not by hand of these four. Bill had Dene's triangle. It had been taken from Dene's dead body. But that didn't necessarily mean that Bill with his own hand had done this; any one of the four, or Stefan himself, might be the one. It meant only that Bill was custodian of that tiny scrap of paper. She knew they were together as one in this, no matter how different was each one's particular duty, no matter what separate alibis they might devise.

Why should they all be working for Stefan? He was the only one who would profit by this. The others would receive nothing but what he gave them. Doubtless he gave promises, but if these were unfulfilled, what could Bill Folker and the Bruces and Guard Croyden do? Nothing—do without. Maybe they trusted Stefan; maybe they didn't believe he would get rid of them when they had outgrown their usefulness to him. And with cold creeping, she realized with certainty that she was in the same boat. She too would know too much, wouldn't be worth salvage when her duties were done.

She stood. "I'll see Lans tomorrow." She excused herself again, crossed to her own apartment. But someone was there, the lights were on in the bedroom. She turned on the living-room lamp quickly and stood motionless, waiting.

It was Anna who emerged, unhurried, unembarrassed. She looked like a musical-comedy maid; her legs belonged on a stage not on duty. Her eyes deliberately lowered as before, she said, "Good evening, Miss. I was turning down your bed." Again the slight accent was noticeable.

Lizanne doubted, although the bed would be turned down. There was something in the girl that wasn't maid-like, something sly. She stood with her hands respectfully folded on her starched apron. But she wasn't respectful; she was almost insolent as she moved away.

The box. But it was untouched there on the closet floor. Lizanne didn't stay more than a few seconds looking at it, not seeing it. Then she closed the closet door, returned to bolt the others. She was too late. Guard Croyden was already standing in the room, frighteningly big.

She began to back away. It was absurd to be terrified, stricken as she was, more absurd to show it. Yet that big brutal mass might have been what Lydia saw coming to her last night. Perhaps her throat too could utter no syllable until it was too late. Strangling was the easiest way. Tobin knew. He was of the homicide squad.

Guard said, "I want to talk to you."

Speech returned but her fright didn't diminish. Her heart was pounding so hard he must have seen its beat through her dress. "How did you get in here?"

Irony was heavy in his voice. "I picked the lock." He walked over to the couch, made himself comfortable. "Sit down," he ordered.

Gingerly, not taking her eyes from him, she felt her way to a chair.

He said, "I'm still trying to figure you in this. The

trouble is you haven't any more known background than poor Lydia had. You might have sprung full-blown from West One Hundred Eighteenth Street."

They had tried to trace her.

"I'm a government man. If you're as innocent as you make yourself out to be, you needn't be afraid to open up to me. If you're something else again——"

"What else would I be?" she defied him.

"Plenty." His eyes shivered through her. "For one thing, you might have been put here to steal the cross-eyed bear, to make certain that it doesn't appear until after the first of April."

Her teeth were chattering. She said, "I don't believe you're a government man."

He said as evenly as before, "It doesn't matter a damn to me what you believe. You're going to answer questions."

She knew that he was right. Here alone with him, she would be afraid not to answer questions. But he wasn't as right as he thought. He didn't know she'd learned in two years to dissemble.

He asked, "Why, did that Leeds girl come here this morning?"

Her answer came with surprising ease. "Mostly I think because of the sensation, because it happened in my old room. You understand. And she was in on it and I'd taken Lydia's job here, and—you do understand?"

He said coldly, "I think she came for more than that. I believe Lydia sent something to you by this Leeds."

She made her voice tiny purposely. "I don't know why you should think that."

His eyes bored into her again. "Because important papers are missing."

Guard had been there. She could hardly make words come. Again she was afraid, afraid of him, yet afraid to try to get away. Her terror sounded although she tried to quell it. "How do you know that?"

He said casually, "I'm with the government. I had permission to go through her things. I want you to hand over those papers."

"I don't have any papers. How could I have them?" she flashed at him. "I didn't know Lydia Thorp. I didn't even know Janet Leeds but casually and she certainly couldn't have known Lydia. I don't see how by any stretch of your imagination you could think we three could have made a contact. And certainly you don't think Janet Leeds searched through Lydia's things for some papers she knew nothing about to bring to me who knew nothing of any of it. It's"—she was scornful—"it's ridiculous."

It was; even he couldn't deny it, stated that way.

She pressed her advantage. "Why don't you believe the murderer took them?" There was only one answer to that. He knew who the murderer was, knew he didn't have the papers. And he did know. She was certain. But he wouldn't say so. "Or do you think I killed her?"

"No, I don't think you did."

She didn't like the way he was looking at her, boring his eyes into her skull. She wasn't afraid that he could find out what lay in secret within her, but it made her uneasy.

"You could have but I don't think so. However, it doesn't alter my belief that you didn't come in here uninformed. I don't know who sent you. For all I know you may have come from the Committee of Three. Or you may be Lans's spy. I wouldn't doubt that, though he hasn't any money to pay you. But there are the Great Expectations." He had noticed her interest in Lans then; she had thought it hidden, made casual. And he didn't like it. It was in the way he spoke. He moved his hands. "You may be working for someone I don't know about. One thing I do know. You're not on the right side. Because that's where I stand.".

"You and Bill?"

"We are working together."

That didn't ring true as did his other words. And she wondered suddenly if he were what he said, if Bill alone were Stefan's man. If he were she could trust Guard, tell him everything, have his help. His shoulders might even be comforting, not frightening. But she didn't dare trust anyone. To trust, to tell, meant stark danger for her.

He smiled, his interpretation of a smile. "If you still refuse to help me out, I'll get hold of that girl. She'll talk to me." It wasn't a threat, but it held certainty.

That hadn't occurred to her. Was her reaction noticeable? She didn't look at him until she could without a tremor. "She knows no more than I."

Mockery remained on his face. She had given away. He knew that Janet Leeds had reason for coming other than gossip. She must reach the music student before he did. The government position he claimed might bear weight; it couldn't help but do so. It would have with Lizanne had she not seen him before, had she not known he was mixed up with murder. If she could get rid of him now, she might reach Janet before he did.

She said through a yawn, "This isn't getting you anywhere. If you really are a government man, all right, but you can pick some time when I can keep my eyes open. Tonight I can't." She stood up. "I wish you'd get out so I can bolt my doors and go to bed. Of course, if you want to sit there and ponder, I can't stop you. You're bigger than I am. Whatever you decide to do, I'm going to bed now." She stood there, pretending bravery, waiting for what he might decide—hoping.

He stared at her, really smiled. "I'll go. And you sleep on it. Maybe you'll decide it might be safer to confide in me. I'll be here tomorrow."

She waited for him to leave, bolted the door, and waited again. Nine-thirty by her watch. Five minutes, ten minutes, for safety five more, although her nerves were edged. He might even now be on his way to see Janet Leeds. She wouldn't phone from here; she didn't know how many devices for listening they had. She didn't know who below, at desk or switchboard, might be a hireling. She put on the beaver coat, pulled the hood over her bright hair. She left by way of the corridor door. She didn't ring for the elevator here on the tenth floor but ran down two flights to eight. She didn't think she was observed passing through the lobby; no one seemed to notice her; and she took the Central Park South exit, walking west toward the Broadway subways. Somewhere she could phone: a red-bordered cigar store, a phone booth; she knew the number. She also knew the Texas voice.

"I've the most horrible cold; that's why I'm home. If you aren't afraid to risk me—you can sit and spray Lysol on yourself, if you like—come on up."

Lizanne decided. She wasn't afraid to risk catching the cold; the other risk was her fear but it must be taken. "I'll come. But if anyone calls before I get there, anyone," she stressed, "even the police, will you tell them you're too sick to see them tonight? Or if anyone should come.

I must see you alone."

"Don't you worry," Janet said. "I don't want to see anyone, especially the police. I don't want any man seeing me with this red nose and flannel around my neck."

Lizanne rang off, hurried down into the subway hole. No one had followed her. She was certain of it now. She was alone walking down the cold stairs, and there were only the usual faces waiting for the uptown express. At 116th Street she got off; there were several others, but no one walked in her direction. No one followed as she turned down West 118th, stopped in front of the dark house. The elevator boy never hurried to answer the bell; the lights were always too dim in the entrance below, too dim on the circular winding steps where she had ascended with Guard Croyden but a short time ago. But she could run up the steps, reach fifth without breath. And she was still alone.

She pushed the buzzer on the door, pushed hard. Janet opened a crack and then wider. She was in old blanket robe, flannel wrapped about her throat, her nose and eyes red-tinged. "Come on in."

Lizanne felt the door closed tight after her. They went into Janet's lighted room, a better room than Lizanne had lived in here, than Lydia had died in.

Janet asked, "What is it? Is it"—she lowered her voice —"something about the letter?"

Lizanne nodded. "It's worse than that. No one knows about the letter yet but even so you're in danger."

The girl's eyes blinked. "But why? What have I done? I called the police the minute I found her."

"It isn't from the police."

Janet understood. She understood too well. Even the red rims of her eyes paled to flesh. "Do you know who killed her?" she whispered.

"I know who might have killed her." She spoke carefully. "I don't think you ought to stay here any longer. Why don't you go home for a while?" She hushed her from speaking. "I can give you the money to get away. I'm getting good money on this job, that's the only decent thing about it; the rest is horrible." She could see Guard Croyden entering through a locked door, his ugly face and more ugly hands, hands that could so easily kill a small thing; Bill's yellow eyes and fingers like fangs; the glass-white hate in Alix's glance. She trembled.

"Why don't you leave it?"

"I can't now. I don't dare. The police on one side, asking questions and not believing anything I say; and these others on the other side doing the same thing. They wouldn't let me leave now." She knew it for the truth it was and terror trembled through her. "But you . . ." She took a breath. "You can go. If you go now before they come to you, you'll be safe. You'll be out of it." She added, "You'd better not stay here tonight. I know you feel miserable, but—maybe you wouldn't get away tomorrow."

Janet could do nothing but stare. "You mean it's that dangerous? Someone might try to stop me?"

"You were here that night when she was killed. The murderer doesn't know what you might remember."

She began to sniff. "You've scared me straight silly, Lizanne. I don't care if it's risking pneumonia. I'm getting out of here. I'm going home." She pulled out a weekend bag from under the bed. "Can I stay tonight with you?"

"That isn't safe. It's even worse. They're all down there and the police in and out." She thought quickly.

"The Martha Washington. They won't let any men in
there. You won't be found. You'll get away."

Janet was throwing things into the bag, jerkily now;
hurriedly she started to dress. "Do you want to call a
cab? It won't take me a minute more."

"I think we'd better walk over to Broadway for one,
where it's light." She didn't say more; she didn't need
to. "Put a scarf over your nose and mouth to keep out the
cold air. I'll ring for the elevator. You stay there in the
doorway till it comes. If anyone should be in it, you can
close the door and be safe."

Her own teeth wanted to chatter the way Janet's did
but she held them clenched. Surely if Guard Croyden had
been coming, he would have before now, or would have
called. There was only the always-discontented slouch
of the boy in the cage. She beckoned Janet and they
descended to first. No one was in the entry; no one in the
dark street outside. They hurried under the shadows
of the university, left them at Broadway, crossing the
still snowy street to the west side.

Lizanne hailed a cab. She drew breath when they were
safe inside, bumping downtown. She lowered her voice.
"I'm going to give you the money now, just in case I can't
get away tomorrow. I'll call you if I'm able, but whatever you do, don't call me. If I get a chance I'll come see
you off but I'm afraid of being followed."

Janet spoke sagely. "I think you'd better go home,
too."

Lizanne said, "I haven't any home. I haven't any
family." And she whispered in sudden stark fear, "I'm
all alone." Lydia Thorp was all alone. And she knew for
the first time why Bill Folker had hired her without
beauty: because she had told him she was all alone.

Janet touched Lizanne's sleeve almost timidly. "Come with me. My family would be pleased to have you."

Lizanne shook her head. "I tell you, they wouldn't let me go." Like Lydia Thorp, she knew too much now. She would never get away unless she could make Dene's murderer admit the truth, not to her alone but to the safe police. And at the moment the police weren't even safe. They could believe she killed Dene! If they could believe she killed Lydia, how much more that she had murdered Dene.

She repeated, "I know they wouldn't let me go."

They were safe at the hotel. She paid the driver, went in with Janet, waited while she was registered. "You'll be all right here. Remember, get away as soon as you can. I'll do my best to get in touch with you but I can't promise."

Janet scribbled an address. "I'll pay you back the loan. And let me hear from you."

The music student had been a slight acquaintance; now she seemed an only friend. Lizanne felt forlorn, lost, as she went out into the dark. It was almost midnight and the night was cold. She crossed the street, waited in chill for the bus. At least, Janet would be away by tomorrow; no one to tell of Lydia's message. For this much longer she herself was saved from death, saved to go on in danger.

Chapter Seven: THE ACID BRAND

TOO WEARIED for more fear, she entered the deserted lobby of The Lorenzo. Tonight's work was done. Nothing mattered now except bed. She walked to the elevator. It was open. And Guard Croyden was inside.

"Oh." It was less a word than a catch of breath. Automatically she took two backward steps, just two.

Guard said, "Going up?"

The elevator attendant said nothing, looked sleepy, dull. She stood, and then she took two steps forward. The cage closed. The elevator stopped at tenth. Guard's steps were behind her as she moved dreamlike to her own door. She took out her key but she couldn't insert it. She held it in wavering fingers. He took it from her, opened it as if it were a simple thing to do. Again he stood aside for her to pass.

It wasn't herself who was doing this. She hadn't been here since she reached the elevator door. She was someone standing outside the frame watching a girl walk deliberately, open-eyed, into danger. The girl didn't have to go up in the elevator with a man who might kill her; she could walk out of the hotel; she could scream for help; she could move so easily to the desk and ask for the house detective. She might be hypnotized for all the volition she had. She stood in her living room watching him turn on lamps. She stood there while he, wordless, helped her off with her coat. Only when he walked back to the corridor door and fastened the bolt did she move, taking a step toward him, her hand flung out in protest.

He said, "We don't want to be interrupted," and her arm dropped, and then he said, "Now that you've had a good sleep, maybe you'll feel more like talking."

She stood there, stupidly telling him, "I didn't get to sleep. I had to go out."

"Had to?"

"Yes."

He said, "I don't suppose there's any use asking where you went?"

"No." She just said it, without emotion, without feeling, not even looking at him.

He was lighting a cigarette. "You might as well sit down. I've some things to say."

"Can't they wait until morning?" She was so tired, half-asleep.

"They cannot. I don't want to be interrupted." He took a chair, made himself comfortable.

She didn't move.

"Would a drink help you?"

She shook her head. "I don't want a drink. I don't want anything but to go to bed."

"I believed that once tonight. You looked so dragged out even I went soft." His face was harsh. "I got out. So you could set about your work. Sit down."

She obeyed. She didn't know why he should insist on talking to her; it had all been aimless. He had learned nothing, nor did she know what he might expect to find out. He knew so much more about it all than she.

He said to the cigarette between his fingers, "I did a little serious thinking while you were out. Sometimes a person gets ideas sitting alone thinking." He was mocking her and something again began to chill her, creeping about her like fog. She sat very still. "One interesting thing occurred to me; sometimes redheaded women don't have red hair when they're born."

She was awake now. She didn't say a word. But she couldn't move her eyes from his.

"There was some girl Dene was playing around with up in the woods. At the time we didn't know about her so we didn't get to talk to her. Later when her name came into it, she was gone." He smoked. "Just an ordinary young girl according to description, nothing out-

123

standing about her at all. She hadn't been there very long and she went away again. It was believed she'd come to New York but no one knew. No one had heard from her since she left. She didn't even come back when her uncle died. Her name was Mary Elizabeth Porter."

She was like a statue.

"We couldn't even begin to trace her, knowing no more than that." He rose then but still she didn't move; she couldn't. She could only wait fearing what was to come, not daring to speculate on it, powerless to stop it. He crossed to the couch table, put out his cigarette. He said, "She didn't have orange hair," and then his voice changed. It wasn't light, mocking, as it had been. It was cruel as the lines slashed in his face. He was in front of her and he said, "Well?"

She pushed back into the chair, holding with damp palms to the arms of it.

He repeated, "Well?"

She jumped then, up and away from him, but his hand caught her wrist and held her motionless a moment. Fear made her alert as an animal. She felt the initial relaxation of his fingers, and she wrenched away, fled into the bedroom; by miracle closed the door in his face, locked it. She was tense, shivering against it, hearing him turn the knob, sensing his weight on the panels.

She whispered because she couldn't make sound, "Go away. Go away. Go away. Go away, or I'll call the police." He couldn't hear her.

He was calling, "Don't be a fool. Open the door. Open that door." The knob was clacking as he spoke.

After long moments she heard his hand removed, heard his receding footsteps, heard the outer door open, close. Only then did she creep away. She was drained of all strength. She didn't know what she could do. To call the police was futile. Tobin believed Guard Croyden a government man. Her word, that no matter what his government status he was working for Stefan Viljaas, perhaps even for The Three, would be to no avail. They would all deny it.

She began to undress with quivering fingers, letting her clothes slide from her, without caring where they lay. The new expensive wool dress, her satin slip. A worse thought smote her: he had entered that outer locked door before. "I picked the lock." She couldn't go out and fasten the bolt; she didn't dare. Yet she must. Anything but wake in the night and find him beside her bed. She didn't wait to take off the satin step-ins, to put on the satin nightgown; she ran blindly into the living room. And he was standing there.

His grin was evil. "The old door-bang gag——" He broke off. It was too late now, to move, to do anything. He had seen the bear. And he hadn't known. She had been safe before.

He was stating a fact to himself. "Dene had the bear." It seemed a long time before he remembered that she was standing there. His head nodded to the bedroom. "Go put something on."

But she didn't go alone. It was like walking in a nightmare; you couldn't move because your feet wore lead slippers, but you moved. She knew now how Lydia had died, obeying him because there was nothing else she could do, because he was bigger, stronger. He followed her; she could feel his bulk behind her, as she had in the corridor. He closed the bedroom door.

She took her robe from the closet, wrapped herself in it.

"Get in bed."

"No." She dared to say it. She wouldn't do that. Even if he were bigger she didn't have to be a sheep, help him set the stage for her murder. "No!" She repeated it, with anger now.

He looked at her, scorn on his mouth. "I'm not Bill. I wouldn't touch you with a ten-foot pole."

That hadn't even occurred to her, only death. Scarlet now flooded her face as he spoke the idea and she was suddenly more angry. But she wasn't to be allowed even anger, only terrible sick fright. For he repeated, "Get in bed. You told me you were tired." She heard in his voice the ruthlessness she had seen on his face. Nothing would stop him in what he intended to do.

The way Lydia had been found. Those thick hands about her throat. She swallowed hard. She touched the edge of the bed. "I'm all right here."

Surprisingly he agreed, "Suit yourself."

He didn't act now as if he were planning to kill her. But how could she know? She'd never faced present danger; before it had been only possibility.

His mouth twirked. "We can really get somewhere now."

Her eyes were wide with fright. She couldn't help jumping when he came over to her, but he only held out a cigarette, insisted, "Take it. Calm you down."

He lit it from a small lighter, went back to his chair and settled himself. He repeated, "Yes, we really can get somewhere now." Then he grinned at her. "You realize your life wouldn't be worth a plugged nickel if Stefan Viljaas knew what I do." He hesitated, suggested, "Or Lans."

She nodded dully, "Or Lans."

"But if you're a good girl, they needn't know." His grin was uglier. Whatever way he meant it, she was too numb now to speak, to care. She could only listen.

He spoke sharply as if he would wake her out of her apathy. "You understand that, don't you? I'd only have to tell them you're marked with the bear, and you'd be found. They aren't going to divide, you know. Not if they can help it. But I'm not going to tell them. Not now. Not yet. You're too valuable to me." He mocked again, "You'll do as I say now because you have to. You realize that, don't you?"

She whimpered, "Yes. I do." She wanted to cry but she wouldn't cry. She'd walked into this on her own feet and she wouldn't give up yet. If he weren't going to kill her, there was still time to save herself.

"I'm glad we understand each other. It's been difficult for me before." She was the mouse but he was not a cat toying with her. He was something worse, something out of a bad dream. "Well, suppose you talk."

"What do you want to know?"

He looked steadily at her. "About Dene."

"About Dene." She didn't know where to begin.

"He's dead, isn't he?"

"Yes, he's dead."

"Tell me about it."

She shook her head. "I don't know about it."

His mouth was a line. "Don't start that again. I don't care now whether you think I'm with the government or on my own in this or a part of the Viljaas crowd. You'll answer me now or you'll go out like a light. I'm through with waiting."

Spirit returned. She flared at him, "I don't know as much about it as you do. I saw you up there. You didn't see me, or if you did, you didn't notice me."

"You were—are—Mary Elizabeth Porter."

"Yes." She must admit that much. But she wouldn't admit to marrying Dene, not unless he knew it and she was certain he didn't. No one did. No one had known but Uncle Will and the old preacher, dead now, and the disinterested witness housekeeper. Better let him think she'd only slept with Dene, that didn't seem to matter here.

"Go on. You know he's dead?"

"Yes."

"You know it?" he insisted, and again she nodded. "How?"

She said, "I found him."

The white of snow everywhere, and he didn't return. He went out and he didn't return that night. All that next day she waited, expecting him to come to her, and because of what he had told, she was afraid for him. Even hating him, she was afraid.

She hadn't always hated him; she had been flattered by his attention; she had been infatuated. And she had pitied him because of what he told that she knew must be true; it was in the halting way he spoke of it, and the tremble of fear beneath the words. Dene hadn't wanted to die. And he had known what would happen, known it while he was wilfully gay, trying to cheat the black groping fingers.

He didn't come back that night, and the hatred and horror of what went before didn't change things. You didn't condemn a man to death no matter what you felt.

"I was afraid he was lost. He'd been drinking and he didn't know the woods. I told my uncle and we went to look for him. My uncle was born and raised up there. We found him."

Uncle Will knew trails that city folk, outlanders, wouldn't know existed. They found him, going in on snowshoes along

128

those secret places, fearing he had fallen from one of the peaks because he was city, because he'd been drinking and didn't know the woods. Because if he'd been on the familiar paths, the Inn folk, city folk, hunting or on toboggans or in sleighs, would have discovered him that day.

They found him. He had fallen from the Pointed Peak. He had fallen, but in the back of his neck was a bullet hole.

She said, "He had fallen from one of our high cliffs—with a bullet in his neck."

Guard hadn't known. If he hadn't known, he hadn't killed Dene. One of the others had.

"You're certain of that?"

She was impatient. "We found him lying there."

"But you didn't go to the police."

"No. We didn't."

There in the frosty night, her teeth chattering from far more than cold, persuading Uncle Will. They couldn't go to the police. If they did, she would be killed. Telling Uncle Will. She was Dene's wife. Whoever murdered Dene would murder her, murder Uncle Will. Because the murderer wouldn't want Dene found. He shouldn't have been found. Telling honest Uncle Will, frantically making him understand, forcing him to understand, with tears turning to ice on her cheeks.

"I was afraid to tell. I didn't want us to be murdered, too. Just because we'd found him. Just because I knew him. I made my uncle see it. We buried him there."

Even the native folk seldom went onto those dangerous, below-cliff paths. They had brought a shovel to dig him out of the snow. Digging through snow into the frozen earth, they buried Dene Viljaas with the bullet in his neck. Perhaps in the spring, boys trapping might come upon the lone grave. If he were found, by then they would be safe. No one would know they had done this thing. No one would connect them with it.

"Could you find the place again?"

"Yes. Of course." What good would that do?

"Your uncle——"

"He died six months ago."

"Then only you know." It might be a warning.

"And now you." Her hands were folded quietly.

"No one found the body?"

She shook her head. "Few go on those paths. Few, even of the natives, know how to climb them. Uncle Will was a born woodsman."

He was silent. He said again, as to himself, "Dene had the bear."

She said, "It wasn't in his pockets. Nor was the triangle." That was truth. If you mixed absolute truth with lies, it sounded true. "Whoever killed him must have taken them before rolling him over the cliff."

"You looked?"

"Yes, I looked." She was defiant. "I thought they'd be gone. He'd told me something of the danger he was living in. I knew if they were missing, he'd been murdered, not shot accidentally by a hunter. They were gone."

He asked grimly, "And you—the mark of the bear?"

She closed her eyes, whispered, "He put it there."

"Why?"

"Why?" And she cried out, "Why do you make me remember it? Do you think I want to remember that?"

Their wedding night. It had seemed adventure that morning; she'd only known him a week. Away in the sleigh to that tiny mountain town where the record would be kept secret, would never appear in print. A secret marriage because he was not yet of legal age. Return to the lodge for dinner, his dark eyes laughing down at her, the delightful unexpected excitement turning her cheeks shiny. She was happy then.

He began to drink at dinner. She had known that he drank; once or twice when they went skating, she'd known he had had too much. Uncle Will had objected mildly but she overruled him. No city boy had paid attention to her before. No city boy had ever come with such looks and assurance, such dash, such charm as Dene Thyg. She hadn't known then that his real name was Viljaas, and even so it would have meant nothing to her.

She had never before watched him empty glass after glass as he did now. But she wasn't upset. It didn't change him. He was gay, charming as ever. After dinner to his room at the end of the long wing, casually letting the waiter hear, "Come on down while I get my jacket and then I'll take you home."

She whispered to Guard, "You ought to know why. You knew Dene Viljaas."

She hadn't known him. Not until he closed the door on them, and locked it; said, "Take off your things." But he hadn't said them as a lover, as a husband; he was a stranger standing there, eyeing her out of black inscrutability. And he said, "You needn't look at me like that. I'm not going to rape you. You think I want someone like you? I can have my pick of New York." And biting off each word, "But I can't stand women."

She had been bewildered, so young then, so un-understanding. "But you married me."

She'd never heard him laugh that way. "Sure I married you. No matter what happens now, it won't go to Stefan. And I'll fix it so no one can doubt your word." She didn't know what he meant.

Holding her pinioned, one hand on her throat, "If you make one sound——" His other hand pressing that acid-eating metal against her body. Agony defacing her, and she couldn't move, couldn't even moan until he stood up, laughing at her writhing there on the bed. Laughing, "My father did that to me when I was five years old. I'm going to get another drink. Stay here until I come back."

After he had gone she was sick, wretchedly sick, in the bathroom. And after that she was afraid to leave, afraid she might meet him in the corridor, afraid of what he might do to her if she didn't obey. It was almost dawn before she dared dress and go, creeping out of the hushed Lodge through the servants' entrance. But she didn't leave that vicious piece of metal there. She poured away the acid and took the stamp with her in the pocket of her coat. He'd never do that to anyone else.

She cried again, "You knew him. I didn't know him. Why do you make me remember it?" She shuddered, her face in her hands.

"Was he drunk?"

When she answered she said, "Yes. He was drunk. I didn't even know that then."

"He had the bear." Repetition again. Telling himself. Trying to puzzle it out.

She said, "He had it. But he didn't have it when we found him. It was gone."

She had hidden it, wrapped in an old handkerchief at the back of the deep stamp drawer. Uncle Will didn't ever clean out the post-office drawers; he left that to her. The men who came asking questions about Dene Viljaas couldn't search the federal post office. After the outsiders went away, she moved it; she hid it with the hated marriage license in her own room. No one to find them, only she and Uncle Will living together above the post office. When she fled from Stefan Viljaas' letter she took them with her at the bottom of her trunk. She didn't know the bear was valuable but she did know that with it she might some day accost the murderer. And she wouldn't chance its cruelty ever being loosed on another. It was as if she had buried it.

Guard shook his head. "I can't see why Stefan hasn't got rid of Lans before. If he's had the bear these last two years, why has he waited until now?" He asked abruptly, "Did Dene marry you?"

She lied now, lied deliberately, coldly. "No." She added the truth, "He didn't come back that night. I never saw him alive again."

She didn't know if he believed her She didn't care. She wouldn't admit it. He knew too much about her now. He might believe she was Dene's wife but he couldn't prove it, couldn't tell Stefan Viljaas that about her. If they knew she was the wife, they might suspect she had the bear.

He began to speak again conversationally. "We've been looking for the girl Dene was with that night. It's funny how we ran into the information. Stefan was in Geneva, incognito, but it was generally known he was Stefan Viljaas. A waiter in the hotel had worked at your Lodge. He was pleased to talk to the son of the great Cross-Eyed Bear. He mentioned the girl. We'd never heard of her before. Bill came over here immediately but when we went up to see her, she was gone." He asked, "Why did you run out?"

She said, "I didn't want to be murdered too."

Again he looked steadily at her. "Then why did you take this job?"

She met his eyes. "Believe me, I didn't know when I came. I needed work."

"You want me to believe you walked into this place by pure chance and found yourself in the middle of what you'd run away from?"

She shook her head at that. "Not quite. I came to New York to find Dene's murderer, and to prove he murdered Dene." She spread her hand on the quilted satin of the gold counterpane. "Until he is found, I'm not safe. Until he is captured"—she knew the word smacked of a detective magazine but it was true—"I'm in danger of being killed too, always in danger of his finding out that I know Dene was murdered, not just disappeared."

"So you came here purposely—detecting."

Again she shook her head. "I didn't know what the ad might be. I came truly looking for work. But"—she faced him—"I saw you and Bill Folker at the theater.

I heard you mention the ad and he The Lorenzo. I knew you were connected with Dene. And when I came, I hoped."

He took a deep breath. "You've more guts than it would appear, Lizanne."

"No. No, I haven't. I've been sorry a thousand times that I did it. But I won't give up now." Now she was confiding in him. It was foolish. For all of his words, he still might be the one who killed. He was working with Bill. She had heard him admit it. *And Bill was working for Stefan.* But for the moment she wasn't afraid of him. And it didn't matter. He knew enough now to get rid of her if he wished. What more she had to say wouldn't make things worse for her. And he'd said he wouldn't give her away yet. As long as he didn't know she had the bear, there was reprieve. She asked him now, "Who murdered Dene?"

"Stefan."

She was impatient with him. "If you know that, if you're really working for the government, why don't you do something about it?"

He said irrelevantly, "I wish I had a drink," and went on. "I'll tell you a little story now. Knut was pretty sure Stefan would try to kill his brothers for their shares. That's why he fixed up the will as he did. Lans left home even before the Old Bear died because he didn't feel safe under the same roof with Stefan. Dene was at school then, and was looked after pretty carefully. When Knut died, Tedford, the Ambassador, had the problem of preventing murder until after Dene was of age and things settled. Lans was looking out for himself. The Ambassador asked me to keep my eye on Dene when he wasn't at school. When he was, Dinky was with him—roommates, inseparables—so there wasn't much chance for a murder there. I went with Dene to the Lodge that vacation. You probably saw me then; you're right that I didn't see you. I gather you weren't hanging around the city folks at that time; it was before you met up with Dene. I was really no more than a bodyguard for him.

"And then——" his mouth was bitter,—"you know that Alix was my wife. We hadn't been getting along. Bill was her lover. I was sure of that but there wasn't anything I could say. He'd been her lover ever since she was a mere child. But he wouldn't marry her, so she married me. Anyway, she wired me asking me to meet her in New York. She'd been in Florida with Bill." His mouth was more grim. "I thought she'd left him there. I used to jump through hoops for her although I knew what she was. I thought Dene would be safe a day or two."

She interrupted, "Bill was working for Stefan at that time?"

His eyes looked deeply into hers. "He is, has always been, Stefan's right hand."

She knew she must remain frozen as she was now until she could escape from this place and these henchmen. She had come to find Stefan Viljaas, to make him answer for what she was certain he had instigated if not actually carried out. Now that she knew she feared to go on, but there was nothing else she could do. She was trapped.

Guard had turned away. "Alix kept me in New York a week. I told you I jumped through hoops for her." He was remembering a dream. "She was wonderful that week. I thought maybe things were going to be

135

right." And then the slashes deepened. "I didn't know she was merely obeying her lover's orders." He shut his lips tightly together, before he cried out angrily, "Why the devil am I telling you all this stuff?"

"You might as well finish now," she said without inflection.

"That's all there is. I went back up and Dene was gone. No one knew anything. The detectives Ted sent couldn't find out anything. Bill might have shown up, or Stefan himself, no one knew, and Dene bolted. He might have gone to join Lans. None of us knew where Lans was. There wasn't any murder, you see. There wasn't anything to be done."

She said, "I see."

"Even now there's nothing to pin it on Stefan. Bill could explain in so many ways his having the triangle. When Dene wasn't heard from in these years, Tedford and I were sure of what happened but without proof. Dinky's been certain all along that Stefan killed Dene." He hesitated. "We all think Alix has proof, in a letter. Dinky claims to have seen it. She denies having it, naturally. It may be destroyed by now although Dink refuses to admit that possibility; says she's always saved every scrap of anything connected with Bill, and all Viljaas business is. And too, we all feel she has some hold over him. He wouldn't be so decent to her if she hadn't. He's always treated her like the devil, except when he's wanted something from her."

Bill Folker had said—she had heard him say it—that he wouldn't be bothered by Alix. Yet he had been, constantly. There must be something to it. Lizanne yawned; it just happened; she didn't mean to.

He looked at his watch. "It's almost three. I'll go. Remember, you're taking orders from me now. You're Bill's secretary; you'll do the things he tells you, but you'll report to me. I may make some changes. And you won't tell him, or anyone," he stressed that word, "anything that is said between us."

She nodded dumbly.

"You haven't any choice in the matter. I've told you one reason why; if it were known about the bear, you wouldn't live." He didn't let her speak. "Here's another thing to think about. I could turn you over to the police for suppressing Dene's death. You know that. And you know I'm working for the government. You'd have no chance, your word against mine."

He didn't know she had heard him admit he was working with Bill, only pretending to work for the government. It seemed now he was double-crossing Stefan's organization as well.

"I'll do what you say," she promised. Weariness was overcoming her. She didn't care what she did, whose puppet she was, as long as she could sleep now.

He said, "Go on as you have, watching Lans. One thing, keep him away from here. No matter what Bill orders about that, fail him. You know from where his orders come. Don't let those two meet."

She assured him, "Lans is as determined as you about that."

He warned her, "You must be wary of Bill Folker. He might have a way that wouldn't appear to be a meeting! He is a brilliant fellow, Lizanne. It's unfortunate that he is entirely bad."

"He's your friend."

His mouth twisted. "I have hated"—he made the word venom—"I have hated Bill Folker from the first day I met him." He stood up. He was calm again. "For twenty years I've been waiting for the chance to get him. It's coming soon."

Chapter Eight: BEHIND THE HOTEL ROOM DOOR

LANS SAID, "Will you marry me?"

She wasn't dreaming; it was ten o'clock on Wednesday morning and she was sitting beside him on a bench in the waiting room at Grand Central. But the question was fantastic.

She laughed out loud. "You're already married."

He asked, "Is that all?" and waited for an answer. She didn't speak. "Because if it is, that can be fixed easily."

She shook her head. "I don't believe in divorce. Besides—that isn't all." Even if he were free, she wouldn't marry him. Even if she felt as she did, wanting to touch his hand, to be touched by him, here in the prosaic gray light of the waiting room, she wouldn't. Before she came to meet him, she had determination; she wouldn't be stirred by his physical presence. Not after the talk with Guard Croyden last night; she wouldn't trust any Viljaas. She wouldn't let herself a second time be trapped emotionally by a Viljaas.

"What else?" He shifted on the bench to look at her.

She laughed again. "What else? I scarcely know you. I'm not in love with you."

"I'm not asking you to be in love with me," he interrupted. "I'm not in love with you. This is strictly business. You understand."

"I'm afraid I don't."

He stared at her. She was uncomfortable. His eyes were too dark to express what he might be thinking.

Then he said, "You were Dene's wife."

She laughed again. It wasn't real but it sounded real. This was too absurd; Guard figuring things out last night, Lans now. But it didn't make for comfort. Bill might be next. And Bill would inform Stefan Viljaas.

He said impatiently, "You needn't pretend. I've known it since the first night. You see, Dene wrote to me."

Laughter went out of her. She looked at him quickly. She asked, "What did he say?"

"He said he'd followed my advice. He'd been married that morning. He said she had eyes like the white plush kitten Alix wouldn't let us touch when we were kids. Like your eyes, Lizanne."

She was silent at that. He wasn't guessing; he was certain. She asked bitterly, "And what was your advice?"

He said, "If we married, Stefan wouldn't get our shares even if he killed us. Our wives would. And he couldn't go in for wholesale slaughter; he'd be sure to be caught. It didn't matter who we married. By marrying, we had Stefan stopped."

"It didn't save Dene."

"No." He sobered. "Stefan killed Dene before he had a chance to discover what he'd done. I was the only one who knew." He added, "Dene was dead before I had the letter."

"You know he killed Dene?"

He shrugged. "No one else had any reason to. And I know Dene didn't just disappear that night. He was murdered. You know he was murdered, don't you?"

"Yes, I know." She spoke slowly. "I don't know who did it. I don't know how. But I know he was killed." She lifted her eyes to him. "You told me you're not admitting you're Lans Viljaas. I'm not admitting I was Dene's wife." She wasn't ever, really. The half-blind old preacher had mumbled words, that was all. "But why do you want to marry me?" Her voice was bitter again. "You have a wife. You have your heir. Where do I come into it?"

He said, "Together we could really stop Stefan." He spoke carefully as if figuring it out. "At least I think we could. We'd be majority. We could protect our interests when the contracts come up. If we're not together Stefan will do us out of our eyeteeth. And you can believe that."

She said, " 'Our interests.' I have no interest in this but to find Dene's murderer."

He looked at her suspiciously. "What do you think you're talking about? You're Dene's heir."

She shook her head. "He gave me nothing. He had nothing to give me, and no time to make a will."

He said, "I don't know whether you're being dumb on purpose or if you're just naturally that way. His part of the check is your share."

"I don't have it."

"You don't have to have it. The money is yours. He didn't need to make a will. You're his wife. You inherit. That's the way the Old Bear fixed it."

She had actually not known it. She was worth one million dollars—if she lived. If she didn't . . . there would be only the two. Suspicion stiffened her. Did Lans want to marry her to get rid of her? And if he did, would Dene's share go to him as her heir? It would. He was a Viljaas, and she moved slightly away from him although she knew he couldn't hurt her here.

"You don't mean this is news to you?" He was acting

140

amazed. "You don't mean you didn't come into this to look out for yourself?"

She set her chin. "I'm going to look out for myself." If she'd had only a little of what had been legally hers, she could have saved Uncle Will. They, in their greed, had let him suffer and die. She couldn't even go to him, be with him in those last days. She would never let the Viljaases have it all now. She would stay in this until they, or she herself, was eliminated.

She said as if to herself, "From now on I'm going to look out for myself exclusively." She wouldn't want to cry if she weren't tired and nervous. It wasn't because Lans had turned out to be true Viljaas; it didn't have anything to do with Lans. She blinked her eyes and looked at him. "I'm not going to trust anyone from now on. Not anyone. I'm going to be on my own. And I'm going to fix things so that if anything happens to me, neither you nor Stefan will get a cent. It will go to those charities." She was warning him, warning him not to kill her. And she'd warn Guard, too; and Bill, when the time came. Let them think she'd leave a letter to the police; but it was true, if anything happened to her, they could do nothing, not without the cross-eyed bear. If anything happened to her, they'd never see the cross-eyed bear. She'd get a safer place for her deposit key, today, tomorrow.

He said acidly, "I hope you haven't been fool enough to trust any of that outfit at The Lorenzo. I didn't think you'd done that."

She wouldn't tell him she'd half-way trusted him before now. Nor that she could never have faith in him again. "And now will you kindly tell me the real reason you asked me to marry you?" Her words were cold.

"And what made you think I might?"

Again he seemed to be working out the answer. "I suppose the real reason was because I didn't trust you, to get you on my side, not Stefan's. But maybe there's something in what I thought was the answer last night when I couldn't sleep. To take care of you, protect you from Stefan."

He looked, he sounded, as if his words were true. If they had been, that ache for him that was somewhere inside of her could have been something precious, not something she would outroot if she but could with clawing fingers. He wasn't arrogant now; he was like a little boy, embarrassed, trying to explain things. She could almost believe in him as he spoke; she knew better. He turned up the velvet collar of his overcoat. She could see where it was worn at the folds.

"I don't blame you for not trusting me. I'm a damned Viljaas. Only—take care of yourself." His hand closed on hers. "I don't know how you came to marry Dene. I don't want to know. But you're too decent a kid to be in this. Be careful." He'd stood up from the bench, was buttoning his coat, about to turn and go.

Hating him as she did, she had to warn him. She jumped up, caught his sleeve, noticed the button missing, the thread still a lump; noticed the broken button next to where it should have been. Sally could sew buttons on his coat; she could do that much for him.

She spoke breathlessly, and softly, as if there were listeners even here. "You must be careful. You're in danger. I don't understand it very well; it's about the mines, some countries that will stop at nothing to get control. They will be highest bidders if it's thrown on the open market, as it would be if you and Stefan were missing on April first, or dead."

He nodded, and he added, "And you, too, Lizanne."

"They don't know about me." But Guard Croyden did. She hadn't fooled him last night. That was what he'd meant about the Viljaases being unwilling to share. Lans and Guard knew; she wasn't safe any more.

"It might not be a stranger representing The Three." He shrugged his coat to better fit on his shoulders. "Well, I've got to go along."

Again she caught his sleeve. "When will I see you again?" She dropped her fingers as quickly. She had sounded like a college girl.

He flicked his eyes to her but he didn't laugh. "Come down to the club tonight." His mouth didn't move. "Do you have the cross-eyed bear?"

She trusted no one. She said, "I do not."

She let Lans go away, waited until he was out of sight before leaving the waiting room and starting to the Forty-Second street ramp. She was barely to the ticket windows when she heard the call, "Lizanne!" Face to face with Janet Leeds, afraid to speak with her lest someone see, yet there was no one to see; Lans was safely gone.

Janet had caught her arm. "I'm as nervous this morning by broad daylight as I was last night. I don't know why."

Lizanne was walking with her. She didn't want to but there was no need to give the girl more fright. And then, approaching the gates, she caught her breath and stopped where she stood. Guard Croyden was standing over there, bulky, frightful. It was a moment before she noted the large toast-brown bag by his heels. He wasn't there to spy on her; he was going away. He hadn't seen her; his back was turned.

As if remembering suddenly, she glanced at her watch, spoke to her companion. "I must run. I've got to get back to work. I'm sorry I can't wait to see you off."

If Janet were surprised, she only let it be reflected in her eyebrows. She said, "Of course, it's all right. Thanks for coming down anyhow. Write to me."

She promised, not listening, her eyes flicking to Guard's back, hoping it would remain a back. She spoke, "Good-by," and fled. Not until she was on the uptown bus was there clarity again in her thoughts. She had behaved like an idiot, leaving Janet there with Guard, leaving her in the immediacy of danger. Danger for Janet meant worse danger for herself. Yet surely, done without thought as it was, surely Guard couldn't have remembered the girl's face, had he ever seen it. Definitely he had not seen Lizanne with her. Recognition came of something else, leaving her with more fear in her bones. The man she had brushed past by the first check stand, as she fled from those dangerous gates, the man whose face under the careless hat had seemed vaguely familiar, was Inspector Tobin. And he, she knew, had seen Janet before. Moreover, he had watched her walk with Janet Leeds to a west-bound train.

Lizanne didn't hear the door open until the voice spoke. There was a face, an elf-child's face, poked through the slight opening. The accent was like Anna's, slightly more so, the voice more piping. "Pardon me, yes," it said. "It is Bill Folker I am seeking."

Lizanne said, "This is his office."

She came in then. She was like a Dutch doll, small and rounded, buttercup hair that should have been in

144

pigtails, not styled by some Emile or Robert. Closer view didn't diminish the look of elf in her slant brown eyes, her tilted nose and chin. Elf-tailored in hunter's green by some Parisian couturier. There was something familiar, more than familiar in the girl. If she would lower her eyes, Lizanne could be certain. But she held them wide. She looked first about the room, second at Lizanne, frankly with curiosity.

Was there a new ad running? Was she about to be supplanted? "What name shall I say?" Lizanne asked. She knew that Bill would be there on the chaise. He had been surrounded by business papers, letters, when he gave her these to type. What she was typing she didn't know; the languages were strange; she only followed the alphabetical order. He gave, as he had from the first, no addresses for the correspondence, no envelopes.

The girl turned her eyes from the left door to the right. "But I shall surprise him." She pointed correctly a canary doeskin finger.

Lizanne indicated affirmation. She wasn't hired to protect Bill Folker from his camp followers, and the girl had been definite. The girl knew which door was his. Lizanne went back to her machine.

"Fredi!" The girl had left his door open a narrow width. Bill's voice was amazed and he called out, "Fredi!" again; the rustle of papers flung away, and silence. There had been more than surprise in the second speaking of the name: a certain tenderness, almost of love, that didn't go with Bill.

After the silence, a soft little laugh. "I surprise you!"

"I can't realize it. Fredi! When did you get here?"

Lizanne had not been mistaken. It was the lover's

voice. She wondered if Alix knew, and what would happen when she did. She listened, unabashed. They had forgotten the door or they didn't care.

"Only this morning. I hurry to you."

"Not very fast." Silence; then in his voice too much casualness, the lover's casualness that believes it conceals the jealousy underlying it. "Is Wolfgang with you?"

Her so soft answer: "But of course, my darling. You would know that." Pause. "He is to me no more than before. I to him no more."

Pregnant pause again. Lizanne wondered if she might close that door without being noticed; it was embarrassing, listening in on a love-scene; it was not what she had expected from Fredi's accent. And then the girl spoke again. "I come as soon as I see you get rid of Lydia."

His voice was harsh. "I didn't get rid of Lydia. She got rid of herself."

"For me you did not abrogate her?"

He repeated, "For you I did not." His voice tautened. "Don't say those things. Don't say them out loud." He spoke in foreign tongue now, and she replied in the same. Another of the rustling silences set in.

Fredi spoke again, but not with the same softness. "The contracts. You have not signed with no one else?"

"Certainly not." He spoke sharply. "I've told you our hands are tied until April first."

She said, "They would not like it if you made new arrangements. It would not be pleasant for us—nor for you."

He was suspicious. "Is that why you and Wolfgang are here? To watch me?"

"But no." She laughed softly. "We are here because

I arrange it this way. I do this myself. When I see what you have done for me I tell Them, Wolf and I will go to this New York and watch out for the contracts. It will be better, quicker."

That voice was the same. If Fredi had come in wearing a maid's uniform, she would have been Anna. A dark wig could cover sleek blonde hair. Eyes downcast hid expression. She could have managed it, avoided Bill's room. There couldn't be such duplication.

Lizanne heard their footsteps moving toward the bedrooms. She waited, then softly closed that opening so slight as to be unnoticed by two engrossed, but wide enough for every word to be audible. She didn't want to hear more. She plunged back to the typewriter, began furiously at the work. She didn't ever again want to hear lovers' voices, not these two with something evil crawling through love. Love shouldn't be that way. It should be as she had loved Dene, blindly, happily, until that night. And now—but she wasn't going to allow herself ever to feel as she had before, certainly not over Lans and his eyes like Dene's. It was ridiculous to be miserable because the unpredictable Bill Folker had a tremble in his voice when he spoke to an exquisite doll-like girl called Fredi or Anna.

She worked. There were but three more pages to be done when the door opened again, not quietly this time but arrogantly. She was startled into immobility.

Could this, at last, be Stefan Viljaas? She rejected the thought. A Viljaas would be wild and black like Dene, like Lans beneath his night-club lacquer. She would know Stefan when he came, the Viljaas evil would be marked upon him. She certainly hadn't seen this man before. He was so Germanic in appearance, the cropped head, the monocle, the military heel and shoulder, but so Oxford when he spoke. "This is Bill Folker's flat."

It was not a question but she answered it. "Yes."

"He is in?"

She said, "I will see. What name?"

"Koppel. Wolfgang Koppel."

The door opened again before she could move. Now came Alix, tawny furred, brimstone and slate, her eyes without any color save anger. "Where is Bill?" she demanded. "Why doesn't he open his door?"

Lizanne told her with the matter-of-fact briskness of a perfect secretary, "I will see if he is in."

"I will see." Again as if Lizanne were doorstop, she brushed past, flung herself into Bill's suite. Her tawny alligator pumps echoed back although the room wore rugs.

Wolfgang Koppel fixed his eyeglass after her. He said flatly, "It saves you the trouble," and sat down in an armchair, with elegance lighted a cigarette.

Too soon came sound, a knob rattled, a panel pounded, beaten with fists, tattooed with heels. Above it were the imprecations, the demands.

The visitor stated, amused, "She is losing her temper."

And then there was one sharp gash of silence with its aftermath a scream of pain, a moan, a thud.

Wolfgang Koppel said in his languid British voice, "I never want to miss any fun." He was through the door so quickly he had not seemed to move. Scarcely knowing that her own feet followed, Lizanne was close behind him. A chill in her could not let her be alone. Another murder. Alix was written down for murder— or had she killed Bill and his beautiful woman?

But this was not death; this was somehow more sickening, humiliation of the proud. Alix was sprawled grotesquely on the floor, raising herself on one arm, protecting the other, ugly red mottling one cheek from bone to chin. Above her, in the doorway opening to his private rooms, Bill Folker was standing. His amber eyes regarded her as if she were something unclean there on his maroon carpet. Behind him peered Fredi's elf nose, her Robin Hood green cap, neither fear nor surprise but delight on her face.

Bill's eyes moved from Alix upward when Lizanne and Koppel entered. They looked down again at the floor. His mouth barely moved. "Get out. And stay out."

No one helped Alix struggle to her tall alligator heels. No one spoke when she pressed the tawny fur across the disfigured cheek. There was no fire; there was menace rather than hatred in her words. "You dare not do this to me. You and your whore." She turned and walked quickly, proudly across the room; the heels ceased as the outer door sounded shut.

Lizanne shrank again behind Koppel as she passed. Because she would not forgive this; no woman could; degraded by her lover in the presence of his new fancy. Certainly not an Alix Bruce. No one who had witnessed this humiliation would be forgotten or ever forgiven.

The closing of the door made movement. Bill came across the room, hand outstretched. Lizanne felt a sudden frightening need to explain her presence. She began as if in introduction, "Mr. Koppel——"

Bill spoke on her words. "Wolf—delighted to see you again."

Wolfgang clasped the hand. He was still languid. "So good to see you, Bill. You were surprised to see Fredi?"

"Bowled over. Let's have a drink."

Lizanne was unessential. She turned to go and Bill seemed to notice her for the first time. He said, "This is my secretary, Miss Steffasson. Baron Koppel and the Baroness. Old friends of mine."

Fredi's eyes were avidly bright acknowledging the introduction. Wolfgang said, "We're practically old friends by now. Mutual experiences, don't you know?"

Lizanne stood very still, but Bill only smiled and Fredi tinkled.

Bill said, "Dress up tonight, Lizanne. We're going to be gala. We'll dine at Jim and Jack's."

It wasn't invitation, gaily as given; it was assignment. Hers to keep Wolfgang amused doubtless while Bill and Fredi held hands, made plans to suck Lans into their whirlpool of evil. She said, "I'll be ready," and returned to the office. She was covering her typewriter when the voices in the next room became audible.

Fredi was speaking. "But why do you have her, Bill?"

"She is useful."

The elf voice was greedy. "You pay her how much money?" She knew the new clothes, the expensive labels; she had unpacked.

Bill laughed. "Chips. There's plenty more. And it won't be for long."

Lizanne was suddenly shaking, her hands pressed on the desk. She hoped he didn't mean what "it won't be for long" could mean. Reality smote her. She could never touch that legacy; all that she wanted was to get out of this alive and free. She should have known that Dene's death was more than just the killing of a man; after she learned he was a Viljaas, she should have known there were dangerous reasons why he must die. She was afraid. She wanted to live. She and Lans.

Bill must have ordered Alix to be present. She wouldn't have come otherwise, have posed there murmuring, "So stupid to have fallen as I did this afternoon. My heels!" The mist blue of pale fox swathing her throat, protecting her jaw line; swathing her wrists where she might favor one as Lydia had favored a limp arm; three too-wide ruby bracelets could easily hide a bandage.

Dinky had already had too much to drink, Wolfgang, too. Bill was unchanged, as always the man who held the strings. "Only Guard is missing from our circle," he stated.

Dinky said, "He'll be back from Washington in a couple of days."

Lizanne looked at him, at Bill. Guard had left from Grand Central *not* the Penn station; the Boston and Albany, change to the Rutland upstate.

It was almost nine before they reached the club. Dinky's tongue was giddy but his hand helping Lizanne in and out of the cab was steady. Lans did not look to the table. Sally did, wistfully, watching Dinky bent to Fredi's pert laughter, eyeing Alix's lovely grandeur to-ward Wolfgang. She didn't come near but she watched. Lans didn't watch. His head was black patent leather in their direction.

While Dinky danced with Fredi, Alix with Wolf-gang, Bill moved beside Lizanne. It was then past one. He said, "We're going to move on soon. You and Dinky stay. Go out with Lans when he's through here. Keep him out as long as you can. Dinky has business with Sally. You can use your rooms."

"He won't go there," she told him pointedly. But, after all, she was working for Bill. And Lans was safe with her. "I'll do something."

The others returned and Bill said, "I'm weary of this place. Suppose we try another?"

Dinky unsteadily spoke on cue. "I like it here. Suppose we stay, Lizanne."

And she said her lines. "Yes. Let's stay a while longer."

The others went away. Dinky walked at once to Sally, surprised to plate-eyes and happy. Lizanne waited for Lans. She was not surprised when he came and she wouldn't be happy.

He mocked, "Nice company you keep. The Baron and his wench."

She didn't defend them. She said, "I want to see you. Shall I meet you at the side-entrance?"

"You needn't bother with that."

She turned her head. He was watching Dinky and Sally cross the floor. Sally's sleazy black velvet cape covered her too-bright green satin. He waited until they were out of sight, said, "I'll be back," and returned to the platform. One more number and he left with the orchestra.

She sat there alone. The room was emptied of all but the help, clearing tables, stacking chairs. She waited, waited. Just when she plumbed absolute failure, he returned in coat and hat. She told him, "I thought you'd forgotten me."

"It's not that easy." He spoiled it. "You don't forget kids you're sorry for, and worried about. Let's get out of here."

The weather had turned, mist lay quietly over the streets, hung in shreds on the lamps. They stood in front of the old brownstone on the now deserted walk.

"Where do you want to go? Where it doesn't cost any-thing." He laughed but it wasn't a laugh. "I'm a mil-lionaire but I can't even ask a girl to have a drink, or a bite of supper, or to come in out of the rain."

She said, "I don't want them. And it isn't raining. It's glorious." She breathed the January thaw, first premoni-tion of spring. On impulse, "Let's walk up into the Park."

She didn't think he would agree but he did. They moved arm in arm to Fifth, up Fifth, turned in to the misty paths. Only then did he speak. "When we were kids Dene and I used to walk in the rain at night, at the Bear's."

"You and Dene were very dear to each other?"

"I don't know you'd call it that." He spoke, thinking it out. "We had to stick together against the others——" He broke off, said angrily, "We didn't have much of a show. The Bear meant well, I suppose, but he was God or somebody, to be seen by appointment only. And Stefan was there. The stable boys had it better than we did." He broke off, looked down at her. "You probably heard about it from Dene."

"He talked some." She had been sorry for him, for his ragged, lonely, and mistreated boyhood, even as she was now sorry for Lans. And then Dene had shown himself as he was, as Lans would show himself if she allowed him to touch her life, interfere with her emotions.

She said, "Let's sit down and have a cigarette."

"Hurt your coat?"

"No."

They sat on a bench under black ragged trees thread-ing mist, claw-like bushes catching at it across the path. Their cigarettes were bits of lighted amber in the dark.

She didn't like the silence, two on a park bench. She laughed, uneasy, made words, "This is better than Grand Central."

He said, "I saw Inspector Tobin when I was leaving."

"I thought I did."

"He was there."

She said, "Lydia's case isn't closed yet."

"It could be."

"Not without proof."

Again there was silence, intimate mist silence. And this time he broke it but not the intimacy. For he said, "You wondered why I was sorry for you."

"Yes, I wondered."

He said as if to himself, "You're a nice kid, too nice to be mixed up in this. I don't care if you were Dene's wife; you're clean and decent—and nice." He repeated the word as if it were strange to his tongue. He turned on her. "I'm sorry for you because you're in it, and I'm worried about you at the same time for the same reason. I don't like you tied up in Stefan's set. I wish I'd found you first."

He put one hand softly against the side of her face and he kissed her mouth. She clung to him for one fierce beautiful moment and then as fiercely pushed him away. She asked, "Lans—why, Lans?" It hadn't been fair. But then he couldn't have known how she felt about him; he didn't know it was unfair.

He looked surprised; surprised, she was certain, not at her rejection but at her first welcoming. He said, "I don't know why. I only know I didn't tell you the whole truth this morning when I asked you to marry me. I'd like to take care of you. I know that. I'd like to know you. I'd like not to have this wall of suspicion always between us. Maybe that's love. Maybe I'm in love with you. I don't know." He didn't touch her; he wasn't Dene, reckless, impetuous, the insistent lover. But again she rejected. Years and events would have made Dene more sober, thoughtful. It didn't mean Lans could be trusted.

She turned his words aside. "You can't fall in love so quickly."

"That's what I tell myself," he said quietly.

And that was what she must keep telling herself. But you could fall in love, as suddenly as thunder in spring. There wasn't any more use pretending; she loved him, the way she had wanted to love Dene, the way in which she had thought she did love Dene. She cried softly, "Lans!" and again he turned to her in surprise. Their lips were together for the moment, another brief moment of beauty, shut in by mist and stark trees.

He said then, "We'd better go. This isn't doing any good—for either of us."

She stood up from the bench, shivered a little.

He said, "Maybe some day. If we get out of this."

They walked down the path, toward the south stone entrance.

She asked, curious, "Why did you marry Sally?"

His answer was immediate. "I couldn't stand her. And I knew Stefan would loathe her. It was a mistake."

They crossed Broadway, awaited a downtown bus.

He spoke, "Come back to my room with me."

She suddenly recollected Bill's orders and she trembled. Had she kept him away long enough? It was almost three-thirty by her wrist watch.

He was saying, "You can take Dinky home with you," but she still wondered if that were the reason she was to accompany him. There could be others; he might fear going alone, fear lest death be waiting for him. It might be to introduce her to death; it was to his benefit that she should be put out of the way. But tonight she would go with him.

He was silent on the bus, on the walk crosstown to the second-rate hotel. They went up in the elevator to eighth, walked down the ill-lit corridor, stale with smell of unaired clothes and cigarette stubs.

She wasn't afraid of him. He put the key in the lock, pushed at the door, said, "Damn it, something's in the way," pushed viciously making an aperture. The light switch was just inside. He snapped it before he stood aside for her to enter. He closed the door after him.

They stood there without moving, without even breath-sound. They saw what had held the door: Sally crumpled on the floor as if she were asleep, but the sleeping do not lie so still. She wouldn't sleep with her head against the door, a hand outstretched as if to reach the fallen gun. She wouldn't sleep in that garish green satin dress with sticky dark stuff across the bodice.

Lizanne whispered, "You've got to get out of here." They had left this for Lans to find, for Lans to be found with.

He said, "Sally." A moan rather than a word. Sally hadn't been anything to him but if he were alone, Lizanne felt he would weep. He said viciously, "God damn him."

Only then did Lizanne see the rest of the room, the disarray, bureau drawers pulled wide, desk drawer open spilling papers, even the bedclothes torn apart. Only then did she see the stupefied Dinky sprawling in the arm chair. But Lans's curse had not been for Dinky, hapless sodden Dinky; she knew that. And she was frightened for him as well.

"You must get out of here!" She cried it out now.

Lans heard. He said dully, "Why?"

"Can't you see? They've done it this way purposely. Don't you see it? We must get Dinky out, too." She went over to him, shook him fiercely, crying, "Wake up, Dinky! Wake up!" She shook him frenziedly with all her strength. "Dinky, Dinky!"

Lans looked at her. "That's no good," he said. He took the water pitcher, quietly drenched Dinky's head.

This time the boy hadn't been simulating. His eyes were glazed, his mouth made unintelligible sound. Suddenly he lurched from the chair, wobbled unsteadily and stumbled doorward. "Sally—Sally—" There was apprehensive anxiety in his voice. He saw her and he swayed, caught the bedpost. His voice was hard, not like Dinky's. "The dirty bastard."

Lans asked curiously, as a child would, "Who?"

He turned, still holding the bed, sat on the edge of it. "Who?" He put up his head painfully. "You don't think I killed her, do you?"

"No," Lans answered.

At any moment someone would come in that door, Inspector Tobin, or worse, Stefan Viljaas. Lizanne spoke again in desperation, "We've got to get out of here before someone comes. Someone will come." She caught Lans's arm. "You're meant to be entangled in this, you or Dinky or both of you."

Lans said, "We can't just leave her here, like this."

"You will have to."

Dinky said, "She's right. You're playing right into Stefan's hands if you don't." He rubbed his neck. "I was hit on some nerve." He repeated Lans's curse, "God damn him. I must have been doped, too. My mouth tastes like rubber."

Lizanne urged—like a talking crow, "Let's go. Before it's too late. We can talk it over some place else."

Lans sat down heavily, and she could have screamed with nervousness. He said, "I haven't any place to go. It'll be worse for me if I go."

"You can come to my apartment."

He didn't scoff at her now. He smiled gently. "You're a good kid, Lizanne." His voice was grim. "But I'd rather not meet Stefan's crew tonight. I might get the chair."

Dinky said, "You won't meet them, Lans. I'll see to that." He stood again holding the bedstead for support. "Get my hat and coat, Lizanne. Give me a hand, Lans."

Lans said with finality, "I can't go there. I don't dare." He didn't move from the chair.

Dinky stumbled to him, put a hand on his shoulder. "You can't let Stefan win now, not after you've fought through this long. You can't do it."

Lizanne pleaded, "If you won't go with me, at least let's go get in a cab and talk it over." She had, for once, an idea. "We'll bring you back, Lans, if you insist. But let's go talk it over."

He seemed to agree to that. At least he followed Dinky and Lizanne past the crumpled figure to the door. He stopped there. Dinky took his arm, moved him outside. It was Lizanne who put her forefinger to the light switch, pressed it; Dinky who said, "You are an unshorn lamb," wiped it with his handkerchief, leaning against the door jamb, wiped also the inner and outer doorknobs. He said, "Prints in the room don't matter.

We've all been in it, no secret to that. But they'll check who was last to leave." He, too, must believe the police would come soon. But no one was in view.

He leaned heavily on them, one on either side of him, as they went down in the elevator. Lizanne wondered why she had put this sudden trust in Dinky. Why couldn't it be that she and Lans were no more than dupes, extricating him from the scene of his crime? Or she alone the monkey, Lans and Dinky together in this. There was yet another thing to fear if Dinky were only playing a part, with Stefan manipulating. How could she know if Dinky were not, with her innocent connivance, leading Lans directly to death? Her head rang with her fear of all of them.

They found a cab quickly at this hour. They helped Dinky first, she climbed in beside him, but Lans did not follow. He stood there on the walk without expression.

Dinky said, "Come on."

He asked, "We'll drive about?"

"Yes, yes," Lizanne told him. They mustn't delay.

He got in then, still obviously reluctant.

Dinky spoke, "Go through the Park." He pushed tightly the glass separating the driver from them. But he was taking no chance. His voice was quiet. "Lans, if you can just see it now. You're safest with Lizanne."

"Folker's secretary," he said bitterly.

"But she's not in this. Don't you know? That's why he picked her."

Lans knew better but he didn't give her away.

"She's not one of his women. I'll vouch for her."

Again Lans didn't speak.

"Stefan's desperate. You know it. It's getting too close and he's not going to share. Not Stefan."

"No." Lans spoke thoughtfully. "No. He's not. I've known that since I was ten years old, Dink. Since he tried to kill me that summer in the woods."

Lizanne held her hands together like clamps. That he could speak so calmly, continue to live a normal life, eat, sleep, work, always in the pathway of death.

Dinky nodded soberly. "It's always been you that's bucked him, Lans. He never worried about Dene. He knew he could get him out of the way easily. Dene was wide open for it. I did my best——" He shook his head.

"Dene was always reckless," Lans said.

Dinky raised his eyes. "You're still the one in Stefan's way. He must get rid of you, and he must do it quickly now, Lans. He's in this business too deeply now to take a chance on you. If he doesn't get those contracts for The Three, he'll be, to put it crudely, bumped off. That's why the Koppels are here, to see that there aren't any mistakes. Fredi doesn't mind a little sex-life with business; but ultimately, pleasure isn't the thing to her. That's why she's as important as she is. The point is you can't let them win. My God, Lans, what's the answer to all the hell you've been through, all of us have been through, if Stefan gets you hanged for murder and collects the whole estate?"

Lizanne sat between them without moving a breath. They might have forgotten her. She didn't know this Dinky Bruce, and she wished she could believe in it as Lans seemed to.

"How is hiding out at Folker's going to keep me safe?"

"Because you're not safe alone!" Dinky stressed it. "They'd ferret you out at any hotel you went to. You'd be wide open to them. Lizanne has bolts on her doors. No one can get in there. You don't have to worry about

160

the hotel dick interfering. Anything goes in Stefan's lair; he pays off well."

"On my money, and Dene's."

Dinky agreed. "God knows how much he's piled up taking over the mines as he has since the Old Bear's death. He lies to the Ambassador, and his reports are falsified. There's never been an accounting—"

"No."

"I'll be across keeping an eye on Bill. You've got to lie low until Guard's back. He'll take care of you then. But right now, when Tobin finds out about tonight, you're in a bad spot."

Lans decided, "I'll go." It was as if he were too tired to offer further rejections.

Dinky pushed aside the glass. "The Lorenzo, driver." He closed it again. He passed cigarettes, flared his lighter, but his hand was shaking. Doubt again stifled Lizanne. Was it relief that he had won a point not his own but Stefan-commanded? Or was it merely reaction from the drug he'd been given?

Following Dinky's plan, leaving the elevator on ninth, waiting for him to come down from tenth with assurance, "Coast's clear." The strain of climbing the one flight of stairs, expecting the elevator to disgorge Bill before they could be safe inside. But they were. And Dinky repeating, "Lay low. That's all you need do."

Lans nodding acquiescence. And then he cried suddenly, harshly, "Why did he kill Sally?"

Dinky spoke slowly. "We must have interrupted a search. The light switch didn't work. I started for the lamp. That's all I know. I don't know why she was killed, and I not. I don't suppose we'll ever know." He started away. At the door he paused. "Don't trust anyone. Don't trust Alix."

Lans said, "I'm not that big a fool twice."

Lizanne bolted the door after him. She went into the bedroom, took extra blankets from the shelf, a pillow from her bed. Lans was still sitting there on the couch —she said, "If you'll move I'll make up your bed."

As in a dream he stood up, moved to a chair. Silence continued. She might have been a complete stranger to him; what had happened long ago in the misted park had never happened. He began to speak tonelessly, saying what he had before, "The Viljaases are damned. Anyone who touches their lives is damned."

He didn't know she was there. "I shouldn't have done it to her. It wasn't fair to let her in for it." Suddenly he came out of his coma. "If I thought Stefan did it to hurt me more, to break me down, I'd strangle him—"

She didn't move. She was frightened again. Lans was a Viljaas. No Viljaas was safe to be with. He said, "Whatever made him do it, I'll pay him back."

She walked to his side, wanting to comfort, but she couldn't now. She wasn't in his consciousness. She didn't touch him, only said, "You'd better try to sleep. It's almost daylight."

He seemed to see her for the first time in hours. He even tried to smile. "You're a good kid, Lizanne."

She said, "Good night," and went into her bedroom closing the door behind her. She had thought the evening might bring meeting with Lans. But not this way. Not irrevocably shut out of his life. She didn't let the tears trickle from her eyes until she was pressed into the dark pillow. She too hated Stefan tonight. Lans had begun to care for her; she had begun to mean something. But now only a tawdry girl on a dust-stiff rug in a cheap hotel had meaning for him. It would be that way always.

Chapter Nine: THE ONE WHO VANISHED

LANS WAS sleeping as a child does, the blanket pulled to above his chin, one arm limp, hanging to the floor. She hated to wake him; he would need what sleep he could snatch. But it wasn't safe to leave him in an unbolted room. She touched his shoulder and he jumped. He blinked at her, explained, "I was dreaming."

She said, "I'm going over to breakfast with Dinky. He called. Lock the door after me. And don't open it for anyone."

"How will you get in?"

"I'll rattle the knob like this." One-two—one-two—three—she had worked it out while dressing. "Then I'll insert my key. You'll know." She added, "Try to go back to sleep. It's only seven."

He told her, rubbing his head, "I'll try. Bring the papers when you come."

Dinky didn't look so young and beautiful, his face was worn at the corners. He was in pajamas and robe, the Thursday morning papers surrounded him.

She asked, "How did you wake so early?"

"Couldn't sleep. Besides I knew there'd be a hue and cry early." He said, "There's fruit, coffee—even toast and bacon and eggs if you can look them in the face." He pushed the papers to her.

Sally's blonde face, like too many other blonde faces, staring out at her. Below, a blur of Sally as they'd seen her last, a white arrow pointing to the tired body. The headlines bellowed, "Night Club Wife Murdered." Inside, a picture of the orchestra, Lans no more than a smudge of profile, unrecognizable. No other of him.

There wasn't much of a story. The hotel detective had investigated in the early hours of morning, not long after they'd gone away, called by another resident of the hotel because of undue noise. That much wasn't true. The room had been left in silence that couldn't be broken. Someone had miscalculated the time; there'd been a mistake there.

She went on reading, "... *the body of Mrs. Lans Vaught, wife of Lans Vaught, pianist with Jim and Jack's orchestra* ..." The husband missing. Look for the husband. The hue and cry had started.

She drank orange juice. "Inspector Tobin will come."

"Yes, he'll come," Dinky said wearily. "They'll know I was with her. Last night I thought Lans was in a spot. Now I know I'm the one. I can't alibi. I was out cold."

She asked now, fearing the answer, but under compulsion to make certain. "Is Stefan Viljaas in this country?"

His eyes somber, his head barely nodded.

She didn't move. And then she cried out, "You know it's his work. You can tell the police that."

He looked steadily across at her. "I don't know anything. And if you mention him, I'll lie."

She knew why. Guard had told her that; they must have definite proof before accusing Stefan. Maybe that was his reason. Maybe Dinky was afraid of Stefan.

She stammered, "I won't say a word, not a word," and then she asked helplessly, "What am I to say?"

He poured more coffee. "I don't know. We've got to have a story before Toby arrives. That's why I called you. I wish I could reach Guard, but I don't know where."

She could help at last. "I saw him at Grand Central

yesterday morning. I think he's gone to Vermont."

For a moment they looked into each other's eyes in full knowledge.

Dinky said, "I'll wire," and then, "There's only one thing for you to tell the police. It may not be much good but you'll have to stick to it. You were never in that room last night." She questioned with her eyebrows.

He went on, "You and Lans came in the hotel about three-thirty or four, whatever time it was; went up in the elevator and met me—outside the room. I was drunk. So you took me home. Simple as that."

She shook her head. "It puts you in a spot."

"I am, anyway. They'll find out she must have been killed while I was in the room. They'll get that close to the right time. There's one discrepancy in your story but you'll have to stick to it, by hell and high water. You and Lans weren't in that room."

She asked, "The discrepancy is why Lans didn't go home at all?"

He said, "No. That's an easy one. He stayed all night with you." He looked at her. "You don't mind that?"

She said, "No." She didn't. If Vermont ever found out, let it think what it chose. No one in New York would care if she had a lover. And she didn't have one. "Then what's the catch?"

"The time lapse between when you and Lans came up and went down again." He lighted a cigarette, on second thought passed the case to her. "We'll have to chance that. Hope the elevator flunkey was tired enough to be foggy about the time. And you can say I was hard to manage. You'll be believed in that."

She nodded. "It doesn't seem fair for you to be the one, when you know."

"I don't know," he told her sharply. "I was out." His mouth twisted. "Maybe she bumped herself off."

"Not Sally." Not that poor unhappy girl who'd never had the breaks, who'd loved and married a man who hated her, a Viljaas. Lizanne suddenly realized only a miracle had saved her from the same fate. If she'd been found in Dene's room after he was killed—but she'd run away in time. She shivered.

Dinky asked, "Scared?"

"No. No. I can tell it that way." And she asked, "Can Guard get you out of it?"

He said slowly, "I'm not worried about that. I'm innocent. But I can't afford to be locked up now. I'm needed."

They re-read the papers. Waiting was hard. And she had nerves. She pushed back her chair. "I think I'll go out to the desk and do some work."

"You have work to do?"

"No. But I can do something. Type the quick brown fox if nothing else. And I'll be out there if anyone comes."

He agreed. "That's not bad."

She sat at the desk and waited, making words, only remembered words: *"O, the blood is spilt..."* Not this. Was there nothing to remember save murder, blood?

Lydia, Sally, why should they meet death? Alix and Fredi. But she remembered with water again in her veins: the dead were the Viljaas wives, the unwanted Viljaas wives. Only she was left. Only one more woman to be murdered. And one more man? Lans? Her fingers stood quietly on the keys. If Guard were what he pictured himself, if he and Dinky were what they pretended, she should be safe. But why should Guard be going to Vermont save to find out about her, to make certain of her marriage that she too might be put out of the way? Her lips set. That she might not be murdered without purpose. Guard wasn't to be trusted.

She knew it was impossible to run away. Inspector Tobin would be after her at once, save Bill Folker and Guard Croyden the trouble. She couldn't go and hide; she'd let herself in for this; there was nothing she could do now but follow it through. Hope, but hopelessly, that she would come out of it alive.

Waiting, one hour, two hours; waiting for Tobin, waiting for Bill; the minute hand on her watch had tortoise feet. Another thought: where was Lans supposed to be now? Dinky hadn't thought of that item. When Lans gave himself up; yes, his alibi was set; he was with her. But she must face Tobin before then and what was she to say? She must find out quickly.

She hastened to the room, entered without knocking, and stopped short. Tobin was there, staring out of the window at the park below. She didn't know how he had entered; perhaps the house detective admitted him. Moore was snooping under the silver cover, regret in his face at frigid bacon and eggs.

She began, "I beg your pardon——"

Tobin turned from the window. "I told you eventually someone would turn up," he reminded the Sergeant.

Lizanne controlled her falsetto. She became the secretary at once although her nails pushed hard into her palms. "Have you waited long? I didn't hear you. I was in the office."

Tobin's hands were in his pockets, his hat set on the side of his head. He didn't look like an ogre.

She came forward one step. "Mr. Folker is out this morning. Do you wish to wait, or leave a message?" She didn't know if she were expected to know of Sally's death; even if she were, she wasn't to connect any of them with it.

"Mr. Bruce here?"

"I don't know." She wondered where Dinky had gone. "Shall I find out?"

"If you will." Tobin turned back to the window.

She went beyond to the bedrooms, her hands still clenched. Dinky's door was closed. Her tap was unanswered; she entered. A moment of fear, seeing him slumped there in the chair, but he hadn't been attacked. He was only asleep. She closed the door, went over to him, and spoke, "Dinky!" He came out of sleep, not frightened as Lans had been but as foggily. "They're here," she said.

"Tell them to go away," he blurred.

"It's Inspector Tobin and that Moore policeman."

He woke then, shaking his head violently. "I'll come. I'll be out soon as I soak my head in cold water. I must have fallen asleep. Amuse them. And don't forget——"

There wasn't time now to find out what to say about Lans, besides she might be overheard. She returned to the living room. "I woke him. He'll be out in a moment." She started to the door, hoping, not expecting to be allowed to depart.

Moore asked plaintively, "This your breakfast?"

She hesitated, answered, "Yes."

"You didn't have much of an appetite."

"I never take more than coffee and fruit."

Tobin raised one eyebrow at her. "You could use something more nourishing."

She flushed a little, didn't speak.

"Who'd you eat with?"

Again she hesitated but answered truthfully, "Mr.

Bruce asked me to breakfast with him, before he went to sleep." She was a secretary, on duty early; Dinky went to bed when working people were getting up. It couldn't seem a conference.

Tobin took a chair. "What do you know about Sally Vaught's death?"

The question came so suddenly, casually as it was spoken, that her breath caught. She didn't know what to answer. The pause seemed long before she said, "I've seen the papers."

He was going to ask another question but the corridor door opened. It was Bill and Fredi, Bill looking as if nothing more important were on his mind than the hang of his tweeds, the roll of his hat. Fredi's elf eyes were bright as copper.

Bill looked surprised. "Good morning, Inspector. What brings you here?"

Dinky spoke from the doorway as if still befogged with sleep. "Morning, Inspector. You wanted to see me?"

Tobin glanced around the room, his stare resting on each one of them. He said, "I want to see all of you."

Bill acted more surprised at that, and Fredi said, "I have not met you, no?"

Bill made introductions. Moore had gone to a corner of the room, idly examining a silver unicorn on the glass whatnot. But his yellow pencil was behind his ear and his hand obviously on the notebook in his pocket.

Tobin said, "Might as well make yourselves comfortable. I suppose you all know that Sally Vaught was murdered last night." Bill said, "No!" as if unbelieving.

Tobin stated, "You were all at Jim and Jack's for dinner. Mr. Bruce, you left with Mrs. Vaught. Let's pick it up there."

He would know; every move he would know about. She and Dinky must feel their way, not certain what the employees of that hotel might have told.

Bill spoke before Dinky could, "Do you need us, Inspector? I promised the Baroness a bit of sightseeing this morning. She's only just arrived from London."

Her accent wasn't of London. And she'd been in the hotel longer than that, but she hadn't let Bill know.

Tobin answered obliquely, "I'd rather like you to stay."

Bill was pleasant about it, even smiled. "Sorry, Fredi."

"I don't mind." She turned big blue eyes on Tobin. "I think it is fascinating." She hissed the *s*.

Tobin didn't pay any attention to her. He said, "All right, Mr. Bruce. You left with Mrs. Vaught."

Dinky bobbed his head as if trying to recall. "Yes, I guess I did. Usually do." He was giving his customary blurred performance, as if he'd been drunk and was not recovered from it. "And we went up to the hotel for a couple of drinks." He turned on a dazzling smile. "I must have had too many. That's all I remember until I met Lizanne and Lans while I was waiting for the elevator. And they made me go home." He sounded aggrieved.

Tobin asked sharply, "Where was Mrs. Vaught when you left."

Dinky continued vague. "I suppose she was on the bed asleep. She usually went to sleep."

"You've been there often with her?"

Dinky was annoyed. "I've taken her home a few times."

Moore asked, and everyone turned to look at him, "Where was her husband when you was taking her home?"

Dinky stared at him as if he were an interloper. "D'you know, I never bothered to ask?"

170

Tobin was sharp again. "Do you actually mean that's all you know about it?"

"About what?"

"About her being murdered."

"Oh, that."

Lizanne could have screamed. Why should he act like a moron? She set her teeth to keep from crying out to tell the truth, to tell them. Why should he not even try to save himself?

"Yes, that." Tobin's voice was dangerously casual.

Dinky said, as if it didn't matter, "I don't know anything about that."

Tobin took a stick of chewing gum from his pocket. He slid off the white wrapper, unwrapped the pink covering, fed the gum into his mouth, said, "Let's start all over again."

Dinky's sigh was audible. "Better give me some dog-hair, Bill. Make it Hennessey."

Bill said, "Right," and moved to the portable bar at the window. "Anyone else?"

Moore mumbled, shocked, "Not in the morning."

Dinky eyed him again. "It tastes just the same." He snickered. "Liquor can't tell time."

Tobin waited until the bulbous glass was cupped in Dinky's hand. "You went to dinner at Jim and Jack's. After dinner?"

"We danced and drank. Very gay. Y'know, Inspector. Party to welcome the Koppels to the great American shores and all that. Oh, very gay."

Dinky was ironic. It hadn't even been relaxation. It had been polite, divided, and taut. Lizanne realized that now. No one had been at ease, save perhaps, Wolfgang Koppel.

"And then?"

171

Dinky sipped. "The others left. Lizanne and I stayed."
"Why?"

Lizanne waited. If he would but tell; Bill's orders, Bill manipulating. But Dinky winked. "We had business." He went on, "And Sally and I——"

Tobin interrupted. "Business. What do you mean?"

"I had a date with Sally. And Lizanne——" He didn't complete the thought, nor did Tobin ask. He would wait for her turn. Dinky held out his empty glass to Bill.

"You went straight to her room?"

Again he was aggrieved. "You mustn't say it like that. It was the Vaught apartment, the Vaught home. She couldn't help it if it was only a room. No matter how humble, Inspector, there's no place like home, y'know." He hummed. His mouth looked as if he were about to cry. Bill handed him the replenished glass.

Tobin said, "All right. Now what happened there?"

"Nothing happened. We had some drinks waiting for Lans, like we always do—did. And then, I went to sleep in the chair, and I guess she went to sleep on the bed. Just like we always did."

Tobin chewed thoughtfully. "And when you woke up, she was still asleep? On the bed?"

"I suppose so."

"Did you see her there on the bed?"

"I suppose so. I don't know. I was kind of hazy. I remember getting my hat and coat and going out in the hall."

Moore asked, "She wouldn't have been lying on the floor there by the door? You'd known if you'd stepped across her, wouldn't you?"

Dinky spoke soberly enough now. "Yes, I'd have known."

Lizanne closed her eyes, seeing as if she'd been a by-stander three figures skirting that crumpled dress on the floor.

Tobin was saying, "You don't remember hearing a shot?"

He could be truthful not evasive. "I didn't hear any shot, Inspector."

"You seem sure of that."

"I am."

Tobin barked, "Yet you're not certain if Sally Vaught was alive or not when you left?"

Dinky shook his head. "She must have been alive. Even in the condition I was in, I'd have noticed if she were dead."

Moore's voice again, "If she hadn't been on the floor, if she'd been on the bed, shot, would you have noticed?"

Dinky answered. "I don't know. I didn't examine her. I just left."

"Without saying good night?" the Sergeant asked.

Dinky nodded.

"Did you——" Tobin began.

But Dinky interrupted. "Can't you understand, Inspector? I'm trying to tell you I was drunk, plastered, if you like. I get that way." He paused to drink and continued, "And when I'm like that, there's no reason for anything to me. It's all vague and lovely. I go along like I've been going along with Sally Vaught, because she asked me to and offered me more drinks. I didn't kill her. I don't know why you'd think so. She wasn't anything to me. I just felt sorry for her, sitting around all night in that smelly club, waiting for her husband. That's why I started taking her home."

"Didn't he mind?" Moore asked.

The case was shaping now. Lans killed his wife because of another man. Only Tobin couldn't believe that. He was too smart for that. He must know it wasn't that simple, must know that somewhere it was connected with the cross-eyed bear.

Dinky answered, disinterested now, "Of course not. Lans and I have known each other since we were children. He knew I wasn't interested in Sally Vaught. He knew she was safe with me."

He didn't mean it that way. The way he meant it she hadn't been. No one was safe. No one would be safe until the estate was settled.

Without warning Tobin addressed himself to Bill. "And what were you doing at that hotel last night?"

Bill took time in answering. He was not prepared for the question. He must have thought, as she herself did, that Lizanne was next. By her watch it wasn't long, but it seemed an endless silence. Fredi was moth-still while Tobin waited Bill's reply.

He didn't make the mistake of denying it; he must have known the elevator boy had identified him. When he spoke it was easily, as if he'd planned the answer carefully in advance. "We were going up to Harlem, the Baroness and I. We thought Dink might want to join us. Being in the neighborhood—we'd been having food at one of those all-night restaurants on Broadway, I couldn't tell you the name, Inspector; I didn't even notice—we stopped at the hotel." Fredi's smile applauded him. "We went up but there was no answer at the door, so we left again."

"You went to Harlem?"

He shook his head. "We were over the idea by then. I took the Baroness to her hotel, the Ambassador."

"And where were you from the time you left Jim and Jack's until you went to the Vaught room?"

Bill said, "We dropped in at the Cotton Club."

Impossible to check that; it was always too crowded.

"Where was Croyden?" Again the unexpected.

"He had to run down to Washington." Bill said it as if he believed it. Guard's destination might have been secret even to him. "What's happened? I haven't seen the papers."

Tobin said, "I'll tell you what I know afterward. I want to find out first what you know."

Bill was almost amused. "But we know nothing, Inspector. How could we? I didn't ever meet her except that day you asked her to come here. What does Lans have to say?"

Tobin stared at him. He said, "I'd like to know that," and he turned at last to Lizanne. "What do you know about it, Miss Steffasson?"

"Nothing." Her voice sounded squeaky, like a rusty wheel. She tried again. "Nothing."

"Mr. Bruce left with Mrs. Vaught. What did you do?"

Lizanne said, "I waited for Mr. Vaught." She caught her underlip in her teeth. "We—took a walk." It sounded absurd, walking on a damp night.

"Where'd you walk to?"

"Into Central Park." That too sounded absurd, as if you were a silly young girl out with your best young man. She went on helplessly. "We stayed there awhile. I don't know how long. Then we went to Lans's hotel." He didn't ask why but she explained, "We knew Dinky would be there and I could go home with him."

Again Tobin asked no questions. He didn't seem very interested, chewing his gum, swinging the chain across his vest. Perhaps he took it for granted that Dinky needed help to get back to Bill's.

She must step softly now in continuing the story. "When we got out of the elevator, Dinky was in the corridor. It took a little time for us to get his coat and hat on him." She hated lying about the real Dinky, the one she had seen for the first time in the early morning hours. But it was by his own express wish. "I couldn't manage him alone, so Lans came along to help me."

Bill's eyes were on her, unwavering. She kept her own turned away, not daring to look at him lest he discover she was lying.

"You didn't go into Lans's room?"

She hoped her look lifted to Tobin wore innocence. "No." She embroidered, deliberately hesitating. "No. Dinky was—noisy. Lans wanted to get him out before there might be complaints about a friend of his."

"You didn't hear a shot?"

She shook her head. "There was no shot." She thought she was on guard against a surprise question but she wasn't:

"Who were you with at Grand Central yesterday?"

She looked quickly at Bill, saw the little leap of suspicion flare in his temples; turned quickly to Dinky, saw his lifted head, his eyes hard and curious. Back to Tobin. "A friend of mine was leaving for the West. I saw her off." Why did Tobin have to ask it here, before all of them? Didn't he know her precarious position? But of course he didn't. However, he did not ask the name of the friend; he had another question:

"You weren't there with Lans Vaught?"

She'd almost forgotten that, the reason why she'd been in Grand Central. She said, "I ran into him there." No one believed her, not anyone in that room. She knew it.

Tobin pounced. "You wouldn't have been making plans for last night—including the train he was to take to get away?"

"No! No!" She beat against his disbelief.

"Where is Lans now?"

"I don't know!" Her voice was too loud, too insistent.

"He didn't return to his room last night."

She cried out, "How could he? He didn't leave here until this morning. It was morning when we brought Dinky home."

Even that didn't alleviate the suspicion against Lans. "Where did he go when he left here? What time did he leave here?"

"I don't know—I don't know——" She knew she was near hysteria. "It was daylight. I don't know."

Dinky's drawl interrupted, "Why pick on her, Toby? You can see she doesn't know anything."

Tobin said, "I'll tell you why. I'll even tell you what's in my head if it'll do you any good. Somebody shot and killed Sally Vaught—Sally *Viljaas*—early this morning. Maybe it was supposed to look like suicide. The gun was by her hand. A nice new shiny gun." His eyebrows quivered. "One we can't check. Made in England."

"Lizanne hasn't been to England," Dinky said easily.

"No? The rest of you have."

"Not Lans," Lizanne breathed.

"Yes, Lans," he snapped. "He played his way around the world in steamer bands, hasn't been long back in this country. All right. It wasn't a suicide. The room was all torn up. And Sally was backing away from someone when the bullet got her, from across the room! That's not suicide. And it isn't suicide when the gun's wiped clean, and the doorknobs, and the light switch. Suicides aren't that particular."

Dinky said, "I'd better have another drink, Bill."

"I'll tell you some more," Tobin went on furiously. "Mr. Bruce, you were in that room when she was killed, according to the time our medical examiner sets. You, Miss Steffasson, and Lans Viljaas must have played a pretty long game of tag with Mr. Bruce in that upstairs corridor, according to the elevator boy's testimony. And you, Mr. Folker, and you, Baroness, went up but you didn't come down. According to the boy."

"That's stupid." Bill spoke quietly. "The boy evidently doesn't remember. There were others in the cage when he took us down."

"O.K. So he doesn't remember your coming down. You, Bruce, must have passed out pretty thoroughly not to hear a gun shot off practically in your ear."

"I must have," Dinky admitted.

"Or you killed her and are lying. Your motive—I don't know. I can't think one up—yet. I can't think of any motive for you either, Folker."

"Or for me," Fredi piped.

"You're out of it, so far," Tobin said. "As for you, Miss Steffasson, I'm not accusing you of killing anybody. But Lans Viljaas had a motive, and that motive is you."

"You're wrong." Tears filled her eyes. They couldn't accuse Lans of this for such a reason. It wasn't true. "You're terribly wrong." And she exposed herself, openly now, without thought of consequences, angry, not caring save that Lans shouldn't be accused. "Can't you see it's a part of the cross-eyed bear?"

Such complete silence followed that her words seemed a series of shrill overtones in the room. She watched Bill

Folker's eyes fill with yellow, this time for her. Her breath caught in her throat like an imprisoned bird.

Tobin raised his chin. He came so perilously near the truth. "I hadn't forgotten the bear, Miss Steffasson. I mentioned that the room was torn up. Sally Vaught could have surprised any of you searching for it."

Lizanne's breathing was loud as a sleeping dog's.

Tobin said, "I haven't closed the books on Lydia Thorp. And I don't intend to close them on Sally Vaught. I have a peculiar distaste for a murderer running loose. Maybe because it's my job to see he doesn't."

It was a warning. He and Moore left on that.

Lizanne just sat there, trying to keep her teeth from chattering in this overheated room. Bill was looking at her quietly, almost pityingly. Fredi's shiny eyes were staring through her. They wouldn't kill her with Dinky there; Dinky would take care of her. But he hadn't saved Sally.

Bill spoke. "Relax. They're gone." He stood up and her fists were tight lumps. But he walked to his bar, poured a slight drink and sipped it. His voice was casual. "You shouldn't have said that about the bear, Lizanne."

She stuttered, "I'm—I'm sorry. But they were accusing Lans and he didn't do it." She repeated, "I know he didn't do it. He was with me the whole time." There were no tears in her eyes but that horrible sound was coming from her.

Dinky said, "Poor kid. She hasn't had any sleep."

Bill urged, as kind-toned as if he were Uncle Will, "Why don't you go lie down, Lizanne? You need rest."

She couldn't answer, the sounds were still coming out of her throat. She stumbled blindly to the shadowy door.

She heard Fredi's light laugh, "She is not used to excitement, no?"—heard Bill's answering laughter.

She remembered to close the door after her before stumbling on across the office to her own rooms. Only then did it occur to her, in her morning hurry she had left her keys inside. It did not matter; there was the signal; but the knob turned under her hand; it shouldn't have opened but it did. It had been left unlatched.

She was quiet then. She went quickly through the apartment; she even looked under the bed, and in the child's-size dumb-waiter. Lans was gone.

She must tell Dinky. How to separate him from the others, she didn't know, but he must be told. Yet she hesitated. Dinky was no more than another hireling. He, too, accepted murder, if Stefan were behind it. All of them were in this together. They might disagree under their breaths, but they worked toward the same ultimate end, the success of Stefan Viljaas. Lans alone was outside the damned circle; he didn't belong. But doubt on noiseless feet crept in again. Was he outside? Or was she alone the one, standing against all of them?

She was still safe: Until Guard returned, gave her away, or until Lans did. She went to the bedroom. She noticed then what she had not before, her purse on the dressing table where she had left it, but it had not been placed there opened, contents spilling from it. She dumped everything out of it, examined quickly. The piece of paper on which Janet had scribbled her address was gone; she should have memorized it at once, destroyed it. Something else was missing, something that made that hollow again come inside of her. Her key ring, all of her keys including the one for the deposit box.

Lans must have taken them. Was it that he might come and go as he pleased? But unless she was out, he knew 'he couldn't enter the apartment. Did he know that one key opened Bill's door? The deposit key—he knew now she was hiding something of value. He might suspect, knowing of Dene, that she had the bear. He couldn't use that key. But if she were dead, maybe he could. The police might believe she'd given it to him; they believed he was her lover.

It must have been Lans. The others were all in Bill's apartment. But they weren't. She didn't know how long Lans had been gone; he might have left immediately after she did. Bill and Fredi could have entered on Fredi's key. Alix was missing with Wolfgang Koppel. Guard could have only been pretending to leave town. There were the police, appearing in Bill's locked place.

She rested her head weakly on her arms. She would wire Janet to take care; no, anyone could wire, sign any name; she would write, airmail; she remembered the address. The Texas girl wouldn't know her handwriting but she could phrase it so that there would be no doubt the letter was from her. Her eyes wouldn't stay open any longer. Fully dressed, she lay down on the bed.

The alarm clock was jangling and she couldn't reach it to silence its ferocious yell. She opened her eyes. There wasn't any alarm clock here. It was the phone ringing. She answered sleepily.

Dinky said, "I was getting worried. I thought maybe something had happened to you. I've been ringing you for ten minutes."

"I was asleep. What time is it?" She fumbled for the lamp. Daylight was almost dark outside.

"It's almost five-thirty. You've slept all day." He said, "Guard's coming in at seven. Will you go with me to meet him?"

She couldn't refuse. It would look suspicious if she did.

"We'll have dinner together. Don't dress. The others left right after you did; I don't think they'll be back. I've been sleeping too. Shall I come over for you?"

"I'll come over there." It was better. She wouldn't know if she were opening to him or another. Always the fear of someone coming in; from the beginning it had been there like a nightmare—Bill Folker, or Guard Croyden—or Stefan Viljaas.

Lans had left without a word. Where was he now? Had the police found him? Would he be gone again for ten years? But he couldn't be. He would return for the closing of the estate.

She showered, dressed, without nerves, but it was only six when she crossed to the other apartment. She didn't knock; Dinky had said he was alone and she doubted if he would be ready yet. There would be no one to hear the knock. But there was. Wolfgang Koppel was stretched out in Bill's place, glass in hand, bored.

"Hullo. Join me in a drink?"

She shook her head. "I'm going out with Dinky."

Wolfgang said, "He's yodeling in his bath. Where is everyone?"

She said she didn't know. She sat opposite him but she was restive, not knowing why. Then, meeting his eyes, she did know. Like the others he wasn't what he seemed. He wasn't aimless, merely trailing in Fredi's wake. Was he Stefan? When he smiled at her, she held her breath.

He spoke softly. "You're a wise child, aren't you?"

She didn't dare answer lest he hear the tremor in her throat.

"You'd be careful not to talk too much, wouldn't you? Bill sees no one save those known to him. The maid who does his rooms, the men who serve him, have been placed in the hotel at his demand. We too have staff friends." He was lighting a cigarette. "It was no risk to watch him. Unless someone should talk."

She had found voice. "Is that why she tried to kill me?"

He shrugged. "I never know exactly why she plans to abrogate certain persons. But it would have been safer if no one took Lydia's place. Or if the place were not taken until we had arrived." She put her lip between her teeth. The box had been placed there, deliberately.

He yawned, pursed his lips. "Everyone's been doing the queerest things today. Won't you have a drink?"

Dinky's voice said, "She doesn't drink. I'll take one, Wolf." He was in the doorway, his hair still damp from the shower. She wondered how long he had been standing there, what he might have heard. "What have you been doing all day, Wolf?"

"The queerest things," he repeated. "Listening to a police officer interview Alix. Fancy!"

Dinky told him. "Lans's wife was murdered last night."

"Now, really! Was that it?" He wasn't interested. "Most peculiar. Alix didn't even know about it. And then seeing her off to Washington."

"Why is she going to Washington?"

"To visit her father."

Dinky said carelessly, "What a lie. She never goes near the old gent."

Wolfgang shrugged. "She said to visit her father."

Dinky set down his glass. "Wonder what she's up to. Must be a new man. Come along, Lizanne."

She moved quickly to him; didn't glance at Koppel. They took a cab to Grand Central. Guard came in on

183

the train from upstate. He couldn't have gone to Texas and back. He hadn't been near Washington. He had been to Vermont. A flicker showed surprise at Lizanne's presence, but he said nothing. They walked out.

Dinky asked, "Where do we eat? Downtown? Lafayette? It's too quiet for Fredi's taste—the Koppels are here."

"So?" He always looked angry; no way to know if the news displeased him. "I haven't had the pleasure in a long time. How's Alix taking this?"

"She's gone to Washington, according to Wolf." He laughed with real amusement. "A sudden interest in the Ambassador, according to Wolf."

Lizanne was curious. "You knew them, Dinky?"

He laughed without mirth now. "Everyone knows Fredi. Worst little tramp on the continent. I met her when I was at Lucerne one winter. There was before she was the Baroness, her mannikin days."

They were seated in the quiet old room, elbows upon the old-fashioned white tablecloth. Guard turned to Lizanne. "Drink?"

She nodded. "Dubonnet."

She was surprised that Dinky didn't order, that Guard did not suggest it. Dinky was studying the menu with delight. "I haven't eaten for so long," he mourned. "The other places all one can do is partake of nourishment, but here——" He smacked his lips.

"What's your wire about?" Guard demanded.

"You haven't seen the papers?"

He shook his head. "I haven't had time. God, I thought I could get away for a day or two. I thought I had everything under control here for that long——" He scowled, and Lizanne stopped looking at him.

Dinky finished the order for the three, withheld answer until the waiter was out of earshot. "Well, hold on to your hat, boy. Our friend got rid of Sally last night."

Without moving a muscle, Guard stated, "You were on her."

"I was, yes." Dinky's face was glum. "Until I got a rabbit punch in the neck, and a hypo in my wrist." He showed the pinpoint mark.

Guard turned on Lizanne and she jumped a little. "What were your orders?"

She parroted, "I was to keep Lans out of the way. For a long time."

"And you did?" He didn't like it.

"They went for a walk in the park." Dinky grinned.

She flushed. "We did. It was a beautiful night, misty. He hasn't any money. And I *wanted* to."

Dinky patted her hand. "That's all right, lamb." His mouth was serious. "Sweet simplicity is so refreshing in this set-up. You ought to realize that."

She didn't say any more. At least he didn't accuse her of being in love with Lans. At least he didn't look at her as if she were in love with Lans and as if it were distasteful to him. No reason for Guard to care where her interest lay: it had nothing to do with the Viljaas estate.

Dinky spoke to Guard again. "We had Tobin this morning, not the casual good guy Toby, but hard as a mallet. He's got it all worked out. Lans did it."

"What does Lans say to that?"

"Nothing. Lizanne's his only alibi and she might be considered prejudiced the way Toby's reconstructing it."

"The way he says he's reconstructing it," Guard amended.

"Maybe. Anyhow I thought Lans better hole up until

you got here. We have him in Lizanne's apartment."

Only then did she remember that she hadn't told Dinky. She was afraid to tell them. Guard would blame her; he always did. But she had to speak. "You're wrong," she said. "He isn't hiding out any more. He's gone."

Dinky's "What?" was so startled that her spoon dropped with a clang into her soup plate. Guard had turned on her, his eyebrows vertical. She stammered, "When I went back, he wasn't there."

Dinky sighed, "Oh, my God. He doesn't have the sense of ducks. Where do you suppose he is?"

Guard asked, his eyes suspicious, "He couldn't have been taken away?"

"Not if he kept the bolts shut," she told him. "No one could have surprised him."

Dinky went on, "Wouldn't you think at this stage of the game he'd stay safe?"

Lizanne spoke for him. "But he didn't think it was safe, Dinky. You convinced him at the moment but he wasn't really convinced. It was too near Bill's for him. You know how he felt." That was probably his reason. It was the one she preferred, not that he'd gone through her purse and then changed his mind.

Dinky repeated, "Not the sense of ducks. You'd think he'd take my word for it. My God, if he had the nerve to go there, you'd think he'd have the nerve to stay put."

She defended him again. "He was too worn out, and sick about the whole thing to argue longer last night."

"We'll have to locate him," Guard said quietly. "We'll take a run up to the club later. Someone in that crowd must know something about him."

Lizanne's heart contracted for Lans. She knew how he felt: trust no one, play it alone. She herself, even now, could feel no other way. Yet she had made her mistake; knowing better she had trusted him. She said, "Maybe they won't know. Maybe he's alone."

Guard nodded, "That's just what I'm afraid of."

Dinky's hand was suddenly hard on her wrist. "You don't know where he is? You're not holding out on us?"

She shrank. Guard was watching. She hadn't seen a Dinky like this and she was afraid for herself now, not Lan's. "No. No. I swear to it."

He released her but he mocked, "I've heard you swear to a lot of things today, Miss."

They sat at a table, Dinky's eyes avoiding hers, both of them turned from that corner where Sally was wont to be; the two of them silent, mirthless, while Guard disappeared with the one called Jim or Jack, and while the orchestra filed out for an intermission and Guard followed them. It was reprieve when he returned, said, "Let's get out of here."

Dinky asked wearily in the cab, "To where?"

"The Lorenzo. No reason to spend the night combing the town. Tobin will take care of that."

"Any news of him?"

"None at all and I don't think they're lying. Kept to himself. They didn't know anything about him. He's played with them about a year."

Guard paid the driver. They walked inside, to the elevators. He continued, "There's not a better place to disappear than New York. He can hide out as long as he likes. Especially when there's no photograph to identify him. Any hotel."

They went into the office. Lizanne said, "Good night," starting to her door, but Guard said, "Just a minute." He spoke to Dinky first, however. "Get off to Washington tonight. Tell Tedford I want to close up the estate now, right away. If he's willing, I'll send the papers a story on it that'll smoke Lans out." He continued, "Make him understand, Dink. God knows how many more murders there'll be if we don't get this thing over with."

"What'll you tell Bill?"

"You're on a bat. As a sideline, see what Alix is up to." Guard's voice was bitter when he spoke her name. Lizanne couldn't understand. Surely he couldn't still care for Alix. Not a man with the strength, whether it was for good or evil, of Guard Croyden.

"A pleasure, a real pleasure." Dinky waved a goodnight and went away.

Guard turned to Lizanne and she jumped. He said, "I'm not going to bite you. I want you to find Lans."

Her eyes widened. He'd told her she must obey and she knew that she must to be temporarily safe. But this was impossible. "How?"

"I don't know," he admitted coolly. "I'll run a personal in tomorrow's *Times*. It's queer how persons who voluntarily disappear keep their eyes on the personal column."

Had the advertisement she had answered really been for that? Was Bill's purpose actually to locate her?

Guard scrawled on the back of an envelope. He read aloud: *"Will young man who occupied young woman's apartment on the night of January eighth communicate at once? Essential."*

She asked, "And if he doesn't?"

"I'll chance it. If he does, you must convince him that it's for his own welfare to see me. It is."

She answered hotly, "I won't trap him."

His mouth hardened. "When are you going to realize that I'm handling a case in this Viljaas business, not working it for my own ends?"

She sighed out loud. "I wish I could believe you. I wish I could believe any of you." And under her breath, "Even Lans." She looked at him. "There's too many numbers that don't add. The whole thing's a network of lies."

He shrugged his great shoulders. "All right. Make it hard on yourself." He fixed his eyes on her. "I made some inquiries about you in Vermont."

He hadn't had the time to ferret out the marriage license. He couldn't have. She didn't flinch from his stare.

"You are difficult to get anything on, Lizanne," he admitted. "Even at the source. The best I could do was to hear from everyone what a nice girl you were and how surprised they all were when you took up with one of the city fellows at the Inn, that Dene Thyg."

She smiled a little, and then it trembled away as he continued:

"You weren't Dene's mistress, Lizanne. You weren't that kind of girl. After he—disappeared, you stayed right there in the post office. No sin on your soul." His eyes mocked. "You hadn't done any wrong in the eyes of God and Middle Peak, Vermont. Had you?"

He didn't know; but he was an investigator, accustomed to figuring things out. She didn't answer.

He said abruptly, "I saw Tobin. You have a deposit box at the Madison bank." She didn't move. "You visited it the morning after Lydia's murder. Two papers were missing from her room. A passport, and a marriage license. I want to know what you put in that box."

She was afraid of the expression on his mouth. She insisted, her voice lifting, "Nothing to interest you."

He spoke quietly. "There's such a thing as getting permission to open a box."

He mustn't do that. "Oh, no!" He mustn't see the bear.

He had it all worked out. "If you were picked up for questioning in the Sally Vaught case, held in custody, it might become necessary to get court permission."

She walked away from him.

"Think it over," he said. "I'm seeing Tobin again in the morning."

She asked, "Why are Lydia Thorp's papers so important?"

He seemed impatient. "Don't you realize we're looking for a murderer?"

"You know who did it," she returned. "Why not pick Stefan Viljaas up for questioning?"

"It's no good without proof. He has plenty of money for the smartest lawyers. He knows the answers. He couldn't be held for five minutes. That should be obvious to you. Do you think he'd still be running around loose if he could be held?" He strode to her side. "Do you think the department likes to spend the time and money it's spending watching him?" He walked to the door. "I'll pick up the answers to the ad."

She spoke after him, humbly. "If you get any—I mean, if he answers—I'd like to see it."

That not-liking-it look was on his face again. It went away. He even grinned, bowed slightly. "You may have that privilege, Miss Steffasson."

Chapter Ten: THE CONTINUING PERILOUS QUEST

THE SATURDAY tab noon editions lay on her desk. The headlines still shrieked the search for the missing husband. An artist's conception of Lans Vaught, looking surprisingly like although it was not he. Rehash. Sally's life, pathetically scant, the wrong streets of New York. A tab's toy—Night Club Wife Last Seen With Son of Ambassador—not there, not a word of that yet. Tobin must be suppressing that item for some reason. For Guard, no doubt. Not a word of Lizanne as yet. Nothing to identify her but the phrase "a young woman" leaving the club with Mr. Vaught. Not the name of Viljaas.

She looked up when Guard banged through the door. She had not seen him since Thursday night. He flung a plain envelope on the desk before her. It had been opened.

The message was brief: *"Young woman should know young man not interested."* Nothing more. She was disappointed, more so than she would admit although the ache inside of her admitted it. What she had expected, she wouldn't say. But it seemed as if he could have given some personal reassurance, something more than this abrupt flip. Not that she blamed him for not planning a meeting; he knew by whom she was surrounded. But she had hoped for it.

She handed back the envelope. "It didn't do any good." She had unreasonable satisfaction in speaking it.

"No. I'm running another tomorrow. *'Young man must be interested. Essential.'* Lans must get in touch with us. We can't afford delay now." He turned to go. "If Dinky calls, tell him to get in touch with me at Tobin's office. He may use the private wire. Leave Bill's door open so you can hear the ring." He looked at his watch. "Bill won't be back until five or after." He went.

She ate a meager lunch in her own kitchenette, returned to the work. Surprisingly much work, all in the strange language—Swedish, Danish, Finnish, or what?

The phone sounded once. "Is Bill there?"

"No. Any message?"

"No." The man rang off. Only then did she realize it had been Lans's voice, disguised only slightly. She stood there, her hand still pressed on the phone. She couldn't summon him back; it was too late now.

She worked on wearily. She didn't like being alone here. Too many of them might come in, do away with her. Her ears ached listening for sound through the clack of the typewriter; she angled her chair where each of the three doors would be visible. She remembered that she must write Janet, warn her not to talk in case whoever had that address should go after her. She put aside work temporarily and began the message.

She had thought there was a rustle, was certain of it now. She took the letter from the machine, laid it in the top drawer under other papers, before starting softly, trembling, to Bill's doorway. A man she had never seen before, handling the papers she had finished. The thought of having to re-do the long tedious pages banished fear. She asked, "What are you doing with those?"

The man turned and stared at her; evidently he hadn't heard her movement into the doorway. But it wasn't his voice that answered.

"He's reading them." It came from someone by the corridor door and she looked in that direction. Ambassador Tedford Bruce was standing there with all of his snow-blue hair, dignity, and importance. The phone began to ring, a silly repetitive sound, but she didn't move toward it. It ceased and the phone in the office took up the jangle, but she didn't move. Ambassador Bruce's eyes were on her, as cold as Alix's.

He spoke as to a servant, "You can go back to your

192

work, Miss. We don't need you here."

She didn't protest. She didn't even say, "Be careful of my work." She returned to the other room, continued listlessly with more pages. If Ambassador Bruce wished to search a room, she couldn't stop him.

The door of the office opened wide, not quietly, Guard striding in. He goggled at her as if she were spectral. "You're here!" He almost shouted it. "Why the devil didn't you answer the phone?"

She said, "Someone was in there."

He walked over swiftly, took a glance. "No one now. I thought something had happened to you." He snatched off his hat, wiped his forehead with the back of his hand. "I thought you'd been——" He broke off. "I can't have any more killings in this case. Bad enough as it is." He shook his head. "Who was in there?"

"Ambassador Bruce and another man."

"Ted?" He seemed disbelieving. "You're sure?"

She said yes.

He took the phone from her desk, spoke into it. "Try to locate Ambassador Tedford Bruce for me. Mr. Croyden speaking. I don't know where. Try all the hotels." He replaced the phone. He looked down at her. "No one knows who you are?"

No reason not to tell him—"Only you, and Lans."

"Lans!" He barked it.

"I couldn't help it," she apologized. "He knew. He said he'd known from the first. He said Dene wrote to him."

"Guesswork. And you admitted it."

She was timid. "You don't think he'd—hurt me?"

"How do I know?" He was angry. "How do you expect me to predict what any Viljaas would do?"

Lans wouldn't hurt her. He cared for her. She said

timidly again, "I think he telephoned."

Guard turned on her as if she were crazy too. "You think he phoned." His inflection was heavy with irony.

She was tired enough to cry. Nothing she ever did suited him. But she flared back instead, "I'm not sure. Some man called and asked for Bill. He only said three or four words. Not until I'd hung up did I think of Lans."

He said, "You make a wonderful operative." He was disgusted. She understood why but she didn't like it, his always blaming her. Her eyes filled now and he said, "You needn't cry about it. That doesn't help. But—"

He was interrupted. Bill was a shot propelled into the room. He was white from rage, not from any other cause, certainly not from any pretended heart trouble. His eyes were danger yellow. Lizanne's fingers held tight to the desk.

"Guard! They've arrested Fredi and Wolfgang!"

Guard didn't seem to know about this. If he did, he could act. He repeated, thunderstruck, "Arrested the Koppels! Tobin's arrested the Koppels? He didn't say anything to me and I've been with him all afternoon talking things over."

Bill was walking circles. "I didn't say anything about Tobin. It's Garth. The Feds."

"Oh." Guard's mouth was an uncommunicative line.

Bill whirled in suspicion. "Did you do this? You're Garth's crack man." His voice grew louder. "Did you have a hand in this? If you did——" He suddenly lunged.

Lizanne screamed. It was a little scream and neither man heard it.

Guard seated himself unperturbed in the best chair. "You're not going to kill me, Bill. Not unless you shoot me in the back. If you try any other way, I'll break you in two." His hands were big, brutal enough to try it. He lighted a cigarette. "Sit down."

Bill sat down. "I didn't have a hand in this. I don't know anything about it. Ted Bruce is in town. He may know why. Tell me what's happened."

Bill said, "We were having a drink in the cocktail lounge. It was done quietly. Plain-clothes men."

"But why?"

"I don't know. Aliens. Spies." He lurched up, began walking again. "Guard, you've got to find where they've taken her, what they're going to do. You must."

Guard twisted his mouth. "They *are* spies then?"

Bill stood quietly, looking down at him as if he still suspected. But he didn't start after him. "They work for their government. The way you do for yours. The way I do for mine. You don't think Ted would do this to me?"

"I don't think he even knows."

Bill said, "Dinky? No. Dinky wouldn't."

Guard told him, "Stop working yourself up. The government is keeping a close check on strangers these days. This is probably no more than a routine pick-up. Don't take it personally. You know that Fredi and Wolf have gone through it in every country they've ever entered."

Bill ignored him. "Lans? Not Lans. He hasn't any drag." Then he smiled, a terrible smile that wasn't a smile. "What has Alix been doing in Washington?" He was quiet now standing there. "Alix. She said she'd even things up." He wet his lips. "Alix. Our dear Alix."

Guard spoke coldly. "Be careful, Bill."

His mouth was vicious. "I'll be careful. I'll take care of this very carefully."

The phone was ringing. Lizanne was almost too weak to pick it up but she did. She said to Guard, "For you."

She didn't move. She wouldn't go to her room, not having to pass Bill, coiled there like a hooded cobra. She let Guard take the call from the corner of the desk. For once his shoulders looked comforting, not fearsome. They blocked her from Bill.

He finished conversation. "That was Ted. I told him we'd come down right away, have dinner with him. Do you want to change?"

Bill said, "No." His eyes were still yellow with hate.

"We'll go, then. Lizanne, any calls"—Guard was harshly emphatic—"any at all, find out who. Relay to the St. Moritz if need be." He touched Bill's shoulder.

Bill followed him as if lost in an evil dream.

Lizanne was bolted in her suite when Guard telephoned back: "We're flying to Washington at once with Tedford, Bill and I. If Tobin or anyone tries to reach us, we'll be back in the morning."

She didn't say anything, thoughts were cantering with such rapidity into her head. It was just seven. If she could reach Lans, she might be able to help him. They could talk it over undisturbed this night, without fear.

Guard's voice broke in sharply, "Lizanne! Are you there?"

"Yes. Yes, I will."

There was a faint hesitation before he said, "Take care of yourself," and repeated, "We'll return in the morning." It was almost as if he were warning her.

She couldn't reach Lans. No possible way to do it; he was hidden too completely, one little man among millions of other little men. However, she herself could relax this night. She turned on the radio; piled the magazines bought during this week but no chance to open them. She made herself comfortable on the couch, pillows stacked behind her head. But it was as if she'd forgotten how to be at ease; she was alert to every imaginary rustle. The stories weren't fiction, what she was living was. Suddenly, as if it had been what she'd been trying to think of, she remembered the letter to Janet, careless in the desk.

She almost ran from the room but she didn't stop in the office. Light was under Bill's door, sound so slight that only with her nerves screwed taut would she have heard it. She tried the door softly; it was locked. She had new keys, furnished by the office when she had explained in a sickening girlish manner that she must have lost hers when shopping. Wisdom warned her from entering his suite, but there was no place in her mind now for wisdom. She was seeking knowledge, and she knew she must find out what was going on behind that door. Even if she walked into the arms of the police, or The Three, or worse, of Stefan Viljaas, she must enter.

Shod in cotton she returned to her room, took the new key ring quickly from her bag, and as softly entered Bill's apartment. The living room was empty, the white geometrics of the table lamp were bright. She had been a fool again, like a boy reading a ghost story at night, fearful for sound until sound was audible. The lamps had been left burning; the rest was imagination.

It was not imagination, that faintest sound from the rooms beyond. She went toward it. There would be no one save those who belonged there, Bill or Guard or Dinky returned; or, with a shiver she thought, perhaps Alix. Yet she went on. Just as if she hadn't good sense, she went on, into Bill's own room where a dim light made color.

The man stood at the desk, his fingers carefully examining one by one the papers in the center drawer. It was only his back and it was somehow unfamiliar, yet she knew. She was immediately washed through with fear for him, immediately knew with certainty that the leaving of Guard and Bill was no more than a trap for Lans. She couldn't make sound come from her throat; she only thought she whispered his name. But he swung around quickly and there was an ugly black thing, blunt-nosed, in his hand. Only then did Guard's reiterated, "Be careful," assume reality. But she had no fear. This was Lans.

She repeated, "Lans," and noticed that her voice held a foolish sort of quaver.

He said almost without recognition, "What are you doing here?" He put the gun into his coat pocket but his hand remained on it.

She said, "I heard a noise and wondered. They're all away for the night." She broke off, "Lans, you can't stay here. It's dangerous for you."

"Why? If they're away."

"Maybe they aren't. Maybe they only said that. And Stefan's in the country. Dinky told me. Suppose he should come." She must convince him; she was convinced. He mustn't stay where at any moment they might walk in on him, kill him as they had Dene and the two unwanted wives. She went over to him, touched his sleeve. His hand tightened in the gun pocket as if even her touch held menace. "Lans, let's go. What do you want here?"

He asked curtly, "What do you think I want? The cross-eyed bear."

"But Bill hasn't it." Her voice must have carried conviction; for the moment he believed her.

"How do you know?" He was suspicious.

She could have told him but she didn't. It was Lans, and Lans wasn't danger for her, but she couldn't give even him that ultimate measure of trust. She was not certain of any of them, whether they carried a federal commission or kissed her in a mist-hung park.

She said impatiently, "If he had it would he employ me to get it from you?"

"I don't have it." His eyes stared into hers as if in a moment he might fathom the mystery of the bear. "But I'm going to get it." His voice was like rock. "For once Stefan's not going to have his own way." He turned back to the desk, systematically began going through it.

"Lans!" She cried it out loud. "Please don't stay here. I'm afraid. I tell you I'm afraid."

He spoke without harshness but without looking at her, as he might to an annoyingly persistent bystander. "You go on then. You needn't stay."

"I couldn't go." She whispered it. "I couldn't go and leave you here alone to face them. They think I know where you've been hiding. Maybe Guard told me they were leaving to see if I'd get in touch with you, bring you here."

"You didn't." But he had listened to her. He fingered the gun and he asked, "Where are they supposed to be?"

"Washington."

"The sweet Fredi?"

He didn't know of that. "The Federal agents took the Koppels into custody today."

His grin was slow but thorough. And it went away. Without expression he said, "They'll get Stefan next."

She was stiff with fear, expecting momentarily the sound of their return, listening, hearing nothing. He finished with this drawer, relocked it with a key, put out his hand to the next. She touched his arm again pleading, "Don't stay here. It's reckless and foolish. Bill wouldn't keep the bear here even if he had it." She added, "Tobin might be watching, might have seen you come in."

"If he did he's taken his time in showing up." He smiled. "I didn't come the gentleman's entrance, Lizanne." But he didn't open the new drawer, only stood there his hand touching it.

The shrill of the telephone leaped between them. She could feel him tighten again; she had jumped as if struck. She reached out her hand to answer but his closed over hers. He said, "Don't," and then he said, "We will get out of here. I don't mind running into Bill"—his hand was a metallic outline in his right pocket—"but I don't want Tobin to lock me up." He asked, "Is your apartment safe or are you still playing the game for him?"

She only answered, "You ought to know by now that I'm not." She led the way, expecting at each new door to see a hostile face. But they were safe within her walls, bolted within. She asked, "Lans, why did you run away from here that day?"

"I couldn't risk staying. Tobin might have found me." He was standing in the middle of the room, looking at her. "You're worn out, Lizanne. I'm afraid this is getting you down. You don't belong in it."

"I'm in it, though."

"Yes." And he smiled at her again, almost pityingly. "Yes. Poor kid." He shook away sentiment. "Want to go out for coffee?"

She suggested, "We could have it here—if you'll stay."

He said, "I'll stay. I don't have the jitters tonight, Lizanne. I don't know. I've a feeling the whole business is going to round out sooner than we think." He walked over to her, looking down at her, asked, "And whose side will you be on?"

She flushed but she answered, "Yours. Always."

He just touched her cheek with his fingers. "You're a nice kid." And then he walked away from her. "How about the coffee?"

"I'll make it." She was nervous, not with fear now; but trembling at being with him, near him, alone and safe.

He sat on the edge of the kitchenette table while she filled the glass container. "I saw Hetty Creighton today."

For a moment the name meant nothing, then she remembered Alix's friend, the rasping one with birds on her hat.."Wasn't that a risk?"

"I didn't tell her who was phoning." He yawned. "I knew Hetty from of yore. I told her I wanted an interview with her for *Harper's Bazaar,* so she turned up."

"Where you're staying?" He hadn't told her that yet.

He said, "God, no. You don't ask the Hettys to view the wrong side of the tracks. I met her for lunch at a Schrafft's. That was safe enough. I figured she'd be more curious when she saw me than anxious to call the police. That's Hetty. She's probably braying to everyone tonight how she lunched with a dangerous murderer."

"She wouldn't believe that."

"She'll tell it." He drank his coffee with relish. He actually wasn't nervous now, nor was she. He was entirely different tonight, the way he should have been if he'd not had an elder brother Stefan. He even looked different; his tweed suit belonged to The Lorenzo not Jim and Jack's; his hair wasn't greased to patent leather. The suit must be new; he had taken Hetty to lunch; somewhere he must have acquired some money. Borrowed on what Guard called the Great Expectations?

He passed his cup for more. "It isn't hard to make Hetty talk, a couple of cocktails and she's wide open. She told me what I wanted to know."

"What Alix knows?" Those talon fingers twisting at the silver sleeve.

"It was when Alix followed Bill to Florida, two years ago. Everyone thought it meant divorce. Hetty was having herself a big time in New York chasing Guard. Suddenly Alix turned up and went back to him again."

This much she knew.

"And then one bright and shiny day Alix asked Hetty to lunch, and told her, 'You can have him, darling, if he's willing. I'm going to Reno.' Hetty was simply slain, to use her own words, and green with curiosity. She came right out and asked why. Guard was big guns even then, and Alix wasn't ever one to give up any of her possessions, whether she wanted them or not. She answered Hetty right out, and just as sure of herself, Hetty says, as if she had the ring on her finger: 'I think I'll marry Bill now.'

"Hetty was slain all over again and being a pretty shrewd gal and the very best friend of our dear Alix, she said, 'You must have something on him.' That drew the blood. Alix white as a gardenia and acting as if she weren't."

"And that's all?" She was disappointed. Nothing to help. Nothing more than Guard had said.

"Yes and no. Hetty's shrewd, I say, and when Dene's disappearance got in the papers, she figured it out that Bill was connected up with the business and that Alix knew plenty about it. So she never misses a bet at goading Alix with it, and it always starts the flutters."

She said, "Dinky is sure there's a letter, or was, with

the proof."

He finished the second cup. When he looked at her, his eyes were steady, shining. "Alix is in Washington, too?"

"She has been."

He spoke slowly. "I think I'll pay her a little visit, tonight." He looked across at her. "Want to come along?"

He didn't mean a trip to Washington. He was reckless now, the way Dene had been reckless. She'd have to go with him; he needed someone to make him remember reality. She didn't want to go. She was breathless at the idea of breaking into Alix's apartment, searching for that letter. She said soberly, "You mustn't risk it, Lans. It is a risk. She may have returned."

"She can't hurt me," he boasted.

"But Bill is looking for her. He thinks she turned in the Koppels."

He laughed out loud. "She probably did, the damned bitch. She tried to snare me once for him." He laughed again. "He can't be in Washington and here both." He shoved his hands in his pockets. "I'm going."

"I'll go with you," she said quietly.

They stood facing each other and he shook his head. "You'd better not. I didn't mean it when I asked you."

She repeated, "I'm going with you. I'll get my coat."

His smile was gentle. "Think you can protect me?"

Again she turned red. She was defiant. "I can help."

It was early, not yet nine, when the elevator let them out on the sixteenth floor. She didn't ask Lans how he knew which apartment. She did ask, "How do you expect to get in?" and he took out a key.

"My friends may not always be reputable, Lizanne, but

they're helpful." He opened the door into the dark foyer.

She whispered; it had just occurred to her, "There may be servants."

He walked inside, switched on the lights. "There aren't. I checked on that." He had planned this search then. "They sleep out. Much more convenient, for Alix."

She followed after him. But she didn't move with security. She didn't like this. She didn't have any business here; she wasn't accustomed to house-breaking.

He began search in the almost toy desk at the far corner of the living room. She sat on the edge of the silver-and-white couch. She was as nervous as Alix herself, folding and refolding her gloves, her eyes on the doorway.

He spoke in disappointment. "I had the wrong dope."

She didn't move but she said, "Pull out the drawer and look beneath. Sometimes women hide things there."

She heard him follow her suggestion, heard a low whistle from him, and in the silence that fell turned her eyes to where he stood. He had a letter in his hand, was reading it. He crossed to her eagerly now. "It's here. Listen to this. 'Dene does not have the bear. I went over his pockets carefully but only the triangle was there. He is out of the way for good.'" He looked at the wall, stressed, "'*He is out of the way for good.*'" He read again, "Lans must have it. Now if you play your part with him——"

In a moment he would know who had it, know for certain. She wasn't afraid of Lans; it was only delaying here that made the cold lump come again within her. But his voice halted suddenly. She too heard the faint sound, a key inserted, turned.

He whispered, "Get behind those curtains," repeated harshly, "Do as I say. There's no reason for you to figure in this." He was fierce. "I can take care of myself better without you."

Only then did she scurry, feeling absurd, like a character in the second act of any drama. She was behind the damask, striped in white and silver, before footsteps were crossing the foyer. She wondered if her shoes were visible, knowing they couldn't be; the heavy drapes lay in decorative folds on the silver carpet. She waited, not breathing, waited until the footsteps were at the door, and Dinky saying happily, in relief it seemed, "You, Lans! I didn't know just whom to expect when I saw the light."

Lans asked, "Has the exodus from Washington begun?"

Dinky drawled, "I'm the harbinger." A different note crept into his voice, the slightest shading but she heard it. "I suppose you came for the same thing I did. Seen the paper?"

"No."

Dinky must have passed it across; she heard it crackle, and in the silence Dinky asked, "Did you find it?"

The paper was flung on the couch. "Yes," Lans said, and, "I'm not giving it up, Dink."

"Did I ask you?" Dinky seemed almost merry. But he was sober.

Lans was suspicious. Without seeing him, she could feel that.

Dinky said, "If you have it, what do you say we go?"

Lans mustn't go alone with him. But of course he wouldn't be alone; she was with him. She would help if Dinky tried anything—but her thoughts stilled as did the two men. Another person had entered, not furtively, but as one who belonged. You heard her open the door, close it. You knew her surprise at lights burning, her suspicion, and rush to the living-room door. And she was saying, "What are you two doing in my apartment?"

"Just paying a little call," her brother said.

She didn't believe it. She wasn't expected to believe it, and her heels went in rush again at that corner desk. Lizanne could see her now, the fawn satin of her evening gown beneath her sable coat. And Lizanne made herself thinner than a damask hanging, without breath.

Alix's voice was now cold as her eyes. "Give me that letter, Dinky."

"What letter?" He was amused.

"The letter you took from this desk."

"Never touched your desk." He almost snickered. He was enjoying himself.

She would be facing Lans now, looking from one to the other, certain that one of them had stolen from her.

Lans wasn't afraid of her. He echoed Dinky's lazy fun. "Haven't seen you for years, Alix. You're looking quite well."

Her voice was stifled. "If one of you doesn't give me that letter at once, I'll——"

"You'll what?" Lans dared her.

"I'll call the police. Inspector Tobin would be pleased to find you, Lans, and I don't believe he'd mind in the least taking your companion"—she underscored it in anger—"with you."

Lizanne looked at her shoe tips in shadow; Alix didn't mean her, she meant Dinky.

He said, "You'd turn in your own father for Bill."

Lans added, "But that doesn't mean you'll get the letter. You've had it too long." He continued with impact, "And you won't call the police."

There was silence that only a pointed gun could bring before Alix spoke again, in a different way. She was begging although her voice wouldn't beg; it was brittle as ever. "You can't do this to me. You know Bill's after me, to kill me. You both know that. If I don't have the letter, I haven't a chance. If it is brought into the open, he'll believe I gave it up."

Alix wasn't inventing; the truth was in her words. The men were aware of it. One was her brother; one had played with her when she was the little girl next door.

And then Lans answered. There was mockery in his voice, a cruel mockery. "We wouldn't think of interfering between you and Bill." And he said, "Come on, Dinky."

They were going. Suddenly in panic Lizanne realized, they were leaving her here, going without her! She didn't know what to do; she only knew she wasn't safe here with Alix. Alix of cold-glass eyes didn't like her; she was in Alix's way. She opened her mouth to cry out not knowing if she dared, if it would be worse for Lans if she spoke.

He remembered, just in time, miraculously he remembered. He said, "Christ, I almost forgot her." His voice was lifted. He said, "Come on, Lizanne, we're leaving."

She didn't see the amazement on Dinky's face, on Alix's. She knew it was there but she didn't look at them or anything. She ran to Lans. She didn't really open her eyes until the elevator had descended to the first floor, and they, with Dinky now, were in a cab, headed again downtown.

Dinky asked, "Why the silencer?"

Lans said, "I'm not going to burn for killing Stefan."

Dinky said, "They're hard to get. Dene tried once."

Lans was thoughtful. "Where's Stefan?"

"He was in Washington."

Lizanne's breath caught. They had gone to meet him. The end was at hand. And she wasn't ready for it.

"But I won't vouch for anything now."

Chapter Eleven: FINDERS KEEPERS

THE cab catapulted through green lights. Lizanne was so close to Lans she could feel his heart beat but he didn't know she was there. Not this night.

He asked, "Where's Fredi?"

Dinky laughed. "Locked up safely, and Wolf. Alix was informer. Not that she gives a damn if The Three get the contracts, but because Fredi is Bill's girl." He laughed out loud again. "For once, that devil sister of mine instead of hindering did something helpful. None of us would have dared do it—yet."

"Is Bill really going to kill her?"

Dinky said quietly, "If he gets to her, he will. And it won't be unpremeditated."

"Is that news story straight?"

"Absolutely." Dinky nodded. The cab was drawing to the blue-and-white awning of The Lorenzo. "Why don't you come up and have a drink, Lans? Talk this over. Two heads might be better than one."

Lans mustn't trust Dinky, not Dinky nor anyone, not now. But tonight he continued Dene-reckless. "I believe I will." But he wasn't trusting implicitly. His arm, the arm her sleeve touched, pressed against the outline of the gun in his pocket. "We'll talk it over at Lizanne's."

"She doesn't have any liquor," Dinky told him. They stopped at her corridor door. "I'll borrow some from

Bill's cellar and be right over."

Lizanne slowly opened the door of her apartment. Always now she would fear a dark, empty room. But no one was there; the room, lighted again, was as they had left it, coffee cups on the kitchenette table, couch cushions with elbow marks in the centers. She stood there wondering. "Do you trust Dinky?"

He looked at her sharply. "Don't you?" He had taken off one sleeve of his overcoat, stood with it dragging.

She shook her head. "I don't trust anyone. Not anyone connected with the cross-eyed bear."

He laughed then, continued to remove his coat. "I don't blame you. You're right, of course." He walked over and bolted the door by which they'd entered. "But Dinky wouldn't do anything on his own. He just takes orders."

She said slowly, "That's it. That's exactly the point. He takes orders from Bill and Guard and anyone."

There was a thump low on the office door, Dinky calling, "Open up, Lans."

She said, "I'll put my things away," and went into the bedroom. If she could but rest there for a moment; if she could but forget that once such a short time ago she had answered an ad which she knew held danger. She wasn't meant for this; she belonged in a little village, sorting mail. But she couldn't stand here mooning into an empty face before an empty mirror. Lans needed her tonight; there was no one else to look out for him. She returned to the others.

They were comfortable; they looked as if they had never been involved in death and the missing key to tabloid-column wealth. Dinky was looped over the chair arm, glass in hand; Lans, slouched on the couch, newspaper opened, drink on the oval table in front of his knees. She seated herself, not near him, at the opposite corner.

He put the paper down, then he asked, "Why has he decided to do this, Dink? I can't understand it."

Dinky said slowly, "I should think that would be clear enough."

"Stefan?"

"Naturally. He's run amok, no telling where it will end if things aren't settled. And then the Koppels, although they're safe at the moment."

Lizanne didn't know their business, didn't care what they were talking about. She took up the newspaper, meaning to idle over it, but the story leapt to her eye. She read on swiftly, *"Knut Viljaas estate to be closed. Meeting of heirs of The Cross-Eyed Bear called by Tedford Bruce for Monday afternoon at the National Bank."* The heirs were mentioned, Stefan, Lans; her name was not there. That much reprieve was granted.

Quoting Ambassador Bruce. His reasons for pushing forward the date. All of it sane; nothing about death, murder. And then Ambassador Bruce said: "We have recently uncovered definite proof that Dene Viljaas, youngest son of Knut, died in a hunting accident in the north woods two years ago."

That was false. Ambassador Bruce must have known he was falsifying if Guard had told him the truth. Perhaps he hadn't been told.

This was what Dinky and Lans were talking about. But she couldn't understand why they were satisfied with Ambassador Bruce's idea. This didn't mean that Lans was safe; on the contrary, it redoubled the danger that he was in. It meant that the mark of death was more certainly upon him, unless he could hide from Stefan until these few days passed. He wasn't hiding, entering Bill's apartment and Alix's; he was courting murder.

She heard him say, "What's the Ambassador going to do about the bear?" She didn't want them to talk of the bear; they might too easily figure that she possessed it. She began to lay down the paper but over the border of it she saw the office door opening slowly, noiselessly, dangerously as a snake preparing to strike. Her breath was caught; she could utter no sound. She remembered Dinky had been last to enter; when he went for the bottles, there had been time to inform.

The door, still silent, was wide. Inspector Tobin was there, behind him Sergeant Moore. Only then did the others notice. Tobin said, "Been looking for you, Lans."

Lans didn't stir. He answered easily, "Have you? No one told me." He turned his eyes swiftly, accusingly, for one brief moment at Lizanne.

Her own met his and she knew he had rejected her again, was believing that she had staged this trap at Bill's orders. She saw his hand move without motion into the pocket of his coat. She had forgotten the gun. But he couldn't shoot it out with the New York police. He couldn't be that wild and reckless even tonight. That would be complete destruction for him, triumph for Stefan. Surely he realized.

He repeated, "Have you? What about?"

"Your wife's death." Tobin wasn't smiling but he spoke softly. "You wouldn't mind coming down to headquarters and answering a few questions, would you?"

Lans stood up, pushing the table away with his knees. "I'd mind very much," he stated. The gun was out by then and even the police were wary, motionless. "I don't intend to. Don't move, Dinky, or you, Lizanne. I'm leaving—alone."

She couldn't have moved even if she wanted to. There mustn't be a false motion, nothing to startle him, to set off that weapon. She watched, statue-still, while he edged away from the couch to the corridor door, put his free hand back to open it. No one rustled. The bolt slid.

She half-whispered, "Lans, don't." They would never believe him innocent now. They would hunt him down as they would hunt any killer.

He said, "Don't any of you start after me for ten minutes." He was gone.

The others breathed now. Dinky poured into his glass. Moore said unhappily, "I could have drawn on him if you hadn't signaled."

Tobin took off his hat, shook his head. "No use shooting it out. Somebody might get hurt." He went over to the couch, sat down, fanned himself with his hat. "I don't like guns." He splashed a glass of carbonated water. "Besides he'll be picked up easy enough. We're watching all the exits."

Moore was still not happy. "I could have done something. He wasn't used to a gun."

Dinky said, "Toby's right, Sergeant. He's crazy enough tonight to shoot wildly. What do we do next?"

Tobin said, "As soon as the boys bring him up, we'll go down to headquarters."

Lizanne wept. "He didn't do it. He was with me that night. He couldn't have done it." All three men looked at her and then through her just as if she weren't there.

Lizanne didn't try to understand the words they were speaking. She just sat waiting there, waiting for them to bring Lans back. But no one came.

Tobin pulled out an old nickel watch. "Wonder what's the delay?"

Moore said, "I'll find out." He felt better now that there could be motion, not just sitting there in an unfamiliar chair brushing the sleeves of his unfamiliar blue serge suit.

Dinky said, "Couldn't you use a drink, Toby?"

"I could." He grimaced. "But I'm on duty. That little punk holding us up with his toy pistol." Now that Moore was out of the room, he didn't like it any better than his sergeant did.

Lizanne begged him, "Can't you see that Lans didn't do it, couldn't have done it? He wasn't there." Dinky was there but Tobin didn't care about Dinky any more. Guard had fixed that. Guard worked for Washington, but he worked for Stefan and Bill, too, and himself. Tobin wouldn't think of that; he wasn't inside the circle.

Moore returned, his eyes painful. "He hasn't left the hotel. I checked with all the men. He must still be inside."

Dinky and Tobin were both on their feet and their faces weren't easy.

Tobin was disgusted. "Hide-and-seek in The Lorenzo." He took a breath. "Well, we'll do the best we can. Get on the phone, Moore, and have some more guys sent up. We'll do a floor-by-floor search. Not that there's a chance in ten that it'll do any good. Too many ways to hide out in a place this size. Get that hick house detective and speak to the elevator men and the maids."

Moore went into the office.

Dinky asked, "What about Lizanne here?"

Tobin took his time thinking about it. She didn't know what Dinky meant; she couldn't even think any more.

Tobin spoke. "Lans must be coming back here. There's

no other reason for him to stay in the hotel. He couldn't have known we had men stationed downstairs. He's after something, and he'll come back for it. We'll have to make it easy for him." He thought some more.

She wouldn't let him be trapped in her rooms, wouldn't let that look that had been in his eyes reappear. She said, "He won't come here. He knows I keep my doors bolted."

Tobin decided. "Take Lizanne to your room, Dinky. No way to get in it except through living room or office?"

Dinky nodded.

"O.K. Moore can stay in the office. We'll leave it dark. Lights out in here. Light in Bill's living room."

Dinky seemed to understand. "I'll go down and check up, see what I can do." He went into the office.

Lizanne put her head into her hands. Dinky said, and his voice sounded sympathetic, "Don't take this too hard, Lizanne. The stakes are big, y'know. Too big."

She only said, "I don't see why I can't stay here. My rooms are safe."

He looked at her steadily. He said, "Tobin's the boss right now. We're lucky not to be sleeping in the jug." Then he sat down again. "Why'n't you get comfortable? I'll wait for you. You can take a nap on my bed until this blows over."

She went into her bedroom without speaking. She understood now. She would be guarded, closely guarded, until they caught Lans. They were afraid she would slip away from them and warn him. She changed to bitter-green slacks, the long coat belted in dull silver, buttoned in dull silver. She had once thought she might be beautiful for him in it. It was all of them against him, all of them, even Tobin who didn't know it, working for Stefan. It was Stefan alone who needed to get rid of Lans;

the others weren't menaced by him. She knew she couldn't elude them tonight. Perhaps Lans could.

She returned to Dinky, caught up a magazine. She didn't expect to sleep.

Tobin and Moore were speaking quietly in the office, planning their campaign against him. Tears without warning covered her eyes again. There was no use repeating his innocence; no one believed. Even Dinky, who had pretended to be his friend on that night when Dinky himself stood in danger, was hunting him down.

Moore asked, "You got a gun, Mr. Bruce?"

"Sure." Dinky's hand touched his pocket, showed it.

Lizanne's eyes were blue amazement. It was a world turning upside down. Dinky armed. And Lans, poor foolish Lans, waving his gun at all of them. They'd only been toying with him all evening then, playing him as a ball on a string, knowing he could do nothing. What were they waiting for? Stefan, of course. Lans couldn't escape now. Let Stefan finish him. They were dogs baying the scent. Stefan must be allowed the kill.

She woke suddenly to unexpected disturbance. Guard must have just burst in. He wore overcoat, hat, gloves, and he was saying, "Have you seen Bill?"

Dinky said, "He hasn't been here. Isn't he with you?"

"Gave me the slip. We stopped at the Stork for a drink on our way up. He went into the men's——" Guard shrugged. "He's on, all right."

"Nobody's safe then," Dinky said.

Guard saw Lizanne on the bed. His face was angry. She kept her eyes slitted. "What's she doing here?" His voice was angrier.

"Safekeeping."

The anger went. Guard said, "Do a good job."

She opened her eyes then. "Haven't you caught Lans yet?" She was bitter. "Haven't all of you together caught Lans yet?"

Guard ordered almost sadly, "Go back to sleep." He asked Dinky, "What about Lans, for God's sake?"

"Waved a gun in Tobin's face and skipped out. We expect him back. He didn't leave the hotel unless he grew wings and flew out a window."

Guard's hands moved. "He's laying for Stefan."

"Yes."

"Are they watching?"

"Moore's in the office. Tobin's somewhere in the hotel directing things. The place is full of his men. And I'm here."

"Alix?" Always he remembered her.

"Alix is alone." Dinky wasn't troubled but Guard was. "She's a fool." Guard turned to the door. "I'll see if I can locate her."

Dinky followed him outside the door. Lizanne closed her eyes. She wasn't safe here. She was not being guarded merely to keep her from Lans; it was that she might not ever have opportunity to tell what she knew. Although it was only Dinky guarding her, it wasn't the Dinky she had known; it was a man with a gun. And she couldn't get away. The windows opened to ten stories of straight wall. They were outside the only door. Dinky came back in. She kept her eyes closed.

When she awoke again, she knew her surroundings. But there was a difference. Dinky wasn't in the chair. He wasn't in the room. There was a slot of light under the bathroom door. She didn't stop for thought. She moved silently as shadow out the door, swiftly down the corridor to the living room. She didn't even stop when she saw Bill bending over that motionless figure on the floor.

He stood straight, looked at her as she ran forward crying it, "Lans! Oh, Lans!" She didn't think about that blood trickling from his temple onto her breast. She didn't even see it. They'd trapped him even as they planned it, killed him. She hadn't been able to do anything. And now she was the only one left in the way. But she didn't think of that, holding his head to her, nor that Bill might be watching, waiting for her to move.

She didn't see him, didn't see Guard burst into the room, stand there motionless watching, as if it were a scene in a play. She heard as if from far away Guard ask, "What——" and Bill say, "I called the desk for Tobin."

She knew vaguely that Guard raised her from the floor, held her quietly against his bulk. She repeated the name as a child might, "Lans, Lans, Lans . . ."

Guard said, "Go on, cry if you want to, but it's better this way." His voice was almost gentle. "Believe me, he wouldn't have done you any good."

The room was all at once alive with voices. Guard's arms weren't around her now, but she stood near him for strength. There was Dinky in one doorway unbelieving; Tobin in another; Moore and strange men, even the ridiculous house detective, craning after him. She saw Bill standing there with incredible calmness, removing his gloves.

Tobin asked flatly, "What happened?" His face was accusing.

Bill said, "I don't know. I'd just come in. He was like that. I bent over him to see what had happened, and then I saw her standing there, her suit covered with blood."

Lizanne heard the little choke in her throat. She felt her eyes stretch like drum-heads. She moved one faltering step nearer to Guard. And she heard him say evenly, "You'd better take her in, Inspector. She killed Lans just as she killed Dene Viljaas."

She was there all day in the narrow gray cell, alone, as in another world where there were no human voices, no human faces. All day thinking, trying not to think. With cruel suddenness in those ghostly hours before dawn, she had hàd prescience of the utter fool she had been, the sightless, stupid fool. She knew Stefan! He wasn't newly arrived; he had been there all along. Guard was he!

None of the Viljaases used the Viljaas name; she had known that. A different mother would account for the difference in physical appearance. He hadn't been working for Bill; Bill worked for him, killed for him. And he hated Bill; for twenty years he had hated Bill. Bill had stolen his wife, the wife who was still his first thought. Bill, too, would be done away with now that he had finished Lans; he wouldn't live to bear witness. Nor would she.

Poor witless fool, believing all along that she would ultimately be safe, that she could win over such as Stefan Viljaas.

Everything was on his side, experience in intrigue, unlimited money, the right government contacts. He was smart; he even knew how to blindfold the smartest man on the homicide squad. Stefan had won. He would have her deposit box opened by now. The cross-eyed bear would be in his hands for the meeting. The contracts would be allotted as he wished. Those on his side, the Ambassador and Dinky and even Alix, would share.

She didn't want the newspapers; she could guess at their story. She didn't want to die; but she should have known when Lydia's letter came that she was doomed to it. That was what happened to a Viljaas wife. She couldn't protest her innocence as she had hysterically to Tobin last night before he took her away. Tobin didn't come now to listen to her.

It was Sunday. Only one week since she had moved into Bill Folker's apartment. It might have been too long ago for remembrance. The days were a blur.

Her watch had stopped at two o'clock. She didn't know the time but it was darkening outside when the uniformed woman returned, unlocked the barred door. Her voice was kind. "Your lawyer's outside."

Lizanne said, "I have no lawyer." There was some mistake. She had no one; she was alone.

The woman said, "He has your release. He's waiting to take you home."

She didn't argue. She didn't say that she had no home. She followed. There was no lawyer. The man was Bill.

He came over to her. The policewoman couldn't hear his words. "I'm more sorry than I can say. I've spent the entire day trying to arrange this. I know, of course, that you had nothing to do with this, but when Guard said what he did——"

She was puppet again, going with him, getting into the chauffeured car with him. There were human beings moving away down the street, leaving her with him. She knew now that she hadn't been released from immediate terror; she hadn't been safe even behind lock and key. He had come for her. *He hadn't finished Stefan's work.*

She sat huddled into the corner of the coat, the fear of him crawling over her skin. She had heard him speaking in this easy, casual way before, while murder churned and spewed from his heart.

"I'm terribly sorry that you were let in for this, simply because you happened to be working for me. I'll do what I can to make up for it, I assure you."

She asked, "Where are you taking me?"

"Why, back to the apartment." He seemed amused.

There was nothing she could say; no other place she might go. They drew up at The Lorenzo, entered the elevator, reached the lighted office.

He said, "I'm sure you'd like to clean up a bit and have some decent food."

She said, "It doesn't matter." Nothing mattered. She could do nothing now but let him play this by Stefan's rules. She couldn't even try to save herself.

He went into her apartment with her, sat on her couch to phone the dining room. She knew she was guarded again. She moved into the bedroom, closed the door. It wouldn't lock, nor would the bathroom; both had been deliberately tampered with. She showered, scrubbing, scrubbing as if she could wash away the grayness that had entered her pores this day. But she couldn't linger forever.

There was yet one faint chance to live. If she could but make him see that his only escape was to defy Stefan, to join with her and convince Tobin who Guard really was, she might not have to die. If she could but force him to believe the hatred Guard had expressed to her of him.

She came out, dressed in the one dress that belonged to the days before Bill Folker had hired her. She hadn't known it would be her shroud.

He looked up when she re-entered the living room, said with careful surprise, "I didn't expect you to dress or I would have changed, too."

It was just a minor lie. He wouldn't have left her alone, not for one moment. Not while she was living. The dining-room service had arrived; the snowy cloth had been spread; the steaming serving table, the iced silver bucket, stood unattended. The men had gone away while she dallied within. She couldn't eat; she pretended to swallow, took tiny and tinier mouthfuls, washed them with sips of champagne. Wine and dine and die. She couldn't endure the even trickle of his voice discussing restaurants, wine cellars. If he would only do it quickly, not keep her here quivering at every move, wondering when his fingers would move to her throat or when the blunt cold black tube would be pressed deafeningly against her temple. Perhaps neither of these. It might be that the next spill of champagne would sear her throat. Now was the time to speak but she kept waiting, trying to find words that would make him heed. And then he turned the subject.

He said, "You didn't come to me in ignorance, did you, Lizanne?" He even smiled at her. "I didn't learn the news until last night from Guard and Dink. Everyone else seemed to realize that you were my brother's wife."

She didn't say anything. The false knowledge she had clutched upon in her hysteria before dawn had been her final misstep. It had delivered her into Stefan's fangs.

"I didn't know you were Stefan Viljaas." She spoke slowly, still trying to realize it. "I knew that Guard Croyden was the man who'd come asking questions about Dene."

She was numb. Now it would happen. But he only went on talking in that quiet way. He was smiling but he didn't know it. Behind the smile was a face, and the face was why her fingers couldn't hold the glass. She set it down. It made too much noise in the quiet of that room.

She said it then. "You're going to kill me."

He said, "I have no choice. It is in self-defense. I kill only in self-defense. Self-protection is self-defense, I believe. I've gambled everything, my very life, to have control of the Viljaas mines. I can't have you in my way." He said it simply as if she were a moth to brush aside.

"You killed Lans."

"Yes."

"Where were the others?" Even now that it had happened, it was incredible that Guard, who had said there mustn't be more bloodshed, had allowed Stefan to do this.

He smiled in scorn of their stupidity. "It wasn't hard to get rid of them. A man seen escaping over the roof. Another man following him. A call to Moore. He was in my office watching. I suppose you know that. A word to Tobin. That idiot Simmons, who calls himself a detective, cooperating with me, not knowing it. Guard out searching for Alix, as if he wouldn't know that Lans was more important to me."

"Where were you?"

"Across the way in a vacant room, long before Guard reached here. I'd rented it months ago—for storage." His smile was set. "That fancy clerk knew but evidently he'd forgotten, or no one asked him. I don't know where Lans was hiding but it must have been on this floor. As soon as Moore was out of the way he went into my room. He had a key. Did you give it to him?"

She said, "No, no!" as if by defending herself in this, she might stay his hand. "He took my key-ring from my bag—without asking."

He laughed as if it were amusing. "Clever of him. I followed him inside. He was afraid of me. He's always been afraid of me." His mouth twisted in more scorn. "I took his gun away from him and shot him. He'd even provided a silencer."

She wouldn't weep again for Lans; she was wept out. But she asked brokenly, "Did you have to kill him?"

"Certainly, I had to kill him." He was cold, matter-of-fact. He added, "It would have been suicide if you hadn't shown up."

"I was running away," she told him. "Dinky was guarding me and I was running away from him. I hadn't heard you."

"No. I didn't think you had. I am a quiet man."

No one heard him in the white woods when he shot Dene. No one heard him go to Lydia's room, leave that room. No one would hear him when he killed her.

She asked out of curiosity, "Did you get Lans's triangle?"

He shook his head. "No. But I will. I will be the only Viljaas left. Lans's effects will be mine." He poured the last of the liquid into his glass. The dark green bottle was empty. And when the glass, too, was empty, he said, "You are the one who has the bear. Is it here?"

"No." She said, "It's in my deposit box at the bank." She might as well tell him. It would be his. He would inherit from her, too. She asked, "Is that why you took me out of prison? To get the bear?"

"No, it would have been easy enough to find it with you gone. But I couldn't take a chance on your being acquitted. Pretty women are often acquitted even when guilty." He smiled at her and the smile was more terrible than his anger. "You are a pretty woman, you know. That's why I'm not going to kill you right away. I'm going to stay with you tonight." His yellow eyes narrowed. "I don't know why I haven't before. I don't know why I've listened to Guard, or why he turned moral all of a sudden. He never cared before what I did."

She bit her finger until it ached, listening to him. And now she was certain. That door was opening as it had earlier, slowly, but definitely. It might be the police coming to rescue her, to return her to the safe Tombs. It might be a hireling setting the stage for her murder. She wouldn't scream; she would go quietly as Lydia and Sally, as Dene and Lans had gone. She wouldn't let her teeth click that way against the glass. She put it down not knowing she had lifted it; began to speak not knowing what she said.

"You would have killed me anyway, wouldn't you, even if I hadn't been——" She swallowed.

The door was open. It was Alix. Rich in gray furs and stiff gray satin, her mouth and nails purple, just as if she were going to a first night, not to assist at a murder. Bill's head followed Lizanne's look and she knew then that Alix was not expected. For anger flooded his eyes.

Alix said, "I suppose this is business, too."

He didn't answer her.

Her voice sharpened. "I suppose this is business. You thought I wouldn't come. You thought I'd be afraid to come now, since she stole the letter for you."

He accused her quickly. "You told me your lawyer held that letter." His fingers became knuckles. "You told me it would be sent to your father if anything happened to you."

"And you believed me!" she scoffed.

He flicked back to Lizanne.

She shrank. "No, I didn't take the letter. Lans took it."
"Lans?"

He had missed it searching Lans? Or Lans had hidden it in those moments when he was eluding pursuers? Alix knew she had made a mistake and she laughed. "You don't have the letter! The letter that will send you to the chair!" She laughed again.

He was without control. He rasped back the chair, would have plunged to her, but she said with authority, "Don't come any nearer, Bill. I'll kill you if you do, and I don't want to kill you—yet."

He sat down again. She must have a gun; he must have seen it. Everyone had guns; they were as common as handkerchiefs. Lizanne was looking at the tablecloth.

"I want you to suffer first as you've made me suffer for years and years." There was a note of hysteria lifting her voice. "But I'm not going to suffer any longer. I'm going to kill you. You never thought I would, did you? You've taunted me for years, telling me that I didn't dare. To-night I am going to kill you. And all that money you've been waiting for won't go to you; it'll go to that snoopy little redhead there. That doesn't make you happy, does it?" Her lips curled. "That hurts, doesn't it? All the rotten things you've done, all the chances you've taken, and you won't get a cent. It'll all go to a stupid little fool who didn't have any more sense than to marry Dene."

He spoke coldly. "What do you want, Alix? What are you here for?"

She moved to a chair, sat down just as if she weren't holding a weapon pointed at him, and beyond him at Lizanne. She even threw back the silver gray of her cape with her free hand. "I told you. I'm here to kill you. I'm not afraid of you now. Even without the letter, I'm not afraid. The others were, all of them. That's why you could kill them. I'm safe from you."

He lit a cigarette with precision. "Stop talking nonsense, Alix. Say what you came to say and go on your way. Lizanne and I have business."

Again Lizanne wanted to scream. To be a part of a nightmare and to be unable to wake out of it. Was he trying now to stir Alix to kill her? But to Alix she was still non-existent.

The other woman said bitterly, "I have much to say, Bill, and I'm going to kill you before I go. I've done things your way so many years, deluding myself that you really cared for me, that once you had what you were after none of the others would matter to you. They've all tried to tell me, Father and Dinky, even Guard, but I went on stubbornly, believing in you. I quarreled with all of them over you. But you opened my eyes that day." She was ice and flame. "That day I found you with Fredi. I knew then."

He admitted, "I lost my temper."

She mocked, "Even the great god Stefan makes a mistake. I told you then you would be sorry. You are, aren't you, Bill? I could have killed you then, you and her, too." Her mouth was acid. "That was too good for her. That is why you had to wait until I got Fredi."

He was ash color. Only his eyes burned.

"And I got her." She spoke with her teeth. "She won't get away, Bill. Maybe in normal times, but not now. There was too much against her. She won't like it, living like a monkey in a barred cage until she grows old and flabby. She won't like wearing rough ugly clothes, eating bad food, working like a servant. She won't like living where there are no men."

He was on his feet again. "Stop it!"

She ordered, "Stay where you are."

He must have known there was nothing else to do, that at the moment she was more dangerous than he. He sat down again.

She continued and her words were like jagged glass. "I've taken it all. One woman after another for you, and you selling me cheap to one man after another, all so that you could be the great Viljaas. I even took your marriage to Lydia. I believed it was to save your life, to keep you from being shot as a spy. I presume that one tale might be true. She wouldn't have appealed to you otherwise, unless she grew dull that way on what you did to her. I believed everything you told me. I did everything you ordered. Until you dared to touch me, and Fredi laughed."

Bill said, and his voice had changed—there was a sureness in it now, "If you're going to kill me you'll have to hurry before Guard and Dinky interfere."

"They can't."

"They are in back of your chair, my dear."

Alix laughed in his face. "That's a stupid trick, Bill."

But they were there, moving slowly ever nearer. Lizanne wanted to warn her, to cry out, but she wouldn't be believed. Alix would think it more trickery, that she was helping Bill.

He shrugged, "Don't turn. But if you're still determined to kill me, you'd better do it. Before Guard takes that gun away from you."

Alix was uncertain. She didn't move her head, but hesitancy flickered like firelight on her face. Bill sat there, at insolent ease, half-smile tantalizing her.

And Guard spoke quietly, not to startle her, "Better give it to me, Alix."

She didn't turn. She shrilled, "I won't! I'll kill him!"

and she fired wildly. There was the sound of three shots before Guard's hand wrenched the gun from hers. Through it Lizanne sat stolidly, just as if a bullet whistling through her hair were a part of every day. She saw Bill rise at the first shot, duck at the second, but it wasn't ducking; he had fallen to the floor. Guard had the gun and Lizanne waited, waited for the fourth sound which would fling her too to the crimsoning carpet.

It didn't come. Guard put the gun in his pocket, said, "Self-defense."

Alix didn't say a word; she was weeping into her furs.

Dinky rose from his knees beside Bill. "He isn't dead. Alix never does things right. You'd better call a doctor quickly, however."

Only then did Lizanne begin to scream, scream louder and louder until the sound of it clanged in her own ears, and there was nothing left in the vacuum of the room save the hideous noise and darkness....

She was in her bed. Guard was sitting on the edge of it, his fingers on her wrist. Dinky's chair was pulled near. And there were other chairs with faces, Inspector Tobin, Sergeant Moore, even a quiet Alix.

Guard said, "She's coming out of it."

Her eyes could see clearly now. She said, "Why am I here?"

Guard took his fingers from her wrist but he didn't move from the bed. "You passed out." His ugly face grinned. "I had to punch you pretty hard on the jaw but you passed out."

She rubbed her chin. It hurt. And she asked, something of horror returning to her whisper, "Bill?"

Alix wrapped her silvery cape about her. "He'll live. I didn't do it right." She spoke to Guard. "Now that she's all right, I might as well go on, hadn't I? You don't need me any more tonight?"

He looked at her. "No, I don't need you now."

She stood then, straight as a tree. She said, "I'm glad I didn't kill him." There wasn't a quiver in her face, her body. Only her words spoke for her. Tobin opened the door and she went away without looking back.

Dinky said, "She'll do all she can to get him off."

"It won't do any good," Guard said. "The Koppels have talked plenty."

"No, but she'll try."

"She won't." Lizanne's voice was husky, as if her throat was sore. "Not after what he did to her."

They all looked at her questioningly and she remembered. They hadn't been there. But she shook her head slightly, said no more.

Tobin spoke, "We'll go along, too. You bring Lizanne down in the morning, Guard, and we'll get it down in black and white."

She closed her eyes. It hadn't been a dream; it was real. Tomorrow she must return to the grayness of a cell. But at least tonight she could sleep, if they'd only go away and let her sleep. But they wouldn't leave her alone. She opened her eyes and the police had gone. She said to Guard, "I promise I won't run away. You can go."

He stated, "I'm staying."

Dinky stretched his long legs. "You don't want my help either?"

Guard walked over to him, laid his hand on Dinky's shoulder. "No. Go get some sleep, Dink. You need it. And thanks. You've had it hard on your first case."

Dinky grinned. "I don't want sleep. I want to get really drunk. Pretending to get that way has made me honest-

to-God thirsty. See you in the morning. Not too early."
He went away too.

Lizanne said again, "You don't need to stay. I promise."

Guard sat down in the nearest chair. "Go on to sleep.
If you have bad dreams, I'll be here to hold your hand."

It was useless to protest to him. He would stay and be
certain that Tobin could have her again in the morning.
Bill had arranged the release; it wouldn't be any good
now that Bill was Stefan. She wanted to be certain, asked
in a small voice, "Do I have to go back to jail again?"

He spoke angrily. "You little fool! Didn't you know
I had Tobin take you in just so you'd be safe? You weren't
even charged. If you'd made any inquiries you'd have
found that out. We figured you wouldn't. I even gave
you credit enough to think you'd understand what I was
doing. Tobin fixed it up with the matron to watch you.

"And what did you do? Walked right out again with
the man that I was trying to protect you from. I didn't
think you were that dumb. Even if he did bring a note
with a poor imitation of my signature on it that fooled
poor old Geraldine, I thought you'd have better sense
than to walk out with him. My God!"

He began to stride the room. "I've never seen such
idiots as in this case. Everyone trying to get murdered!
First Dene. Knowing Bill wanted to kill him, he went
out at night alone for a confab with him. Lydia skipped
off to where Bill sent her and didn't let any of us know
where she was. Sally——" His face hardened. "She didn't
have a chance." He took another breath. "Lans wouldn't
let us put him away where he'd be safe. No, he had to
play it his way. Even when Dinky pulled a fast call to
Tobin to save him in spite of himself, he stuck a gun in
Tobin's snoot and waltzed out alone to find Bill. And

then you——"

He broke off, sat on the edge of the bed again. "What do you think we've been doing the past eight months but try to keep certain people away from Bill until the estate could be settled? Why do you think Dinky or Ted or I never let him out of our sight if we could help it? Because we craved his company? My God!"

He strode away again, returned to the chair, lit a cigarette noisily. "Well, you're left," he told her. "Not through any cooperation on your part, only because Alix thought she was smart enough to kill him. There's plenty of folks underground who've thought that through the years. If we hadn't had a tail on her since last night, and if I hadn't dropped in at the Tombs to see you this evening, you wouldn't be lying here now blinking those big blue eyes of yours up at me. I thought we had you safe, locked and barred from him, or I'd have come around sooner." He was furious with her.

She tried to exonerate herself. "I didn't know he was Stefan Viljaas." She cried out, "Why didn't any of you tell me he was Stefan?"

He said, "Bill—he has always been called that, never Stefan—was here strictly incognito. He didn't have time for The Three or any other governments until he got Lans and Dene's girl out of the way. When you first came, there was no reason to tell you; presumably you were an outsider; one name or another wouldn't mean anything to you. And after we found out you were in, we didn't dare let you know for fear you'd run to the police and spoil everything before our case was set. Even Lans must have been afraid you'd talk. And he wanted the kill himself."

She was quiet again. "I had to go with him when he

came for me. I couldn't do anything else, could I?"

He shook his head. "I should have known you wouldn't know what to do. And I should have known after we had to tell him last night about you and Dene that he'd go after you."

"Did you have to tell him?"

"Do you think he'd have swallowed your arrest otherwise? He'd figured out finally that we weren't playing the game by his rules. I knew that when he skipped out on me after we returned from Washington. If we hadn't given him a reason for accepting his accusation of you, he'd have known it was just a blind, running you in. He'd have known that we knew what we did, that he killed Dene."

She still couldn't understand. "But why not arrest him for it when you knew?"

"I told you before, he was a slippery customer. We knew but we didn't have a grain of proof. Not for any of his murders. We didn't even have him circumstantially. If he was ever seen near the scene of his crimes, there were always too many other interested parties also there."

He lit a cigarette for her. "But there's been more for us to do than just catch him on murder. Even now he might get out of that rap. He's smart, I told you that, and he's built himself a vast fortune taking over the mines, as he has since Knut's death. He has plenty to spend and he knows how and where to spend it. But we've got him on something that he can't escape from. Treason."

"Treason," she repeated.

"Yes. Espionage and conspiracy against the government. He's an American citizen. He was naturalized because Knut wanted it, when he first came over after his mother's death, when he was playing up to Knut to get the fortune. Bill hated his father because of the way he'd treated the mother; he always said Knut killed her, by neglect, and the divorce. And of course he hated the second wife's sons; he would have, even if they hadn't stood in the way of his collecting the full estate. But his hatred of all that Knut stood for went too far. Some of the things he's done for The Three and against his own country have caught up with him. We've decoded those papers you typed after the Koppels arrived. Those things mean curtains for Bill."

He took a deep breath. "We've got him now but it's taken time. Investigators here, and crawling all over Europe, and being hampered by the war. It's taken too long." He eyed her as if it were all her fault. "And while it's been going on, it's been my job to keep Bill amused and lulled in a sweet dream of his own security, pretend to be helping him out, doing things his way, so he wouldn't escape from us."

She was trying to gulp it, understand it. It didn't fit with a quiet Vermont town.

He spoke angrily again. "I should have looked in on you sooner. But we were trying to get everything set; we knew he wouldn't sit around much longer waiting for us to nab him, now that he was on to us. And we had plenty to do today. Getting the bear from your deposit box before he could, and Lydia's stuff. Anyway you're safe, with all the Viljaas millions in mind. But I suggest you let Tedford and me handle the contracts."

She shivered, "I wouldn't touch a cent of it. I don't want it. I don't even want to talk about it."

He eyed her. "It's yours. You can be one of the glamour girls, feature articles about you, one of the ten richest girls in the world——"

She sat up but she lay down again quickly before the room swirled too fast. "I tell you I won't have it!"

He said pacifyingly, "All right, all right. Don't get so excited. You don't have to take it." He charged up again from the chair, walked to the door, back to the bed, looked down at her.

She looked up at him.

"Why didn't you let us help you? Didn't you know the danger you were in hanging onto the cross-eyed bear? If Bill had known that——"

She asked, "Why didn't anyone suspect that I had it?"

"We did suspect that Dené had given it to the girl. But we were so sure that if he had, she'd have shown up before now to claim her share. That was before you came into the picture. And after you told me your story—well, I believed you." His mouth was angrier. "My God, I should think you'd have wanted to help us out in stopping Bill's activities, instead of making us practically hire wild horses to drag any information out of you, and then making it false."

She said timidly, "I didn't know if you were really what you said you were."

He interrupted. "Such is fame. You knew I was Guard Croyden. I don't suppose that meant anything to you. But what the hell did you want, an affidavit from the President of the United States?" Then he broke off.

She couldn't help the tears streaking down her face. "I never do anything to suit you." She was really crying; it was anger that made this happen.

He was beside her before she finished the words, his hands closing over hers. She didn't know his voice could be gentle, his ugly face distressed. "Don't cry, Lizanne. Don't you see? It's because I've been so worried for you these days, ever since I first saw you, sitting there in Bill's apartment with your eyes scared sick and your chin up. That's why I got Dinky up here to take care of you. Don't you see, Lizanne? I wanted to protect you. Oh, God, I'm talking like an old fool to a kid like you!"

He stood up again but she held tight to his hands. They were protection. "No, you're not." She still held tight and he didn't move. "You'll see that I don't have to have anything more to do with anything Viljaas, won't you? You'll see that I don't have to take their money, that it goes to all those societies and things where Knut planned for it to go?"

"If you want it that way."

"I don't need it." She thrust out her chin again. "I can work. I'll find another job."

He grinned at her. "I think I can find plenty to keep you busy." He patted her hand, went to the wall and turned off the overhead light. The lamp on the bed table was a dim glow. "Stop talking and go to sleep now. I'll be right here."

He sat down in the chair again. He was big and ugly; he didn't make your heart ache as Lans had; but his shoulders were comforting. She was safe knowing he would be there. Remembering Dene and that faraway night; even Lans, not knowing now, not ever to know whether the moment in the park was real; remembering Bill and the horror of that moment before Alix came, she murmured content, "You wouldn't touch me with a ten-foot pole."

When he answered she wondered if he were smiling. He said, "Not tonight."